PEELER AND PATRIOT

One man's journey form enemy to patriot

FIACH MAGUIRE

Copyright

Historical accuracy

This book is based on actual historical events and people. All of the main characters in the book were real people. Some events, characters, conversations and timings have been created or altered for the purposes of dramatisation. The Prologue is an amalgam of a number of events.

Visit the website

Please visit www.fiachmaguire.com for memorabilia of the life of Francis Maguire, pick up some free short stories and send your feedback on Peeler and Patriot. Many thanks for buying this book. I hope you enjoy it.

Cover photographs

Front cover photograph: Chief Superintendent, Francis Maguire, An Garda Síochána, April 1924.

Back cover: Francis and his wife Teresa with their first child, Annie, Belfast 1911.

You see my kind of loyalty was loyalty to one's country, not to its institutions, or its office holders. The country is the real thing, the substantial thing, the eternal thing; it is the thing to watch over, and care for, and be loyal to; institutions are extraneous, they are its mere clothing, and clothing can wear out, become ragged, cease to be comfortable, cease to protect the body from winter, disease, and death. To be loyal to rags, to shout for rags, to worship rags, to die for rags--this is loyalty to unreason, it is pure animal; it belongs to monarchy, was invented by monarchy; let monarchy keep it.

MARK TWAIN

A Connecticut Yankee in King Arthur's Court

DEDICATION

For Judith, my loving wife and patient ear.
My dear children Heather and Rachel.
And my uncle Frank, may he rest in peace.

PROLOGUE

The muffled sound of the smack of a rifle butt on the back of a human head is somehow unmistakable, even when heard for the first time. The range of outcomes from such a blow is narrow. A hard blow to a soft skull is likely to be fatal. However the blow at issue here was not what killed the young man, shivering in fear for his life and mumbling a prayer to his all too absent God.

Whether it was his mumbling or uncontrolled shaking which provoked the strike in the first place is not clear. Actually the cause is much less important than the effects which were immediate and dramatic. The young man fell forward and his face smacked into the wooden boards which made up the floor of the Dennis three-ton lorry, in which our murderous crew was travelling. As his hands were tied behind his back he could not reach out to break his fall and there was a sickening crunch as his nose absorbed the impact and flattened against his cheek. The only good that came of all of this was that the young man passed out. A trail of bloody saliva and snot ran down his chin and onto the floor of the lorry.

As the lorry rumbled on into the darkness and rounded a headland on the coast road, a harvest moon appeared in the sky. The moonlight turned the black roadway into a snail's trail snaking across the countryside. The driver's job was now much easier but he did not relish the improvement. Deep lines of concentration furrowed his face and through clenched teeth he muttered to his companion, ‘Bloody sitting ducks we are on a road like this, keep your eyes peeled, we don’t want to get killed on this God forsaken bog.’

A patch of darkness ahead on the hillside heralded the approach of a copse of trees. The driver’s companion rapped twice on the partition separating the cab from the canvas-covered lorry. At his signal two men rolled up the canvas curtain enclosing the back of the lorry and moonlight flooded into the interior which allowed a clear view of the group of men being carried into the night.

The young man with the broken nose was not the only prisoner. There were two others, hands tied and wearing the look of doomed men. Neither was as young as their bruised and battered companion, lying still on the floor of the lorry. Their captors, eight in all, were uniformed in a mixture of khaki and dark green topped off with jaunty tam-o-shanter caps. The prisoners were wearing the rough woollen clothing commonly worn by farm labourers.

§

The lorry slowed and swerved sharply left onto a track leading uphill into the trees. The driver ground the gears in his efforts to coax the lorry up the steep incline, the vehicle rocked violently in response to the rock-strewn surface. The men in the back held tightly onto their benches amid some shouting and swearing aimed at the unhearing driver. Then, as suddenly as the bumping and rocking had started, it stopped and the lorry came to a halt in a small clearing.

The tailgate banged open and a large moustachioed man, with sergeant's stripes on his forearm, jumped down and barked into the lorry in a hard-edged voice, 'Right then, everyone out. Prisoners first if you please, gentlemen.'

The shuffling and grunting which followed was punctuated with a protesting shout of, 'Leave-off ye scum, can't ye see that he's hurt enough already!' At that moment the still unconscious body of the young man was rolled off the end of the lorry and landed heavily on the woodland track.

The uniformed man who'd pushed the young man off the lorry turned to the protester and said, 'Shut up you Fenian bastard or you'll get a taste of the same.' He paused a moment and added to the pair remaining in the lorry, 'Jump down both of you, or fall down. It's all the same to us.'

In the semi-darkness, their minds clogged with fear, it was no small matter for the young man's friends to jump out of the back of the lorry. The fact that they had their hands tied behind their backs made the task all the more difficult. But encouraged by the prodding of bayonets, jump they did, and inevitably both fell forward on landing so that all three prisoners were sprawled on the ground across the track.

The sergeant was wearing a Sam Browne belt across his tunic. At his command his men formed a loose phalanx along the uphill side of the track. The sergeant then stepped forward and trod on the left leg of the lad with the broken nose. He unfastened the brass and leather clip on the holster carrying his side arm.

'Oh sweet Jesus and Mary mother of God, save us,' whispered one of the young man's companions.

'The mother of God will be of no help to you here tonight fella. But, if you are sensible, you may just be able to help yourself. We know you boys are Fenians. And we also suspect that you know the fellows who were involved in the barracks raid last week and made away with a Lewis machine gun.

'You might wonder how we come to be so well informed. And I don't mind telling you that our information came to us courtesy of one or two of your lamentably deceased former comrades.

'But that is neither here nor there. Let me explain why we've dragged you out here and what it is that we'd like to talk about.' The sergeant paused here as if checking that he still had his prisoners' attention.

He then carried on, saying, 'Now as you all know it is our job to drive about these parts and return them to a civilised state of law and order. It makes us a tad anxious to be out on these roads and wondering if that machine gun might be turned on us at the next bend. In truth, it is making some of my boys really jittery and that makes my job of looking after them all the more difficult.

'So it's all quite simple really. We just want you to tell us where the gun has been hidden and come along with us so that we can get it back and all will be right again.'

As he finished this little speech the sergeant bent down and, grabbing hold of the unconscious young man's jacket, he dragged the boy across the track and propped him upright against the side of a large ash tree. A pair of tan leather gloves was folded over the waist belt of the sergeant's uniform. He removed these and slapped the boy's face, first on the right and then back again across the left.

'Come on now Mick wake up and talk to us.' After a little more coaxing the boy woke up and then retched and spat a bloody ball of phlegm onto the ground at the Sergeant's feet.

'Mick, you forget yourself.' The sergeant stepped again onto the boy's leg. As he did so he removed his pistol from his holster.

'Now Mick,' he started, but the boy interrupted him with, 'Fuck you. My name is Seamus.'

'Of course it is Mick. But you see, as I was just explaining to your friends over there, it's not your name which concerns us this splendid evening.' With that the sergeant levelled his pistol and shot Seamus twice through the top of his head.

'Ah you evil piece of shit!' wailed one of Seamus' friends. 'He was only seventeen, may you rot in hell.'

Stepping away from the shattered remains of Seamus's body, the sergeant walked casually to the protestor and whipped him across the face with the barrel of his pistol. He didn't speak and his silence frightened even his own men, who shifted back a step from the mayhem. The sergeant moved towards the third man who had not uttered a word but was staring with ice-cold eyes at the Black and Tan officer.

'You've just signed your own death warrant, Sergeant. As sure as I'm sitting here you're a dead man.'

The sergeant gave the speaker a thin smile, 'As I suspected, you're the hard man here, aren't you? Rather burn in hell than talk to me, eh? You know of course that whatever happens, you and your friend there are going to die tonight. No one can stop that now. But what you can do is die slowly and screaming or you can die quickly and in no pain, like Seamus over there. The decision is entirely yours.'

The third prisoner said nothing more but continued his hard stare. 'Of course you won't talk will you? We could slowly roast your mate alive and there'd not be as much as a peep out of you would there?'

The sergeant turned to his men, 'Gag this one,' he said, pointing to the "hard man", 'and string him up by his heels from that big tree there. Get a fire started under him. Then we'll see if our loud mouth is more talkative.'

Before the gag was applied, the man about to be tortured shouted, 'Michael, don't tell these whores anything.'

'So its Michael is it?' asked the sergeant in an almost friendly voice. 'Well now Michael, what's it going to be? Will you tell us what we want to know and spare us all a lot of unpleasantness or are we going to have to hurt your friend there badly enough to loosen your tongue?'

CHAPTER ONE

The migrant returns

From the mid-19th century on, the lack of economic development in Ireland meant that it was the norm for many young Irishmen and women to go to England, or further afield, in search of opportunity. Ireland had been governed directly from London since the closure of the Dublin parliament following the Acts of Union in 1800. The Union had been imposed on Ireland following the crushing defeat of the 'Patriots' (United Irishmen) 1798 rebellion. The political scene in Ireland in the last quarter of the 19th century was dominated by Charles Stuart Parnell's Irish Parliamentary Party but their desired Home Rule for Ireland had been repeatedly rejected in London.

My grandfather Francis, the third child of Roger and Annie Maguire, was born in Manchester, England, on the first day of the new year in 1874. His father, Roger, was a twenty-nine-year-old police constable at the time of Francis' birth. Roger's impressive physique made him well suited to the role of a policeman. At six-foot-three inches he was the tallest policeman in Manchester but he was not the luckiest. Roger was born on a farm in County Fermanagh, Ireland, in September 1844, just one year before the Great Famine which claimed the lives of a million or more of his countrymen. At the age of twenty, he had taken his farm-grown broad back and strong hands to Lancashire to seek his fortune. A couple of years labouring broadened the young man's back further and made him an attractive candidate for the Lancashire constabulary which recruited Roger in 1866, when he was twenty-two years old. The now long-standing practice of growing large policemen on Irish farms seems to have begun early.

Roger had the good looks of the 'Black Irish' – dark grey eyes, dark complexion and curly black hair. He was the proverbial tall, dark and handsome stranger who swept young Annie Gaffney off her feet. Annie too was beautiful but her slight frame and short stature made her bird-like next to Roger. She bore him four children before she succumbed to cancer of the womb, just two months after Francis' tenth birthday. So Roger, then forty years old, found himself a widower with four young children to care for. A difficult task for any man, but an impossible one for a policeman in Manchester in the 1880s.

Roger was a good policeman and had been twice promoted in his first six years on the force but after an unfortunate misunderstanding, involving a dispute with a senior officer, he was stripped of his seniority and demoted back to first class constable.

Following his demotion, Roger found himself back on the unruly streets of Manchester at closing time on a warm Saturday night in August 1884. The Old Nag's Head on Jackson Row attracted the usual assortment of mill workers, weavers, bargemen and market traders, drawn to the city's less than salubrious drinking establishments. The imbibing habits of the regulars often bought them into the not-so-tender care of Roger and his colleagues. It was commonplace for a number of these inebriates to spend a night sobering up in the cells of the Bootle Street police station. Many seemed to regard this as a preferable alternative to the row they would get at home for drinking away a larger than considerate portion of their week's pay packet.

Roger's own imposing physique would occasionally provoke a challenge fuelled by an excess of Boddingtons Bitter and a misplaced need to prove an ability to knock a large policemen on his back. Roger, it must be said, was not an entirely reluctant participant in these scuffles. His relative sobriety and the fact that he was adept in the use of his nightstick was usually sufficient advantage to allow him to subdue any challenger and progress them onward to a night in the cells.

The kick from Frank Broadbent which ended his policing career did therefore take the unfortunate Roger by surprise. Not least because Roger and his fellow police officer, Tommy Fearing, had just moments before clubbed Mr Broadbent to his knees in the back bar of the Old Nag's Head where he was making a nuisance of himself by punching all and sundry. When Roger and Tommy bundled Broadbent out of the pub door, Broadbent lost his hat so Tommy turned back into the pub to retrieve it. Thinking Broadbent a spent force, Roger loosened his grip and turned to look back into the pub and shouted after Tommy to hurry up.

But Broadbent had recovered from the clubbing he'd had in the bar and spotted his opportunity to break away. He swung a vicious roundhouse kick into Roger's groin. When Tommy reappeared on the street, Roger was on his knees throwing up into the gutter and Frank Broadbent was running away down Jackson Row towards Deansgate.

Tommy was not as tall as Roger but, on his feet, he was faster than most. When he realised what must have happened he became very angry. With a roar he charged after Broadbent and just before Roger passed out he was delighted to see Tommy's club come down hard on Broadbent's head ending his break for freedom.

Roger's injuries lasted a lot longer than his memories of that fateful evening. A persistent groin hernia, coupled with extensive varicose veins, meant that Roger's value to the Lancaster constabulary was in rapid decline. He was invalided out of the force in April 1885, just six months after the incident outside the Old Nag's Head. He was granted an invalidity pension of two shillings and sixpence per week which was scarcely enough to cover the rent on the family home.

All in all Roger's luck was at rock bottom, but it was about to take a bittersweet turn. The following month his father, John, himself a widower of many years, died after a short illness leaving Roger the family small-holding in Tempo, County Fermanagh. While they would never be well off, the farm was large enough to support a small beef herd and with a vegetable patch and some hens they would have enough to eat and a secure roof over their heads. So in the summer of 1885 Roger returned to Ireland with his motherless children.

§

Young Francis tried to be helpful but, in the end, his excitement got the better of his nervousness and he raced up the gangplank onto the steamer while his father struggled with their luggage and Francis' little sister, Annie. Meanwhile Francis' older sister Susan and brother John, both in tears, clung onto Grandma Gaffney on the dock below.

A couple of days spent with Annie's parents in Southport had been a welcome haven following their departure from Manchester. Roger's colleagues turned out in large numbers to see them off and the party had been a rowdy affair. As the evening got started, the station Sergeant, a big soft-hearted man from Newcastle by the name of Brian Dawes, banged an empty bottle on the table to get attention. 'Gentlemen a bit of quite please.' An appreciative rumble, calling for silence, rolled through the bar and was followed by a couple of ribald shouts, 'Keep it short Sergeant, there's beer to be drunk.'

The Sergeant continued undaunted. 'Now Roger, I'm pleased to tell you that a collection has been taken up and every man in the station, including the district inspector, has put his hand in his pocket and contributed to this gift for you and your children. It's no king's ransom but we hope it will help you get settled in your home in Ireland.' Roger received the gift and waved his thanks to his colleagues. A tear sprung to his eye which he brushed away.

'Thank you Sergeant and thanks to you all, lads. You have all been very kind.' He had to stop himself talking as he was choking up. He waved again at everyone in the room and raised his glass in salute; he swallowed hard and drained every drop.

Sergeant Dawes said, 'Men, raise your glasses, please. A toast to Roger and his wee barins. May they travel with God's speed and find the very best of luck and good fortune in their new life back in Ireland.'

§

The brand new SS Caloric, pride of the Belfast Steam Ship Company, was tied up at the Princes Landing Stage next to Albert Dock in Liverpool. A seething press of bodies on the dock jostled for position in the queue to board the steamer for the overnight sailing to Belfast. This fluid mass contrasted sharply with the immoveable sturdiness of the dockside which exuded a self-deceiving sense of permanence.

Roger, who was something of a history buff, reminded himself that these docks were no stranger to great sorrows. During the course of the Great Famine, almost half a million Irish emigrants passed through this very same dock. A hundred years before the famine Liverpool had facilitated the transportation of one and a half million African slaves to the Caribbean and the Americas.

Roger realised that his children, standing on the deck of the steamer next to him and waving goodbye to their grandparents on the quayside below, were too young to appreciate the insignificance of their journey relative to the sea of humanity that had passed this way before them, nor could they know what lay ahead. Roger wondered how his children would adapt to rural life. The remote farm tracks of Tempo were a far cry from the noisy, filthy streets of Manchester.

The throbbing in Roger's leg intruded into his distracted thoughts. His varicose veins, agitated by the effort of hauling the family's belongings on board the steamer, hurt badly. The two older children, sat on top of a small pile of suitcases and duffel bags, had subsided into a state of nervous fidgeting, their tear-stained faces sullenly accusing.

John was a frail child; his lungs never fully recovered from a bout of pneumonia he suffered about the time Francis was born. While Susan was the eldest at fifteen, she had her mother's delicate frame and could hardly have been described as robust and so neither she nor John were much help with the luggage.

The eleven-year-old Francis, the strongest of the children, was nowhere to be seen. As soon as the ship slipped her moorings and chugged out into the estuary, he had run off to explore the boat. Roger shouted after him not to run on the ship's wet and slippery gangways and ladders. Little Annie, three years younger than Francis, and his favourite from the moment he set eyes on her as a newborn baby, took off with Francis who, as usual, had taken on the role of her protector.

The third class cabin where the family finally settled was arrayed with rows of narrow bunk beds offering little privacy. They shared the cabin with an odd mixture of people. Weary families like themselves, working men carrying the tools of their trade and a couple of evangelical preachers, already on their knees, saying their night prayers. The air in the cabin was a rich mixture of cigarette smoke and coal dust, combined with all manner of pungent body odours.

Susan and Francis whispered and giggled about the preachers. Annie complained about the smells and John wrapped his head in his coat to drown out the hammering of the steam engines on the deck below. As the ship gained the mouth of the Mersey estuary, the large waves of the Irish Sea rolled her alarmingly. Annie cried out and Francis took her into his bunk and cradled her until she slept. 'Hush now Annie, there's nothing to be afraid of. It's just the sea rolling under the ship. We'll be fine, I promise.'

A little less than eleven hours later, the SS Caloric nosed into Belfast harbour to deposit her cargo and complement of groggy and travel weary passengers. The family had not slept well but the children's tiredness was quickly dispelled by the bustle on the landing stage. Along with all the other third class passengers they waited until the 'quality' folk from the first and second-class compartments boarded their carriages and charabancs for their onward passage to the grander homes in Belfast and beyond.

Francis made himself more useful at this stage of their journey. He'd noticed that his father's limp was much more pronounced and made a point of taking charge of the heaviest bags.

A thunderous steam engine barrelled the family along the Great Northern Line from Belfast to Enniskillen via Armagh, the ancient ecclesiastical capital of Ireland. Ned Brown, a friend of Roger's father who lived on the farm adjoining the Maguire farm, was waiting at the station at Enniskillen. He'd brought a pony and trap to take the family to the farm at Edenmore, next to the village of Tempo, nine miles east of Enniskillen. As they headed out of Enniskillen Roger distracted his children by telling them heroic tales of the Maguire kings and chieftains of ancient Fermanagh. Pointing to Enniskillen castle, rising up behind them, Roger told tales of a land where the Maguires used to be kings. The castle they passed had replaced one that was originally built during the reign of Tomas Mór Maguire, by his brother Hugh the Hospitable, five hundred years earlier. Roger told his children, 'The Maguires ruled these parts for hundreds of years and were visitors to the courts of kings of Spain and of popes in Rome.'

Worried that the children might feel out of place in their new home, Roger added, 'When someone asks where you are from you should say, '"I'm a Maguire and the Maguires have lived in Fermanagh for six hundred years." Remember your link to the Maguire history and be proud of it, no one should be allowed to tell you that you are not from around here.'

Francis' natural uneasiness about all of the change happening about him was not greatly helped when Ned Brown played a joke on him and his brother. Ned told them that they'd better be quiet when they pass any Irish boys, because, if they heard the Maguire boys' peculiar English accents, they might very well throw stones at them. Francis and John spent the rest of the journey hiding under a horse blanket in fear of drawing unwanted attention to themselves.

As the children settled down, Ned turned to Roger and said, 'It's good to see you again Roger. It was all a bit frantic when you came over for your father's funeral. We are still sad about losing him. John was a good friend to Phyllis and me and we miss him greatly. But it's great that you've decided to come home with your children. You will all find a warm welcome in Tempo.'

'Thanks Ned, as you know, I didn't get the chance to visit my father very often. I'd not been over since before Francis was born. He was a tough man who'd had a hard life. I sometimes wonder why I didn't come home before now. I hope I can make a decent fist of the farm. It's been a long time since I raised a calf!'

Roger allowed a silence to develop which was only broken by the pony's iron shoes clipping against the rough roadway and the noise of the cartwheels grinding the stones beneath them. Unfamiliar smells wafted across the lane. Country smells that took Roger back to his youth but to the children, more familiar with the pungent smells of the city, the sweet smells of the country were strange and even exotic.

Ned tried a broader topic, 'Parnell's Irish Parliamentary Party looks like it has become an irresistible force. The talk is that they will win big in the elections this year. If as seems likely, the Liberals get back into government with a slim majority, then Parnell will be able to force Gladstone to introduce Home Rule in Ireland.'

Roger groaned inwardly but turned slightly towards Ned. 'To be honest, I care little for Irish politics, Ned. In my early years in Manchester I saw the hanging of the Manchester Martyrs. A climate of anti-Irish hysteria surrounded their trail and I was treated with suspicion by both my colleagues in the police and the local Irish community. Since then I have resolved to stay out of all conversations concerning Irish politics. No offence intended.'

'And none taken, Roger.' said Ned, unconvincingly.

Roger added, 'Ned, my apologies, I have no wish to be rude. In truth, I have read a lot about Mr Parnell in our newspapers in Manchester. It has always struck me as curious that Irish Nationalists are again being led by a member of the Protestant landed class.'

'I'm not sure why you should think it strange, Roger. We Presbyterians make natural anti-establishment types. We may have no truck with Rome but we're none too fond of the Anglicans either! Think of great leaders like Wolfe Tone, Robert Emmet or Henry Joy McCracken, all Protestants and fearsome Irish Nationalists.'

'By God, Ned, I'd never have put you down as a patriot.'

'As the old saying goes, Roger, "Live long enough and you'll see it all."'

CHAPTER TWO

Man and boy

The Gaelic League (Confadh na Gaelic) was founded by Eoin MacNeil and others, as a non-sectarian cultural body to promote the revival of the Irish language. This movement was part of a broader cultural revival which gathered pace at the turn of the 19th century and was led for the most part by Anglo-Irish intellectuals and middle class professionals such as William Butler Yeats. On the political front the Home Rule movement was in disarray following the toppling of Parnell. John Redmond had taken over the leadership of the Irish Party but their influence in London had been significantly reduced. Home Rule provoked fear and loathing amongst Unionists, especially in Belfast where many people had been killed in riots, as the Home Rule debate waxed and waned over the years.

A loud cheer went up from the crowd as the *sliotar* curled into the top right hand corner of the makeshift goal. Pat Donnelly had flipped the ball off the end of his hurl and slammed a volley with such force and determination that his shot was too high and fast for the goalkeeper to have any chance of stopping it. The goal effectively settled the match which was the first ever organised Gaelic hurling match in Tempo. The small crowd could not know that this match marked the beginning of a sporting dynasty which, while occasionally interrupted, would survive far into the future and give rise to one of the strongest Gaelic sporting clubs in County Fermanagh, the Tempo Maguires GAC.

Francis watched disconsolately from the sidelines as his friends celebrated their victory. He was solidly built and a strong runner but he had been unable to master the art of Gaelic hurling. His early years in Manchester exposed him to football which, although popular in Ulster, now faced competition from Gaelic sports as a rising cultural confidence gave flower to a resurgence of interest in more traditional sports.

The Francis Maguire watching this hurling match in 1891 and wrestling with his distracting sense of 'otherness' was seventeen years old. He and his family had been working the Edenmore farm in Tempo since their arrival from Manchester six years earlier.

Francis' thoughts wandered back to that fateful day when he and his brother and sisters dismounted from Ned Brown's pony-trap and listened agape as their father was greeted in Irish by his old friends and neighbours. Ned had stopped the trap outside the village post office and Roger was immediately engulfed by a group of older men and women all obviously delighted to see him. '*Failte abhaile,* Roger' sang one voice '*Míle failte roimh*' shouted another. A big burly man with a weather beaten face pushed through the crowd and threw his huge arms around Roger, smothering him in a bear hug and roaring, 'What in the name of God has happened to you?' To Francis' astonishment the big man had tears in his eyes and when the man caught the startled look on Francis' face he released Roger and turned to the children. 'And these are your *leanaí bochta*?'

Francis remembered standing in front of his siblings with the biggest hand he had ever seen in his life waving in his face. 'You must be John; *Cead mile failte!'* Francis was shaking his head in confusion when Roger intervened. 'No, Seamus, this is Francis, my younger son, and here is his older brother John and Susan our eldest, and this is little Annie. Say, "Hello" to Mr O'Dowd children.'

O'Dowd snorted, 'Hello my arse! Have you not taught these poor wee hallions how to properly greet an Irishman? You can't have them going about sounding like bloody rent collectors. John, Francis, girls, your father has clearly neglected your education but have no fear, your Uncle Seamus will soon put that right. In fact, there being no time like the present, why don't we make a start right now. So, this is the proper way to greet a gentleman in these parts. Repeat after me.' O'Dowd then removed his cap and in a slow and deliberate voice said, '*Dia duit a dhuine uasal*. So can ye say that?'

The children's murmured repetition of this phrase provoked a roar of laughter from O'Dowd which frightened Annie and startled the others.

'Holy God.' said O'Dowd, 'Well it's a start but we have a very long way to go before anyone will be mistaking ye for locals!'

Francis smiled at these memories. Seamus O'Dowd went on to play the role of benevolent tyrant in the Maguire household. Regardless of his rather overbearing manner, Francis had become very fond of Seamus and now missed him greatly as Seamus had drowned earlier that year in a boating accident on Lough Erne.

Following the commotion on the High Street Ned Brown had ushered the family back into the trap for the last mile of their journey up the hill behind the village to the family farm at Edenmore.

Everyone was more than a little frazzled and Ned Brown soothed nerves and settled anxieties by announcing that his wife Phyllis would be waiting at the farm cottage with a welcoming meal and a warm fire in the hearth.

Roger wondered to Ned if it were not a bit warm for a fire.

'When we opened up the cottage yesterday we found that there was a bit of damp about, so we built a fire to ensure that when you and your family arrived the cottage would be dry as toast. But don't worry, Phyllis will have opened the windows and doors to let the fresh air blow through the place.'

The farm cottage was approached along a steep and narrow lane up from Tempo. The lane was hemmed in by high hedgerows so little could be seen, even from the perch atop the trap. As the lane opened into the farm yard the hedgerow gave way to a clearing centred round a thatched cottage and large wooden hay barn. The cottage looked back down the hill the family had just climbed. A small black and white dog scampered in front of the pony yapping. Francis remembered their excitement about the dog and then their disappointment when they found out that the dog belonged to the Browns.

The farm yard smells, which had become so familiar, were very strange to the family when they'd first arrived. Long summer evenings were a favourite of Francis' and he remembered well that first evening when the sun remained high in the August sky and a red kite circled soundlessly above their heads before darting away down the hill in pursuit of some unseen prey.

Below them, the roofs of the houses in the village were just out of sight and the view stretched to the curve of the hill opposite, which, in turn, rolled itself into the receding distance. Beyond the horizon lay the forests and lakes of Fermanagh and west of that stretched the sandy beaches of County Sligo pounded clean by the crashing waves of the North Atlantic.

As the kite departed skylarks rose and swooped to feast on swarms of midges. Wood-pigeons cooed from the branches of the birch and elm trees which marked the boundary of the farm.

While Ned went in to announce the family's arrival, Roger gathered his children around him and told them that first thing the next day they would make a sign to hang over the fireplace and it will say *'Nil aon tintean mar do tintean fein'* which means, 'There's no fireside like your own fireside.' Francis realised now that his father had been trying very hard to be both father and mother to his children. He remembered his father drawing them all together and whispering, 'Welcome to your new home children.'

A shout from the field brought Francis back to the game he was watching. He drew in a long breath and smiled again to himself. The thought had dawned on him that he was very happy with his life as a country boy. He decided that he needed to stop feeling sorry for himself and just accept that he was never going to be very good at hurling.

§

The girls giggled together in the corner and threw furtive glances over their shoulders at Francis as he made his way across the dance floor. Rosin O'Leary turned away from the group and whispered to her friend Catherine Mulally, 'Don't you think that boy Francis Maguire is gorgeous?'

'Rosin O'Leary, you should be ashamed of yourself,' said Catherine pretending to be scandalised. 'And for goodness sake don't let him catch you looking at him.'

'Oh, give over. You're worse than the bloody nuns.'

The girls were at a harvest festival Ceili at the end of the summer in 1895, four years on from when Francis watched the hurley match. Instead of noticing the attention of the girls Francis was heading across the hall to talk to Reverenced Clancy, the local Church of Ireland minister, and a leading member of the Gaelic League. Francis wanted to find out if there were plans to start Irish language classes in Tempo village.

Roger and Annie both spoke Irish with some fluency and had managed to pass this on to Francis' older sister, Susan, who had a musical ear. Francis had not been inclined to bother to learn the language, believing it irrelevant, as Ireland and the broader British Empire approached the new century. But the mood of the country was changing. There was considerable growth in cultural self-confidence, and Francis, like many others, had discovered a growing fascination with his country's cultural heritage.

Francis had turned twenty-one that winter. He was working the farm with his father, older brother John and younger sister Annie. John had suffered another prolonged bout of TB and Francis had stayed on the farm after finishing his schooling as he was needed to do the heavy lifting that neither his father nor brother could manage.

That spring his father had remarried a local woman, Ann Murphy, who had been coming in for some years to help with the housework and, more importantly, to help raise the children, especially the girls. Susan, the older girl had married and moved to Belfast. Susan's husband, Frank Murphy, was her stepmother's brother, which made her husband both her father's son-in-law and brother-in-law, and in time her father would become both grandfather and uncle to her children.

Francis, beginning to feel that he was in the way, was growing restless and searching for a new role in life. As the younger son he knew that he would not inherit the land and besides the farm was too small to provide anything but a subsistence standard of living. He began to wonder if there might be a way out of Tempo and an alternative to his confined existence. He worried that he would never be able to marry and start a family of his own while living on the family farm in Edenmore.

After exchanging pleasantries Francis found his conversation with Reverend Clancy took an unexpected turn. 'As a young man interested in your Irish identity I assume you have an opinion on the Home Rule question?'

Francis had developed the natural reluctance of farming folk to offer opinions on anything more controversial than the weather and tried to duck the question with one of his own. 'Well now, Reverend Clancy, isn't that a queer question to be asking me?'

The Reverend smiled in a bemused way as he challenged, 'Oh come on now, Francis, don't play the *amadan* with me. We both know very well that you have a fine mind and a bright intelligence so please don't insult us both by pretending otherwise.'

Francis looked at the Reverend directly but did not immediately offer a response.

'OK,' said Reverend Clancy. 'You are quite right Francis. In these increasingly febrile times it is unfair of me to put you on the spot.

'What if I tell you that, unlike most of my Protestant brethren, I'm extremely annoyed that their privileged and self-satisfied lords have overturned the wishes of the government and rejected Mr Gladstone's Home Rule Bill a second time?'

'Well Reverend Clancy, I can't say that I've given the issue much thought. But I will say that we seem to be travelling a road which will divide us, and in that regard I'm not entirely sure that I support Home Rule.' Francis paused, he had not articulated these thoughts before and he surprised himself by what he'd said.

'If I may say so, Francis, that is an astute observation but do you not think that both communities on this island of ours could find a way to run the country together more effectively than our distant masters in Westminster?'

Nodding his agreement Francis added, 'There seems little doubt that while the Union has been good for Britain, it has been largely a disaster for Ireland bringing poverty and misery for many people. Granted, the Land Leaguers won many concessions on land reform but an Irish Parliament would surely have moved faster to relieve the misery inflicted by landlords on their tenants over the years.'

'Go on please,' murmured Reverend Clancy in agreement. But before Francis could do so they were interrupted.

'Excuse me, Reverend Clancy. Francis here is needed on the dance floor,' said Francis' friend John McCormick as he dragged the reluctant Francis away. John and Francis lived on farms opposite each other on Edenmore lane and had picked up together as soon as Francis had shown up in Tempo.

'Francis, let's continue this conversation another time,' offered Clancy to Francis' receding back and turning to his neighbour, Tom McHughs, said, 'Quite a remarkable young man that.'

'Who's that, Reverend? Francis Maguire? Well if you say so, but he can't play hurling to save his life!' Tom chuckled at his own joke and offered to buy Reverend Clancy a bottle of porter.

'No thank you, Tom, but I'd not say no to a wee dram of Bushmills.'

'What were you talking to Reverend Clancy about?' asked John as they made their way across the dance floor.

Francis did not immediately answer. Instead he reflected on what the Reverend had said about Home Rule and he wondered why he had been evasive. The truth was that he was a lukewarm supporter. But he worried that Home Rule would divide the country and he was not sure that such a price was worth paying.

Francis reflected, *Reverend Clancy is a good man but he's a bit of a dreamer and he is certainly out of step with many of his co-religionists*. Francis decided that there was little to be gained from worrying about it for now. He shrugged off his thoughts and turned to John who was watching him expectantly and said, 'Oh nothing of any importance.'

'Fine then, don't share if you don't want to. You always like playing the man of mystery.'

'Oh come on now, John, petulance does you no credit. If you must know I was simply asking about the Gaelic League and if I could get any lessons in the Irish language.'

'Well you are the queer one and no mistake,' snorted John. 'Why in the name of all that is holy would you want to waste your time with that nonsense? Is it an Irish patriot you're wanting to be? Besides couldn't you just ask your own family to teach you? Don't your father and sister both speak Irish?'

'It's poetry and not politics that interests me and I don't want to ask my family as I'd rather surprise them. Besides, if there are classes to go to, they will get me out of the house which, if I'm honest, is getting a bit crowded since Ann Murphy married my father.'

'Well now, Mr Maguire, aren't you turning into the right intellectual?' laughed John. 'How about we forget all that nonsense for the moment and have a dance with some of those pretty girls over there? If I'm not mistaken, that Rosin O'Leary has eyes for you and no one here but you, and you haven't even noticed her, the poor lass. So come on now and let's dance this polka.'

CHAPTER THREE

The Royal Irish Constabulary

Policing in the British Empire developed on two quite separate models. Robert Peel's police forces, hence Peelers, on the British mainland were unarmed and 'civil' in their nature. In contrast, policing across the Empire reflected the paramilitary model developed in Ireland by The Royal Irish Constabulary (RIC). However as the 19th century drew to a close and the Irish Land Wars were largely, but by no means entirely, settled, the RIC was moving steadily closer towards a civil policing role. The force's paramilitary structure and background was reflected in the fact that police stations were referred to as 'barracks'. The training of new recruits took place in Dublin. A once grand Georgian city, Dublin had been in steady decline since the 1800 Acts of Union and the abolition of the Irish parliament, when legislative power transferred to the imperial parliament in London.

Even in the depths of winter Francis spent most evenings tramping about the countryside with a handful of friends, stopping to gossip at neighbours' cottages. The group developed a certain local renown, and when a neighbour wrote a little ditty about them, they became known as 'The boys from Edenmore':

Curls on their moustaches
Caps down on their eyes
They'll sometimes settle at a windowsill

Sometimes at the door
But you're sure to hear the latest from
The boys from Edenmore.

When out on their ramblings, they frequently bumped into the local district inspector of the Royal Irish Constabulary, who was also given to tramping about the area and delighted in any opportunity to sit and chat with the young men. This police officer had the rather unusual name of George D'Amyralde De Montmorency Edwin Dagg. Happily, he was known to all in the district as Inspector Dagg.

Besides his name, Dagg was unusual in several other respects. He was highly educated, having studied philosophy and law at Trinity College Dublin. He graduated with honours, earning a degree in law, and was also elected to the university's senate council. About the time that he had become acquainted with the boys from Edenmore, he had recently completed a project to publish a 'road book' of Ireland; a mammoth task involving the mapping of every road and byway in Ireland. Dagg was also a fluent Irish speaker and active member of the Gaelic League. His road book was published in 1893 under the title 'Devia Hibernia' and included the subtitle: *'Triallanri timcheall na pfodhla: Let us wander round Ireland.'*

Inspector Dagg shared his love of Ireland with the boys and also excited them about Irish mythology, reminding them of the great myths of Irish folklore. Dagg told them that he had learnt Irish in order to read these wonderful stories in their original language. He was an adept story-teller and regaled the boys with tales such as the *'Táin Bó Cúailnge'* and 'The Children of Lìr.' Francis became hooked. He developed what was to become a lifelong commitment to self-improvement and a deep appreciation for Gaelic and English literature.

DI Dagg often talked about the value he had found in studying law and how that study had led him, not as his family expected to the life of a barrister, but to that of a policeman. One summer's evening, in 1895, Francis asked Dagg why he had joined the RIC. Dagg smiled ruefully, 'I can't tell you how many times I have had that conversation with my father. In truth, I saw, and continue to see, policing as a way of doing some good, helping people in a very direct way, and, of course, spending a considerable portion of my time outdoors rather than in a stuffy court room.'

Dagg continued, 'Without question, I find the philosophy of the law fascinating but for me the law in action is a much more dynamic beast where, as a policeman, I have to make daily decisions which directly affect the lives of ordinary people.'

Needless to say, such a man was bound to have a profound impact on a young, bored, but ambitious, farm labourer like Francis. Excited by Dagg's eloquence and full of admiration for his commitment to a civil police force, Francis began to wonder if the police could offer him the future he was seeking.

As if reading his mind, Dagg asked, 'Francis, your dad was a policeman in England, was he not? Why don't you think about joining the RIC? We need men like you.'

The taciturn Francis did not offer much by way of a response, 'Thank you very much for your suggestion, Inspector, I will certainly give it serious thought.'

During the remainder of the year Francis became increasingly desperate to find a way off the farm, until finally, a conversation with his father swayed his decision. 'Son, not long ago the police were reviled by the peasant population across Ireland. In the famine era any evictions granted to landlords were enforced by bailiffs and the police were, often as not, present to enforce the law. During the Land Wars in the 1880s the police were again called on to protect the rights of landlords at the expense of their tenants. When I got the opportunity to join the police in Manchester I was happy to do so but I don't think I would have joined the RIC. But things are different now.'

'In what way do you see things as having changed?'

'For one thing, if you watch what the police actually do on a day to day basis, it is clear that their former status, as a paramilitary force, has evolved into a force which looks to me very much like the police in Manchester. That is, protecting the public from thieves and brigands.'

'But what about the farm?'

'Let's be honest with each other, son. We could not have survived without your help these last few years. But, we both know that your heart has never been in farming. With Susan and her family around to help, we'll be just fine. It's time for you to find your own road, son. We will miss you terribly when you go but I'm sure that go you must. And I have a feeling that you will make a much better policeman than farmer.' As he finished his little homily Roger was smiling broadly at his son. He stood and offered to take Francis' hand.

'Francis, you are a man now and it's time for us to send you out into the world. Go with my blessing but watch out for the Frank Broadbents, they are unpredictable and dangerous!'

The next local intake was due to be enrolled at the Enniskillen barracks on the 21 January 1896, just three weeks after Francis' twenty-second birthday. By coincidence, Francis' father had been twenty-two when he joined the police. By the time Francis had decided to join the police, he had grown to be a tall young man with square shoulders, a barrel chest and a strong jaw. He knew that he had the physique the RIC preferred for recruits. He was also armed with a recommendation from DI Dagg. With that, and given his father's position as an invalided former member of the Lancaster police, he was fairly confident that he would be accepted.

§

Francis rapped on a gate to the side of the main entrance to Enniskillen barracks. ‘Yes?’ barked a voice from within and a grill in the gate slid back to reveal a glowering face topped off with an intimidating peaked cap.

Francis was never easily intimidated and with an assured voice he replied, ‘Francis Maguire, reporting for enrolment.’

‘In that case, young man, you can call me “Sir!”’ barked the cap as a bolt was thrown back and the gate swung open allowing Francis to enter a large courtyard.

‘Thank you, sir,’ said Francis without the slightest hint of irony and despite the absence of any officer’s stripes on the gatekeeper’s uniform. *No point in making enemies,* he thought to himself, *Even if this fellow is clearly a buffoon.*

In this fashion Francis found himself reporting, along with twenty-five other young men, for the commencement of his training. Somewhat nervous and unsure of what he might find, he was relieved to discover that all of the other new recruits were very much like himself; young Catholic men from small farms across Fermanagh.

The barracks in Enniskillen was a brooding and forbidding stone fortress structure, but this did not discombobulate Francis, as he knew that he and his colleagues would not stay long in Enniskillen. The next day they would head to the National Depot in Dublin for their six months of training.

A sergeant called the recruits to order. “Attention, gentlemen, and I will tell you what you can expect to happen this morning. Our process of enlisting new recruits is efficient and not too uncomfortable. First up, you will all be put through a rigorous physical and health check. Strip down to your underpants and place your clothing on that table. Wait until the doctor calls your name and then step forward. When the physicals are complete, you will all take an examination in the Three Rs: reading, 'riting and 'rithmetic.'

The room was cold and the men shivered despite their attempts to ignore the chill and hide their embarrassment. When his name was called, Francis stepped forward, feeling mightily relieved to be getting on with things, but mostly he was just looking forward to putting his clothes back on.

The doctor checked his vital signs, listened to his breathing and asked a host of questions about his health. Once satisfied the doctor then asked Francis to step onto a set of scales which measured height and weight. 'Six feet and three quarters of an inch, and thirteen stone and five pounds,' called the doctor to an orderly who had been recording Francis' answers. 'Chest measures forty four inches,' called the doctor as he swiped back the tape measure with which he had deftly captured Francis in a practiced flick. 'Well young man, I'm pleased to say that you certainly measure up to the RIC's requirements.' From the pained expression on the orderly's face, Francis surmised that this was not the first time the doctor had deployed his corny pun. But he maintained a respectful demeanour and simply nodded, 'Thank you, doctor.'

With the medicals completed, Francis and his colleagues moved through the hall to a second chamber, set up very much like a school classroom where they were tested in the 'three Rs'. While all of the recruits passed the physical checks, one unfortunate failed the 'three Rs' and was asked to leave. Francis felt sorry for the lad as he watched him gathering his things together before being escorted off the premises.

After a break, and a strong cup of tea, the men reassembled back in the large hall where they had been medically examined. The sergeant in charge formed them into two rows and barked at them to stand to attention. A tall, distinguished officer strode purposefully into the hall, took the sergeant's salute and turned to address the recruits. 'Gentlemen, I'm Inspector Charles Robertson, and I'm the County Inspector for Fermanagh. From this day forward, when you encounter any officer of the Royal Irish Constabulary, you will offer him a salute.' This mild reprimand provoked a slight shuffle of embarrassment from the group. 'Never mind your failings now, gentlemen. You are about to embark on six months of training by the end of which, I can assure you, there will be no doubts in your mind as to how to conduct yourselves with honour and dignity and indeed how to show that honour and dignity to your fellow constables, senior officers and most importantly, to the members of the public whom you will serve.'

The inspector was then handed a green, leather bound, book which he held up for all to see. 'This, gentlemen, is the Constabulary Manual.

'The Sergeant here will hand each of you a personal copy. Treat this manual with great respect, and keep it readily to hand at all times. Whenever you are in doubt as to what to do or how to handle yourself, this manual will be your most trusted guide.'

There was a moment of bustling as each of the men stepped forward in turn to be handed a copy of the manual. The inspector continued, 'Now gentlemen, if you will open your manuals at page four, you will find your Oath of Office. Please raise your right hands and repeat after me:

"I do swear that I will well and truly serve Our Sovereign the Queen in the office of constable without favour or affection, malice or ill-will; that I will see and cause Her Majesty's peace to be kept and preserved and that I will prevent to the best of my power, all offences against the same; and that while I shall continue to hold the said office, I will, to the best of my skill and knowledge, discharge all the duties thereof, in the execution of warrants and otherwise, faithfully according to law; and that I do not now belong, and that I will not, while I shall hold said office, join, subscribe, or belong to any political society whatsoever, or to any secret society whatsoever, except the Society of Freemasons. So help me God."'

Francis, along with the other men, spoke the words of his oath clearly and without hesitation. Little did he realise, when he spoke these words, how much angst and anguish his oath would cause him in the future and how ultimately it would guide his actions.

As the last words echoed around the hall the inspector added, 'Well done men, you are on your way to becoming part of the best police force in the world. The RIC are the envy of the Empire, and have been replicated in countries as far flung as Canada and New Zealand. I sincerely hope that no man here ever takes any action that besmirches the good name and standing of the RIC. Dismissed.'

'Men', shouted the sergeant over a rising din, 'You will be assigned a bunk in the barracks for tonight and your journey to Dublin will begin at six in the morning. Meanwhile, you are permitted to leave the barracks until curfew at ten o'clock tonight. Remember, you are on probation for your first month, so behave yourselves.'

Francis managed to fall into step with a fellow from Enniskillen he thought he'd recognised earlier. 'Tommy Kirk? It is you, isn't it? How are you? I didn't know that you were joining the police. It's nice to see a face that I recognise. I'm Francis Maguire. We met at a hurling match in Tempo a year back.'

'Well if it's not the bold Francis Maguire. When I saw you earlier I thought I knew your face but couldn't put a name to it. So we're both going to be Peelers. I assume that the princely annual salary of thirty nine pounds is not what is attracting you.'

'No indeed it's not,' laughed Francis. 'No, I need a change and something with a bit more of a future than being a farm hand. I want to be able to look to the future with some confidence and to be able to think about starting a family of my own. Honestly, and don't go repeating me, I hope I might even do a bit of good along the way.'

'How did you manage to kit yourself out?' asked Tommy.

'For a good while I thought I might not be able to manage it all. The contribution we have to make for our uniforms, and the shirts, suit, hat and such, along with the two pounds we're to have to tide us over to the first pay packet all added up to a big problem for me. But I was lucky, my father insisted on paying the costs, which he said were small recompense for my loyalty to the family over the years. What about yourself?'

Tommy squirmed a bit before he answered. 'Well, to be honest, the shirts and suit came from my father's brother, who died last month, and I've hardly got tuppence, never mind two pounds, in my pocket. I'm hoping I can live on our rations until we get paid.'

'Come on Tommy, I'll stand you a pint of porter and a bite to eat tonight and you can return the favour one night in Dublin.'

§

The next day Francis and his colleagues found themselves on a train bound for Dublin. Francis, ever studious, used the journey time to closely scrutinise the Constabulary Manual. He was particularly impressed with the preamble and underlined and memorised the following extract:

'Let it be remembered that the repression of crime – its prevention if possible, its detection when committed – is a vocation which there is none more honourable or useful; none more essential to the well-being of society; none more certain of securing, in the right discharge of its duties, the approbation of every right-minded person in the community.'

The manual also described the kind of behaviour that was required of all serving officers but most especially any who seek advancement in the force.

'Courtesy and politeness to the general public should be the special study of every policeman desiring advancement.' These attributes were emphasised above all others to the extent that all officers not displaying these attributes were, *'to be specifically excluded from promotion regardless of their capabilities.'*

Francis mused to himself that this was all a far cry from the hostility that had existed between the police and the population at large during the long years of land reform, when the police were often called upon by landlords to help evict troublesome tenants.

On arrival in Dublin, Francis and his new friends were ferried to the Depot in horse-drawn police tenders through the city centre and up the hill through the grand entrance to Phoenix Park.

On his first morning Francis was woken by a beastly roar which was quite unlike anything he had ever heard before. Unnerved, he slipped out of his bunk to peer out of the window but there was only the empty parade ground silently reproaching him for his childish fears. But just as he turned away scratching his head, the roar was heard again.

A shiver ran down Francis' spine and he crossed himself muttering, 'Mother of God, pray for us.' A number of the other recruits began stirring in their bunks.

'What ails ye, Francis?' asked a soft, sing song voice from out of the semi darkness. Francis recognised the voice belonged to Michael O'Connell, a gentle fellow, from the city of Cork, who Francis had met for the first time the night before.

'Did you hear that frightful noise, Michael?' asked Francis, 'What in the name of God is out there?' At which point, as though to mock him, the roaring outside was repeated.

'Ah ye fecking eejit, Francis. Do you not realise that these barracks are right beside the Dublin Zoological Gardens! Sure that roar is the king of the jungle demanding his breakfast from the Zoo-keepers. And there was me thinking that you were the smart boy in our group.'

Francis, in a failed attempt to hide his embarrassment, grabbed his wash bag and towel and headed for the latrine, tossing a nonchalant, 'Of course I did, Michael, sure I was only trying to wind you lot up.' Francis realised that he was fooling nobody, but happily for him, Michael was too much the gentleman to rub Francis' nose in it any further.

For the next six months the recruits took all of their meals in the Mess Hall. That first morning, large pots of scalding tea sat on the long rough tables bracketed with wooden benches, in rows, down the centre of the mess hall. The men soon realised that the roaring of the lions might well prove to be the most soothing sound they would hear each morning. A cacophony of voices, stamping of heavy boots, banging of pots and bustle of men, rose to the ceiling above their heads, making it necessary to shout just to be heard.

The recruits learnt about basic police work, investigation techniques, small arms firing and, as Irish towns had no separate fire brigades, fire fighting, and how to operate a fire tender. Their training schedule was busy and the men were only allowed one day off each fortnight.

§

As Francis rolled his borrowed bicycle through the gates of the barracks he paused to admire the open pastures and mature trees of the Phoenix Park. He was about to enjoy his first day off after two weeks of intensive training and classroom work. He had been in close confines with his fellow recruits for twenty four hours a day since his enrolment in Enniskillen, fifteen days before, and had decided that he needed to get away on his own and explore Dublin, a city he had never visited.

Pedalling past the Dublin Zoo and out onto the main thoroughfare which bisected the park's north-south axis, Francis marvelled at the sheer size of the park which was one of the largest urban parks in Europe, encompassing nearly two thousand acres of pasture, woodlands and playing fields. He stopped to watch the early morning mist rising slowly off the frost-whitened grass. An elderly gent, walking a large black dog, greeted Francis as he passed.

'A grand day isn't it, officer?'

'It surely is, sir. It surely is.'

'If you wait there a moment, I think you might see the herd of Sika deer coming across the playing fields opposite,' offered the old gent.

'Thanks for the tip, but I better keep moving. The cold is already getting to me.'

'Indeed, you'll be wise to keep warm, Constable, the weather may be dry but it is bitterly cold.'

When he passed through the gates and down to the north bank of the River Liffey, he encountered the rude bustle of commerce along the quays. He stopped beside a man leaning on the parapet and looking across the river.

'Hello there mister,' said this fellow when he noticed Francis.

'What's happening over there?' Asked Francis.

'Do you not know? Be japers you must be the only man in Dublin who doesn't know that you are looking at the St James's Gate Brewery. That, me young bucko, is home to Arthur Guinness and Sons, brewers of the eponymous stout.'

'Each of those barrels being lowered onto the barges contains thirty-six gallons of Guinness. What do you make of that? I've been counting the barrels and I reckon that between them three barges, there is easily eighty thousand pints just floating right there in front of us. Now isn't that a bloody marvel?'

Just as Francis agreed with his new acquaintance, steam billowed from the stack of the small train engine into the cold air.

'That little train belongs to the brewery and it brings the barrels out from those big gates and down onto the quay-side.'

'Now watch what happens. They will load a barrel into the canvas cradle and the crane will swing out and lower the barrel on top of its cousins. And do you know what, young fella? In all me years I've never seen them drop a barrel into the river.'

'Where do the barges take the beer?' Asked Francis.

'Jaysus, you really don't know nothing, do ya? Them barges will take the stout the mile and a half down the river to the Guinness ships, waiting at the port just the other side of Butt Bridge.'

Francis had a moment of déjà vu as he recalled a similar but opposite scene from his childhood when he had watched the unloading of barrels of Guinness from barges on the Manchester Canal, from where they were dispersed to public houses around the city and consumed by men just like the fellow who had injured his father all those years ago. Francis smiled wryly to himself at this thought. *Goodness me I've been living too long in close proximity to Presbyterians and Puritans. I'm starting to think like one.*

He promised himself a pint or two in a pub he had just passed, Ryan's of Parkgate Street, once he had finished his exploration of the city. 'Will I get a good pint of Guinness in that pub behind us there?' he asked his self-appointed tour guide.

'Oh now, indeed you will. Ryan's is famous for the quality of its stout. If you like, I'll come over with you and you can buy me a pint. It'd be no bother to me now.'

'Very kind of you to offer, it's a wee bit early for me. But thanks all the same for your offer. I must be off now. Cheerio.' And with that Francis remounted his bike and pedalled away.

A short sharp hoot from the steam engine across the river caught his attention. He watched with interest as the train slowly reversed on its narrow gauge tracks back through the gates of the brewery. Once the train was clear the huge black gates slid closed across the entrance.

The drill sergeant had advised Francis to simply follow the River Liffey all the way to Ringsend where the port opened out into Dublin Bay.

'You'll find that the River Liffey flows through the centre of the city creating a north-south divide,' added the sergeant. 'The south side is typically wealthier and contains elegant Georgian squares, municipal buildings and both of the city's universities, the renowned Trinity College, largely Protestant, and its mainly Catholic local rival, University College Dublin. The north side of the city has seen grander days, but its Georgian town houses have become slum tenements. Some of the poorest and most wretched people in Europe live in those slums. Filthy cess pits best avoided.'

When he reached Sackville Street Francis was impressed by the bridge there which was broader than it was long. A steady flow of jaunting cars crossed the bridge in either direction, being careful to avoid the horse-drawn double-decked trams. These much larger vehicles seemed to be the backbone of the city's public transportation system.

They ran on tracks laid into the cobbled streets and were pulled by large dray horses. The lower decks were enclosed, but the top decks were open and reached via a steep curved stairs mounted on the rear of each tram. A poster on the side of one tram advertised the electrification of the Dalkey tram route which Francis knew, from studying a map of the city, was a distant suburb on the most southerly tip of Dublin Bay. He promised himself that he would take a ride on this modern marvel as soon as it started running.

The busy cosmopolitan scene which presented itself to Francis made him feel very much the country bumpkin. But he was energised and excited by the bustle and hoped that when he finished his training that he would be assigned to a city rather than a rural posting.

A hawker, standing over his flaming brazier, was selling roasted chestnuts nearby. He was shouting at passers-by in a nasal accent barely intelligible to Francis' ear. Francis wandered over to warm his hands and buy a packet of chestnuts. The hawker looked Francis up and down said 'Let me guess, you are a trainee Peeler, up from the Bog, to be trained at the Phoenix Park Depot. Am I right?'

Francis smiled and said, 'Well the new great coat is a bit of a giveaway, but I'm an Ulsterman not, "up from the Bogs".'

'Oh, no offence intended, me bucko,' laughed the hawker.

'But I have to warn you, you won't like the famous Dublin wit if you're so touchy about where ya come from. Anyone who's not a Dub or a member of the gentry is automatically a Bogman in these parts.' The hawker paused and added, 'Forgive me for saying so, but you don't sound much like an Ulsterman, more English than anything I'd say meself.'

'You're not the first man to say so,' Francis replied. 'I was born and raised in Manchester, but in an Ulster family, and we returned to Ulster when I was still a wee lad.'

'Well now, fair play to you,' said the hawker, but before he could add more, he was interrupted by another customer. Francis took the opportunity to escape and wheeled his bike to the east side of the bridge and continued his exploration of the city.

A little further east, having passed under an imposing railway bridge, Francis watched live cattle being loaded onto one ship and coal being unloaded from another. He could see from their markings that both ships were out of Liverpool. Huge cranes, with grab buckets driven by steam engines, hoisted the coal out of the ship's hold and dropped it onto the dockside in great shining black mountains. From there it would be transported to domestic and commercial customers on the back of large horse-drawn carts.

Francis watched a group of street urchins dodging in and around these carts and picking up any lumps of coal which fell onto the street. A young policeman, in the uniform of the Dublin Metropolitan Police, was unsuccessfully trying to chase them away. When he spotted Francis he wandered over, 'Mother of God, what a stupid way for a grown man like me to be spending his time,' opened the policeman.

'Why bother?' asked Francis.

'Well, last week one of those scallywags knocked open the tailgate of a cart just as it was heading out along the quays. The driver didn't notice and we had a near riot as several hundredweight of coal was spread along the roadway. Every pauper in the city seemed to get wind of it and descended on the place to grab what they could before they scarpered back to their hovels.'

'Can't say I blame them, what with it being so cold and all. But still stealing is stealing and mustn't be tolerated.'

CHAPTER FOUR

Empire and Trades Union

When Queen Victoria celebrated her Diamond Jubilee, in 1897, the British Empire straddled the globe at the height of its power. But social and political changes were coming in the decade ahead. Trades Union developed and by 1907 Jim Larkin had emerged as the hero of the working classes in Britain and Ireland.

Following the completion of his training Francis was packing for a brief visit home to Tempo. Finishing top of his class allowed him the privilege of requesting the location of his first posting. He wanted to balance his new-found fondness for city life with proximity to his family so he asked to be stationed in Belfast, Ireland's second city, where his sister Susan lived with her husband Tom Molloy. Belfast was also less than a couple of hours by train from the family farm.

'Here's the top man,' said Michael O'Connell, as he wandered into the bunkroom. 'So you turned out to be the clever one after all, Francis.'

'Good morning, Michael, how are you this morning?' replied Francis, refusing to take Michael's bait.

'Grand as any man might be allowing for all the porter we consumed last night. Thanks be to God that we don't have any marching around that parade ground to do this morning.

Square bashing has to be the most futile and boring thing they made us do these past six months.'

'I agree Michael. But the passing out parade was great craic yesterday wasn't it?'

'To be honest I could have lived without it. All turned out in full dress uniforms to take the salute of Commandant Pennington. Like a bunch of tin-pot soldiers.'

'You know, Michael, that as Commandant Pennington only took up his post this year, our passing out parade was his first such ceremony. It's hardly surprising that he wanted a big show.'

'I have to admit,' responded Michael, 'the mounted troops were resplendent in their dress uniforms. Riding Master Tyson was clearly eager to impress Pennington, and in all fairness, he made sure that the horses were groomed and brushed to a shiny gloss. I thought it was a bit over the top the way the mounted troopers drew their swords and waved them in the air in salute when we were dismissed.'

'I suppose you are right Michael. It was all a bit militaristic. Still, you have to say, the pomp and ceremony was a bit of fun.'

§

Two men stepped out of the rear entrance of McHugh's Restaurant in the centre of Belfast. They looked furtively back over their shoulders as though to check to see if they were being followed. They didn't notice the police constable walking towards them on the other side of the street.

Francis was out on his first solo patrol. He had been assigned to Musgrave Police Barracks, in the centre of Belfast. The barracks was only a few years old, having been built following the murderous riots which had swept through Belfast during the passage of the 1886 Irish Home Rule Bill. Belfast was growing rapidly into one of the most important industrial cities in the United Kingdom and consequently suffered from a housing shortage. To house the expanding police force, the barracks was large and included a range of accommodation from single rooms for officers like Francis, to large family quarters.

Francis remembered his surprise at this domesticity when he first arrived at the barracks. By now he was used to the barracks courtyard being perpetually strung with lines laden with drying clothes, and having hordes of children scampering about and playing with family cats and dogs. He had come to appreciate that this domestic activity gave the otherwise austere barracks an almost cosy and comfortable atmosphere.

Francis had settled quickly into his new home and enjoyed living at close quarters with his extended 'police family'. The sectarianism which afflicted much of the city was absent in the barracks and the policemen and their families rubbed along well together regardless of their religious or political persuasion.

Francis was making his last loop of the city centre when he noticed the furtiveness of the two men. The Albert Memorial Clock tower, which he had just passed, told him that it was ten minutes to midnight. The city was calm and peaceful, the weather warm and the early August night sky hardly dark. Francis walked quickly but silently across the street and slipped his nightstick out of the loop on his belt. When the men turned to walk towards the clock tower they were somewhat startled to find a tall policeman standing in their way.

'Good evening, gentlemen.'

'Officer,' nodded one of the men as they both tried to keep walking.

He stuck out his nightstick to block their path and said, 'I'm sorry to have to bother you. But I must say that you both seem very nervous. Is there anything wrong?'

'No, sir.'

'Well then you won't mind if I ask you to turn out your pockets, will you?'

One of the men reacted aggressively. 'Why should we? We are just leaving work at McHugh's there,' he said indicating the premises from which they had emerged with a raised thumb. 'We are both waiters in the restaurant and you have no cause to be bothering ordinary working men like ourselves.'

'Well as you ask so politely, I will tell you why I'd like to see what you have in your pockets. Firstly the way you were sneaking out just now made me curious; secondly I'm wondering why you are both wearing large overcoats on this lovely warm evening and thirdly you are on my patch and you'll do what I say. Now if that's all clear enough for you, I suggest that we step into McHugh's, where we can settle this matter quickly.'

Francis pressed his nightstick into the chests of the two men, making it clear that this last remark was more of a command then a suggestion. Resignedly the two men turned and Francis rapped his stick on the restaurant door.

'Jimmy? Donald? What's up?' enquired a young woman's voice, as the door to the restaurant was slowly opened from within.

Francis stepped forward and said, 'Excuse me for knocking so late Miss. Do you know these gentlemen?'

'Yes, they are, or I should say were, waiters here. Mr McHugh sacked them both this evening,' answered the girl, who had been interrupted in her cleaning of the premises.

'And is Mr McHugh about?'

'I'll fetch him from the cellar. He's down there counting the night's takings.'

'Thank you, Miss,' Francis waited a moment before turning to the two men. 'Now gentlemen, would you oblige me by emptying your pockets onto that table there, please.'

Reluctantly, and with a sorrowful glance at each other, the men began dropping silverware onto the table. A heavy tread on the cellar stairs alerted the room to McHugh's approach.

'What are you two blackguards doing in my restaurant? Didn't I tell you both never to darken the door again?' McHugh raised an eyebrow in Francis' direction, 'Officer, may I ask what this is all about?'

Francis stepped aside so that McHugh could see the pile of silverware now stacked on the table. 'Why you thieving so-and-sos,' McHugh roared advancing on the now cowering pair.

'Steady, Mr McHugh,' commanded Francis. 'These men are in my custody and I'll not allow you to harm them. However if you will press charges I'll be more than pleased to take these fellows back to the barracks under arrest.'

McHugh stopped short. 'Flogging will be too good for these thieves. I fired them half an hour ago because I suspected that they were pilfering from me. Arrest away, and get them out of my sight.'

'Very good, Mr McHugh. I will come back tomorrow afternoon to take a statement from you. I assume you can confirm that the silverware here belongs to this restaurant? I'm afraid that I'll have to take it with me, so it can be recorded as evidence. I will bring it back tomorrow, if that is acceptable.'

Francis cuffed the two men together and escorted them around the corner to the police barracks. He felt compelled to ask the men, 'What possessed you to do something as stupid as stealing from your employer? Don't you realise that if I'd not caught you tonight, Mr McHugh would have figured out tomorrow what had happened when they set up for lunch?' He got no response and shook his head ruefully as they made their way to the station.

Denis Shanagher, the desk sergeant, smiled broadly as Francis came through the door with his first arrests in tow. 'Well, Constable Maguire, have you really bagged a couple of bad uns on your first patrol? The grin on Francis' face was all the confirmation the Sergeant needed. 'Well done lad. Bring them round here and we'll find a cell for them while you give me the details and I'll fill in the log.'

§

Six months later a letter arrived for Francis from Commandant Pennington at the Depot in Dublin. He, Pennington, had been asked to nominate recent recruits to add to the ranks of a contingent which would accept Queen Victoria's request for an RIC escort for her Diamond Jubilee celebrations in London in the summer of 1897.

One criterion which had been set to guide Pennington's nominations was that all of the police officers in the escort should be a minimum of six feet tall. So, less than a year into his career as a policeman, Francis found himself with a central part to play in the queen's grand parade through the streets of London.

Francis' journey to London began late on the evening of Friday 18 June via a ferry from Belfast to Liverpool, reversing the journey he had made with his family eleven years earlier. At Liverpool he joined with the RIC mounted troop that had arrived the same day from Dublin. The troop, drawn from all around Ireland, had spent the prior week training for the parade at the Depot in Dublin. The mounted policemen, their horses, and their escort then travelled on from Liverpool to London on a high-speed train, which thundered through the countryside, arriving in Euston Station in London on the Saturday evening.

The Jubilee parade was to take place on the following Tuesday, with the RIC in the place of honour, immediately to the rear of the queen's escort. Francis and his colleagues, marching on foot, would provide a security flank for the mounted officers as they passed through the streets of London.

The Mounted Troop Commander was DI John Tyson, Riding Master at the Depot in Dublin. He remembered Francis from his time at the Depot and following a mess dinner in the Wellington barracks, where the RIC contingent were billeted, he invited Francis to join him and some of the other mounted officers for a few celebratory beers in a public house nearby. Mounted military and police officers from around the Empire had come to join in the celebrations. Francis met Indian

Cavalry officers, Canadian Mounties and Australian Troopers. A Canadian officer regaled Francis with heroic tales of lone officers pursuing murderers across hundreds of miles of empty wilderness. Francis had the time of his life and was immensely proud to be part of this worldwide gathering.

Monday found Francis and his colleagues pressing uniforms, polishing boots and shining belts and buckles. Once finished they had time to do some sightseeing and see the preparations being made for the big day.

And what a day it was. Following the parade, the queen wrote in her journal, 'A never to be forgotten day. No one ever, I believe, has met with such an ovation as was given to me, passing through those six miles of streets, including Constitution Hill. The crowds were quite indescribable and their enthusiasm truly marvellous and deeply touching. The cheering was quite deafening and every face seemed to be filled with joy.'

Francis spent that evening celebrating in a London pub with his new friends from around the world. 'Gentlemen a toast,' was the phrase most often repeated.

Everything was toasted; the Empire, the queen, this and that regiment, the RIC, the Canadian Mounties, the parade, the Jubilee, and so on it went late into the night.

When the landlord called time there was little question as to what the last toast would be. A tall sergeant-major from the Horse Guards, made the call in a huge baritone voice, his bristling moustache quivered as he bellowed, 'Officers, gentlemen, please be upstanding and join me in a final toast.' A loud rumble of chairs being pushed back accompanied the clomping of many military boots containing unsteady feet, arms were thrown about shoulders. 'The queen,' barked the sergeant-major and he was immediately echoed by the whole company. 'The queen.'

As Francis climbed into his bunk that night, he felt sure he had consumed one too many. He mused to himself as to how far all of this was from Tempo and wondered what his old friends, the boys from Edenmore, would have to say if they had seen him this evening. He has toasted the Empire, the Queen and much else that his Nationalist friends would sneer at. *But,* he thought, *the Canadians I met have their independence and are more than happy, indeed they are clearly proud, to be part of this great British Empire on which the sun never sets.*

§

He visited his sister Susan in Belfast regularly and the rest of his family in Tempo as often as possible. His brother John succumbed to tuberculosis in January 1901. The funeral was a sad, grey and cold occasion. Francis' father Roger was disconsolate. 'It's neither right nor natural for a father to bury his son. Keep well and keep strong Francis, for I could not bear to lose you as well my boy.'

Francis had offered to resign from the police force and return to Tempo to help on the farm. 'Don't be daft son,' was his father's reaction. 'We will miss your brother greatly. He was a kind and gentle soul. May he rest in peace. But, in truth, son, John was not much by way of a helping hand about the farm. Annie, Patrick and myself can more than cope. You get back to Belfast and continue to make us proud.'

The day in day out job of policing the streets of central Belfast occupied Francis for the next ten years. He progressed in seniority through the ranks, following a system of examinations, first to Acting Sergeant in December 1903 and then full Sergeant in September 1906.

Francis was as disciplined in his approach to physical fitness as he was to the development of his knowledge of policing. His studies and his work schedule were managed so as to accommodate plenty of exercise. Early in his time in Belfast he was pleased to be 'invited' to join a local rugby club, Sydenham RFC. The desk sergeant, Denis Shanagher, who assisted Francis with his first arrest, more or less bullied Francis into joining the team. 'It will do your fitness the world of good lad,' he told Francis. 'With your size, your height and speed you're a natural. Besides, it will be an advantage for you to literally rub shoulders with some of our Unionist brethren on a regular basis. The top brass hereabouts are quite keen on rugby these days.'

§

Francis was running hard and gasping for breath. Several large men bore down on him. A gap opened in front of him and he barged through and accelerated away from an outstretched hand. Then he leapt so high into the air that it seemed his life depended on what happened next. Turning as he jumped, Francis created a cradle with his hands and forearms and the arching oval ball dropped safely into his grasp even while he was still several feet in the air.

Landing on his stronger right leg Francis pivoted to his left, surprising the other players who were turning in the opposite direction, which was where they clearly expected him to run. He cut a diagonal line towards the far corner of the pitch but despite his fitness, he was running out of steam. The opposition fullback looked sure to run him down before he reached the try line. The defence had also turned to follow him across the pitch. Confident now that the defence was committed, Francis flicked a deft pass back inside and behind. His teammate, George Deacon, had come off the left wing and was there to receive the perfectly weighted ball, which he gathered with ease. George had a clear line to the posts and ran in an unopposed try. The subsequent conversion kick, taken by the reliable Sydenham fullback William Andrews, sailed between the uprights.

This score created a five point advantage which Sydenham maintained to the final whistle. The victory helped to earn Sydenham the 1907-08 Divisional title. The following season Sydenham would play first division rugby.

Francis was glad to have rugby to distract him, especially in 1907, which was otherwise a very difficult year, not just for Francis but for the whole of Belfast's police force and for that matter, most of Belfast's working men and women.

§

James Larkin climbed onto the back of a cart which served him as a platform. A cold, biting January wind rushed in off Belfast Lough. A large crowd had gathered in Sailortown, Belfast's waterside village, which was home to over five thousand people crammed into tiny, airless, row houses hugging the docks. These were Belfast's labourers, cigarette makers and mill workers, unskilled and, unlike members of the Trades Union, unrepresented. Larkin aimed to change that and was attempting to organise these workers as members of the National Union of Dock Labourers. The gap between the pay and conditions of Belfast's skilled and unskilled workers was wider than anywhere else in the UK.

'Brothers and sisters,' boomed Larkin. 'The great appear great because we are on our knees: Let us rise. Get up off your knees and look your oppressor in the eye. Belfast will forever remember this glorious day. Today is the day when we say enough. Today is the day we join hands together. Today is the day we refute the sectarianism which divides us. A division which does not empower us, but empowers those who wish to keep us subjugated. Today is the day we find strength in our unity. Today is the day the National Union of Dock Workers says to our brothers and sisters in Belfast: "We are with you. Join us and together we will fight our oppressors."'

Francis was standing at the edge of the crowd. He was wearing the sergeant's stripes he had earned the previous September and was supervising a large patrol of policemen who had been assigned to ensure that the gathering was peaceful and law abiding. The slum dwellers tended to avoid contact with the police and most gave Francis a wide berth.

Larkin's huge hands waved above the heads of the crowd. He spotted Francis who got a jeer from the crowd when he said, 'I see that the police are here in force today. Now do you suppose that they are here to protect you, or are they the unwitting lackeys of the rich and powerful, sent here to protect privilege and keep the likes of you and me in our place?'

Francis judiciously decided not to make any notes of Larkin's speech. He was entirely sympathetic to the miserable lot of these workers and was actually delighted to hear them encouraged to set aside their sectarian differences and unite in common cause to better their own and their families' lives.

What no one, including Francis, anticipated was just how successful Larkin would be in his recruiting. By April he had over two thousand members. The summer saw strikes and lockouts, union members dismissed and replaced with 'blackleg' labourers, brought from the mainland, by Belfast's employers.

These blacklegs needed police escorts to protect them and the Belfast police found themselves under huge pressure, working long and difficult hours without any overtime pay.

When Francis got back to the Musgrave barracks after a routine patrol in mid-July the barracks was buzzing. 'What's happened?' He asked the desk sergeant.

'A constable by the name of Barrett refused to escort a blackleg worker this morning.'

'I assume Barrett was suspended?'

'Naturally, but he's popular and there's a lot of talk about how he should be supported. Everyone has been scurrying around like headless chickens. A meeting has been called for next week and everyone up to the rank of sergeant is being asked to attend. Will you go, Francis?'

'I don't know. I'll have to think about that.'

One week after PC Barrett's suspension eight hundred police officers, about two thirds of the city's entire force, attended an angry meeting at Musgrave barracks. Francis attended so that he might at least have a say in whatever decisions were made. The mood was angry. Voices spoke up for the beleaguered strikers and others complained that the police were being asked to protect the rights of the bosses but without any compensation for all of the extra hours.

'Why should we be party to efforts to subdue ordinary working people?' asked one constable.

An older sergeant, bristling with anger, shouted, 'It's not our place to question our orders. You youngsters have no idea what you are talking about. What do you think will happen if we don't do our jobs? I'll tell you, there'll be mayhem on the streets. Riots and looting and God knows what. If there are no police to maintain order, the bosses will employ their own security. Then you just watch what happens to your "ordinary working people". You lot are dangerous idiots. I want nothing to do with you.' With that he stormed out of the meeting.

A momentary silence was broken only by murmuring. Eventually another officer spoke up. 'But it's hardly fair that we take on all of the extra work and not be paid any overtime. Is it? And who benefits from our efforts. Belfast's workers or Belfast's bosses?'

Francis listened but did not speak. It was clear that the majority of the men wanted to take some action to demonstrate their level of frustration. Ultimately, the meeting voted to give notice of a strike. A county inspector who had been watching the proceeding from the rear of the hall tried to intervene. He was manhandled in the midst of the crowd and hustled toward an exit. Outraged, he barked at those nearest to him, 'By God you'll regret this. Take your bloody hands off me.' He swiped at one constable with the back of his hand. Francis stepped between the senior officer and the constables nearest to him.

'Allow me to escort you, sir,' he said, indicating a side door, and gestured for the senior man to walk in front. The officer composed himself as best he could, nodded an acknowledgement and marched stiffly to the door.

Telegrams to Dublin alerted the authorities to the threat of anarchy. A hastily convened meeting, between Earl Aberdeen, Lord Lieutenant of Ireland and Colonel Sir Neville

Chamberlain, RIC Inspector General, quickly descended into a shouting match.

'What kind of people have you been recruiting? Bloody Bolsheviks in the bloody police! I'm dumbfounded. And what did I read in my paper this morning? Jim Larkin suggesting that the police should form their own Trade Union.' Bellowed the Earl. 'Your head is on the block Inspector General. The Prime Minister wanted to know why I had not sacked you already. But I told him that you would fix this problem and I meant permanently. Now get out of my sight before I change my mind. Send the General in when you pass him. He's waiting in the outer office. I'm going to declare martial law in Belfast until this mess is cleared up.'

That same evening Earl Aberdeen had a secret dinner in Dublin Castle with William Baird, owner of the Belfast Telegraph.

'William, good of you come down so swiftly. I want to get your counsel on this bloody mess in Belfast. Some are saying that we have been too tolerant of Mr Larkin and his ilk but quite frankly, the government sees these strikes as a private matter between Belfast's employers and their workers. We have been somewhat surprised that things have been allowed to get so far out of hand.'

'There's a whiff of popery about all of this my Lord. We have had bona fide Trades Union in Belfast for some time representing our skilled tradesmen, fine upstanding Protestants in the main. Larkin's new Trade Union is made up of unskilled rabble, the majority of whom are Roman Catholic.'

'Are you implying that there is a Nationalist element in all of this?'

'That would be over simplifying, my Lord. Despite the preponderance of Catholics, a large percentage of the strikers are Protestant and loyal but their Trade Union could be weakened if, for example, a newspaper managed to insinuate that Catholic strikers are being favoured by the Union when it comes to strike pay.'

'Ah, I begin to follow your drift. Divide and conquer, eh? Very good. A bit of sectarian scaremongering to bring our Presbyterian brethren to heel. Will it work?'

'It always has in the past, my Lord.'

'Then I shall leave the matter in your capable hands. We would not want any suggestion that the government was interfering with the freedom of the press, now would we? Another port my friend?'

The next day the army were sent into Belfast and for all intents and purposes the city remained under martial law for the rest of the summer. As distressing as this was to a law and order man like Francis, he was even more distressed by how the establishment, especially the press, used sectarian scaremongering to break the strikers' unity.

Following being labelled Nationalist trouble-makers by the press, the strikers were as good as defeated by September. The police force in Belfast was substantially reorganised, with a quarter of the force reassigned to stations away from Belfast. By the autumn of 1907, the city's sectarian divisions were back in place.

CHAPTER FIVE

Marriage and children

Officers in the Royal Irish Constabulary were not allowed to marry until they had served ten years on the force and then not without the permission of the local district inspector.

Early in the new year of 1908 Sergeant Shanagher issued an unexpected invitation to Francis to come to tea and meet the family. The Shanagher family lived at 4 Alameda Terrace, on the Falls Road, a staunchly Catholic and Nationalist enclave. Francis wore his religion lightly, devout but not demonstrative, so as he walked up to the front door of the Shanagher home the following Sunday afternoon, he was a little apprehensive about just how Catholic he needed to be to pass muster.

The door was opened by Mrs Shanagher, 'Sergeant Maguire, how lovely to meet you. Do come in please. We have been looking forward to meeting you. Denis has talked about you very often and, you know, it's not easy to impress my husband.'

Francis felt the genuine warmth in Mrs Shanagher's greeting and was immediately at ease. 'The pleasure is all mine, Mrs Shanagher. Your husband has been a great support to me since I arrived in Belfast twelve years ago. I'm delighted to finally meet his family.'

Mrs Shanagher showed Francis into the front parlour where Sergeant Shanagher greeted him equally warmly and introduced him to the Misses Shanaghers, all of whom were charming, but none of whom were married. Francis was introduced in turn to Margret, May, Teresa, Getta and Kathleen. He also met the youngest member of the household, Denis, named after his father, and a strapping fourteen-year-old youth who scarcely managed a polite 'Hello' before he dashed out to who knows what distraction. The eldest brother, Edward, was away working in England.

All of the young women were striking but Francis found himself intimidated by the older sisters who were somewhat austere. Teresa, on the other hand, with her smooth oval face and direct but open gaze, immediately captivated Francis. Her hair was worn high on her head and scraped back off her forehead. Her dark curls seemed to be fighting the obvious efforts which had been made to restrain them. Her long and slender neck was encased in the high ruffled collar of her white blouse. Francis realised that he was staring and had to consciously pull his attention elsewhere in the room. Teresa, who found this tall dark and handsome man the very picture of her ideal man, was delighted to notice that she had caught his attention.

Unintentionally breaking the slight tension which was building in the room, Mrs Shanagher entered with a large tray laden with crockery and the other accruements of afternoon tea. She set her tray on the sideboard, under a framed picture of The Sacred Heart of Jesus. Her daughters assisted in the production of plates of scones, tea cake and sandwiches.

'Sergeant Maguire, may I offer you a cup of tea? How do you take it?'

'With milk and two sugars please, Mrs Shanagher.'

Francis caught Teresa glancing at him a number of times. She did not blush when this happened but smiled briefly and then looked away. He was not used to this kind of directness and self-confidence in a woman. He felt a powerful urge to get to know this beautiful and daring creature.

Francis became a regular guest at the Shanagher household. He liked the family but had to find a way of dealing with the difficulty of bypassing the older sisters in order to pursue Teresa. The Shanagher women were very strict about such niceties and Francis found it difficult to get time with Teresa without the chaperoning company of one or the other of her sisters, or her mother. There was also the delicate matter of courting the younger sister of two older and unmarried sisters.

Francis decided to broach the subject with Sergeant Shanagher.

'Denis, may I have a quiet word?' Francis asked one evening as he and Denis were finishing a shift at Musgrave barracks.

'Of course, do you want to step into one of the interview rooms?'

'No, I think I'd rather buy you a beer. How about the Garrick on Chichester Street?'

When they had settled in the pub Francis decided to dive right in and opened with, 'Sergeant Shanagher, I have a very delicate and personal reason for asking to talk privately with you.'

'Oh? Must be bad if you've starting by calling me Sergeant?'

'No, not bad, but definitely delicate.'

'Well, spit it out man.'

'I want to ask for your permission to "walk out" with Teresa.'

Denis burst out laughing. 'My God man, I thought you were going to tell me you were having an affair with the county inspector's wife! Of course you can "walk out" with Teresa, as you so quaintly put it. Although I have to warn you that her mother will insist on a chaperone at all times.'

'You don't think her mother or older sisters will object? After all Teresa has just turned twenty and her older sisters are both in their mid-twenties.'

'Elizabeth and I were beginning to wonder if any of our girls would ever find husbands. But May has started talking about joining a convent. So the issue of your bypassing her older sisters to court Teresa is not as big a problem as it might otherwise have been. Besides, Elizabeth likes you and that is more than half the battle. Come on, let me buy another round before we go back and tell her.'

And so began Francis' relationship with Teresa. All of the niceties of a post-Victorian courtship were duly observed until a year or so later when a minor scandal was created. May spotted Francis and Teresa walking without a chaperone across the open fields behind Alameda Terrace. 'Mother come in here and look out that window. I've said more than once that you give that sister of mine too much leeway and now look she'll bring disgrace on all our heads.'

'Oh for goodness sake May, you are already displaying the rigidity of a nun. They are just walking out in the open. I'll have her father have a word with Teresa.'

That evening, his hand forced, Teresa's father admonished her for being so 'immodest.'

When Francis heard this from Teresa as they strolled around the Botanical Gardens, Teresa's mother and her sister Margret keeping a discrete distance, he said 'Well, Miss Shanagher, there's only one thing for it.'

'And what might that be Sergeant Maguire?'

'I'm going to have to ask your father for your hand in marriage. Otherwise you and your sisters will have to live the rest of your lives in purdah.'

'Francis, be serious now and don't make fun of my family.'

‘Teresa, I have never been more serious in my life. I want you to be my wife and the mother of my children.’ Francis paused, hearing himself being pompous and presuming. He stopped and turned towards Teresa taking her hands in his. ‘Teresa, I love you and I would very much like you to do me the honour of becoming my wife.’

It did not surprise Francis that Teresa did not immediately accept his proposal. ‘Francis, I love you but we should wait until you have spoken to my father before we talk more about this.’ But there was warmth in her eyes as she spoke and she allowed herself to caress the backs of his hands with her thumbs.

‘About time too, young man.’ Was how Denis responded that evening, in the front room at Alameda Terrace. ‘Let me shake your hand my dear boy. I’m delighted and I have no doubt that Teresa’s mother will be too.’

Once their engagement was announced Francis and Teresa were allowed a little more privacy together. One of their favourite things to do was go ballroom dancing. Francis delighted in twirling Teresa around a dance floor and enjoyed the admiring glances the elegant couple got from the other dancers.

However, as the year progressed, Francis worried that Teresa might not fully understand what life with him would likely entail. He was very aware that the RIC routinely moved senior officers around the country.

'Teresa as a policeman's daughter you have some understanding of what life might be like married to me. But I'm not like your father; he was happy to stay at the rank of Sergeant as that meant that he would not have to move his family around the country. But I have plans, Teresa. I want to progress up through the ranks and if I work diligently and pass all of the exams, I hope that I might make it to the senior ranks one day.'

'Francis your ambition is one of the things I love about you. Why do you think it might worry me?'

'You have been fortunate in as much as you have lived your whole life in one place. If I'm promoted we will be moved around a lot. Perhaps every couple of years.'

'It will be an adventure, Francis. And I look forward to sharing your journey with you. But just one request please.'

'Anything, my love.'

'If we are blessed with children and I pray to God that we are, then I would like to come back here to Belfast for the births of those children and be with my own family.'

'Of course, my dear. I would want nothing but the best for you and if you will be happiest having our babies here, then here is where you shall be. I promise.'

The following summer, on 21 July 1910, Francis and Teresa were married in St Paul's Church on the Falls Road in Belfast. Denis, proud father of the bride, was not in uniform as he had retired from the police the year before. Francis was thirty-six when he married and Teresa twenty-one. After the ceremony, Elizabeth Shanagher, Francis' new mother-in-law, said, 'I can't tell you how pleased I am that you are now part of our family, Francis.'

'Mrs Shanagher, this is the happiest day of my life. I have got myself a beautiful wife and a beautiful mother-in-law. What more could I wish for?'

'You are an incorrigible flirt, Francis. But you are now a married man and need to behave like one. Now go and greet your father, he is trying to catch your eye.'

§

'Sergeant Maguire, you and your patrol will be in charge of crowd control at the main gates. The shipyard will be responsible for checking tickets but be sure to position enough men around the gates so as to discourage any gate-crashing. Remember, we are expecting a very large crowd. There should be no reason for any disturbances, but let's not take any chances.'

Francis and his colleagues were being briefed on the operational plans for the management of what was expected to be the largest crowd ever assembled in Belfast. The date was 31 May 1911. Belfast was about to give birth to its most famous offspring, RMS Titanic; pride of the White Star Line and the largest ship ever built in the Harland and Wolff Shipyards.

Recounting the experience to the heavily pregnant Teresa, Francis said, 'What a pity you could not have seen her launched; and to have felt the excitement of the crowd. It was estimated that over one hundred thousand people watched the launch. That's one in every three people living in the city!'

Teresa, holding her bloated stomach said, 'Francis all I want for now is to launch our own little ship,' as she shifted her weight in a failed attempt to find a comfortable position. Francis laughed loudly and swept Teresa up in his arms and danced her around the parlour. 'My song and dance man,' smiled Teresa holding Francis tightly as he two-stepped the pair of them around the room. 'You could give Vernon Castle a run for his money. You know that the only reason I married you is because you can dance. Now put me down you ridiculous man before you do the baby a mischief.'

Francis and Teresa lived the first year of their marriage in family quarters at Musgrave barracks. But barracks life did not suit Teresa's sensibilities. She was uncomfortable living cheek by jowl with so many families and the natural rough and tumble of communal living was not to her liking.

Francis was entirely supportive. 'Don't let it bother you, my love. I will get permission to move out of the barracks. To be honest, having lived here so long myself I'll be more than happy to have a place of our own.'

So, just one month after the launch of the Titanic, their first child, Annie Teresa, was born and the family moved into a small terraced house at 16 Agincourt Street. This was close to the Botanical Gardens and Queens University and a short distance from the centre of the city. Their second child, a boy, Rory Joseph, was born in January 1913 and their third, Denis Patrick, in August 1914. Denis was always called by the Irish version of his name, Donagh, to distinguish him from his grandfather and his uncle.

These early years of the new century's second decade were joyous times for the Maguire family but they were tumultuous years for Belfast, the United Kingdom and for Europe. And Francis, willing or not, was soon to be dragged into the mire.

CHAPTER SIX

Home rule is Rome rule

In the UK general election in January 1910, The Irish Parliamentary Party won the majority of seats in Ireland with 85 MPs. The Liberal Party lost the large majority it carried into the election but remained the largest party across the UK by winning 274 seats. The Conservative Party, when combined with the Liberal Unionists, who opposed Home Rule, won 272 seats and Prime Minister H.H. Asquith was therefore reliant on the support of Irish MPs to form his new government. Home Rule was back on the political agenda.

The Ulster Unionists recruited Edward Carson, a Dublin barrister, to lead their opposition to Home Rule. Five hundred thousand Ulster men signed the Ulster Covenant, pledging allegiance to the United Kingdom and vowing to resist Home Rule by "all means necessary." Over one hundred thousand men joined the Ulster Volunteer Force (UVF), a paramilitary group formed by Carson to add muscle to unionism. In response the, at first scornful, Nationalists, formed their own paramilitary force, the National Volunteers.

Francis was standing in the rain outside a polling station in central Belfast, on a cold and wet December's evening in 1910. He was wearing a large waterproof cape over his great coat, but he was none the less wet and cold and feeling a little sorry for himself. A young constable standing with

Francis tried to make conversation. 'Sergeant I know that the police are not allowed to vote but I was wondering, just out of curiosity, how you would vote if you could?'

'Well now, Constable. There are good reasons why policemen can't vote, but even if we could my instincts would be to keep my opinions to myself. I find the sectarian quality of all candidates standing here in Belfast a bit disturbing. But as the saying goes, we get the political leaders we deserve. God help us.'

After a few minutes, Francis added, 'This election has been called because The House of Lords rejected the so called "Peoples Budget" proposed by the government. It is to my mind nonsense that a small number of men of privilege, sitting in an unelected chamber, can ride roughshod over the wishes of an elected government. So I would like to see the Liberals on the mainland get a clear majority with which they will be able to remove the veto power of the Lords. As for Ireland I have no doubt that the Irish Nationalist Parties will sweep the board as usual.'

§

A little more than a year later in February 1912, Francis was on duty outside the Grand Hotel in Belfast. He had a large and heavily armed patrol of RIC officers in his command. His Head Constable had been given the responsibility for the security and safety of Winston Churchill, who was visiting Belfast to speak in favour of the Home Rule Bill. Francis was put in charge of the patrol which had to secure the area around the hotel.

'In short,' Churchill reasoned, 'the protections offered in this Bill safeguard the religious liberty and industry of Irish Unionists and remove all of the dangers, real and perceived, of Home Rule.' With his usual flair for the apt phrase Churchill went on to say, 'As far as the broader governance and security of the whole of the United Kingdom is concerned, this Bill, when enacted, will right the wrong where the Irish have too much power in Britain and not enough power in Ireland.'

Churchill had been addressing a largely Nationalist and supportive audience at Celtic Park. Not everyone in Belfast was appreciative of his intervention. As the car conveying Churchill and his wife Clementine, returned to the Grand Hotel it turned into Berry Street to approach the side entrance. A large and hostile Unionist crowd had gathered outside the hotel. They hurled abuse at Churchill: 'Popery,' 'Rome Rule,' 'Shame on you,' 'No surrender.'

Berry Street is narrow and as Churchill's car negotiated the corner the police line was broken by a surge from the crowd and the car was suddenly surrounded by angry men banging on the roof and violently shaking the car. The driver made a terrible mistake and stopped the car for fear of running over some protesters. The crowd was delighted and began rocking the car so violently that it nearly tipped onto its side.

'Batons,' called Francis drawing his own. 'Clear a path in front of the car now,' he roared to his men. 'Follow me.'

He charged forward swinging his baton. A few heads were split and the crowd parted in front of the charging policemen. Francis shouted at the driver, 'Drive now, and don't stop for anything.'

As the car swept past, the remarkably composed face of Mrs Churchill peered through a side window. Beside her, Winston Churchill tipped his hat to Francis and the car turned safely into the hotel entrance. With Churchill's departure the fight went out of the crowd which dispersed without further trouble.

'By God, that was close,' said a voice behind Francis, who turned to find his Head Constable looking ashen. 'Well done, Francis. Your quick thinking saved the day. I dread to think what might have happened if the car had been turned over. I dare say the brass would not have been impressed.'

'Honestly, sir,' replied Francis. 'If that car had gone over we might have had a murder on our hands. I think we were lucky. The crowd relented when they realised that Mrs Churchill was in the car.'

'Thank God for small mercies, Sergeant. Let's get the streets cleared and get back to the barracks.'

Churchill sent a letter of appreciation to the RIC officers at Musgrave Barracks. He expressed appreciation for their professionalism from both he and his wife who, Churchill confessed, was the cooler of the pair during the incident. The district inspector had the letter pinned to the general notice board. Given the political sensitivity, the authorities chose to gloss over the incident and no commendations were issued. Francis later regretted not asking if he might keep the letter as a memento.

§

Eighteen months had passed since the incident involving Churchill in Belfast. At Carson's beckoning Ulster Unionists had organised a series of 'monster rallies' culminating in this 'Ulster Day' in September 1912.

Edward Carson, reviewing the huge crowd assembled in Belfast to protest against Home Rule, turned to James Craig, leader of the Ulster Unionists and said, 'Jim, did you ever imagine we would get this much support? It is really quite overwhelming. The government can't ignore us now.'

Craig responded, 'Edward, we have your extraordinary oratory skills to thank for our success. And of course your idea for an Ulster Covenant. With five hundred thousand signatures who would dare ignore us? Your master stroke was the formation of the Ulster Volunteer Force. Look at them forming up out there. Once they are all armed no one will oppose us. How many have joined?'

'Coming up on one hundred thousand Volunteers,' answered Carson.

'Whatever about Asquith and his Liberals, I'm sure that we can rely on the Conservatives,' said Craig. 'Did you read what Andrew Bonar Law said last week about our Ulster Volunteers? He said that he could not envision any steps which might be taken by Ulster's Unionists which he would not be prepared to support.'

'Do you worry about Redmond's National Volunteers?'

'They don't have the political support we have on the mainland and they will find it much harder to raise enough money to buy arms. Our friends in high places will make sure that the army won't oppose us but they will clamp down on any efforts by the Nationalists to arm themselves in any meaningful way.'

'Churchill has ordered the army and navy to strengthen their presence in Ireland. I believe that he plans to arrest the leaders of the Ulster Volunteer Force. However, my sources tell me that a large number of senior officers in the British Army in Ireland will resign their commissions before carrying out any government orders to oppose our men. We are fortunate that the head of the army, General Talbot, is a fine Ulsterman. He will see to it that the army are not deployed against us. The government will have to back down.'

CHAPTER SEVEN

Francis walked, 1914

A few months after Ulster Day, The Ulster Volunteers were unimpeded when they imported thousands of rifles and other arms into Ulster. When the National Volunteers responded by bringing arms into Howth Harbour, north of Dublin, the authorities reacted by sending an army patrol which attempted to stop the Volunteers marching with their weapons in central Dublin. Shots were exchanged and two men were killed by the military. This double standard exhibited by the authorities was not lost on the nationalist population. By the spring of 1914 Ireland was teetering on the brink of a civil war and a major constitutional crisis, provoked by the threat of an army mutiny, faced the British government.

Francis walked. He walked amongst Belfast's crowds. But his walking amongst crowds was a front, for in truth, he walked alone. As he walked he talked to himself. He didn't trust himself enough to talk to anyone else.

The law. That's what matters. Without the law there will be chaos. The law protects the governed from the government, the weak from the strong, and the individual from the mob. It is the glue which binds us together. The law must be strong but not inflexible, otherwise it will be broken.

Francis walked.

These people around me think I'm the law. But it is they who allow me to be the law. I have sworn to protect the law of the sovereign. But these people have now sworn to reject that law. Five hundred thousand of them have signed the Ulster Covenant committing to use whatever means prove necessary to oppose the law. A hundred thousand have joined Carson's private army and with their weapons they plan to violently oppose their sovereign's law.

Francis walked. He saw several Royal Navy ships moored in Belfast Lough.

The government has sent the army and the navy with threats to crush this lawlessness. But the officers, who like me, have sworn loyalty, have said that they will refuse to fire on Ulster Volunteers, if that is what it takes, to enforce this law.

Twenty-five thousand German rifles and a million bullets landed at Larne and we're told not to interfere. Twenty-five thousand rifles in the hands of loyalists and pointed at His Majesty's army.

'Ulster will fight and Ulster will be right.' Who said that? I can't remember.

No surrender. Home Rule is Rome Rule. No surrender. What are these people so afraid of?

But who will Ulster fight if there is no one willing to enforce the law? Who will decide; the law makers or the law breakers?

Francis walked.

Redmond's National Volunteers? Will they fight Ulster to keep Ireland united? That would be daft. That would be civil war. Where would that leave the police? Caught in the middle? Impossible. The army will have to engage. But how? And against which side?

Saints preserve us!

Francis walked.

CHAPTER EIGHT

Tragedy and rebellion

When the Great War started in September 1914 it rescued the British government from the constitutional crisis it faced over Irish Home Rule. The Ulster Volunteers joined up and formed their own regiments, as did the bulk of the National Volunteers. Curiously the leaders of both organisations encouraged their members to enlist in the British Army believing that doing so would ensure that they each would get what they wanted on Home Rule, once the war with Germany was over.

The National Volunteers were split on this logic and a new organisation called the Irish Volunteers was formed. They opposed supporting the British war effort and were strongly in favour of an Independent Irish Republic. The Irish Republican Brotherhood (IRB), a highly secretive revolutionary group, effectively controlled the Irish Volunteers. They planned a rebellion against British rule in Ireland.

Sitting in a pub in Belfast on a cold March evening in 1916, Francis shared a few drinks with his best friend, John Boyle. John had been the best man at Francis' wedding. They met through their shared interest in amateur dramatics. A rehearsal for their drama society's next production had ended an hour earlier. Their drama group was planning on staging a production of *Hamlet* in April to mark the tercentenary of Shakespeare's death. Francis was to play the role of King Claudius and he was fretting about how he would cope.

'Don't worry Francis. You'll make an excellent Claudius. All that fratricide, intrigue and corruption; sure you were born to it,' laughed John.

'Very funny,' said Francis, feigning outrage.

'You know Francis, I was thinking earlier that if Ireland were a bit more like Denmark then we might be shot shut of all of these Royals as they'd stab and poison each other.'

'You seem to be forgetting that the Norwegian invaders take the Danish crown and Fortinbras installs himself as King of Denmark.'

'Would we be worse off with the kaiser instead of the king?' asked John.

'Hush now or I'll have to arrest you for treasonous talk. Let me get another pint and then I must get home to Teresa and the children.'

'Fair enough. But you'll have to admit that two years ago, before the war started, there was something very rotten indeed in the state of Denmark.'

When Francis returned from the bar with their fresh drinks, he picked up where John had left off. 'You know I was convinced that there was the very real danger of Ireland sliding into war. What with the Ulster Volunteer's sabre rattling and Churchill's insistence that threats would not be tolerated and warning that force would be met with force, I felt sure it would come to bloodshed.'

'Well,' said John, 'we were spared that and in fairness to them, the Ulster Volunteers said they were for King and Country and when the call came they were not slow to sign up to go and fight the Huns. How many will make it back I wonder? Tell me Francis, what about the other lot. Do you think John Redmond was right to encourage the National Volunteers to join the British Army?'

'No question about it, the Germans must be stopped and every right thinking man ought to be doing his bit. You know that my brother-in-law, Denis Shanagher, joined the Royal Irish Fusiliers. He was in Gallipoli last year and fought at Suvla Bay. His regiment is currently somewhere in the Balkans.'

'Mind you, the split in the National Volunteers has left a bit of a vacuum. I fear that the extremists will emerge to fill that void. Eoin McNeil's splitting group of Irish Volunteers is not as benign as many seem to presume. There are darker forces at work behind the scenes.'

'Do you mean the Irish Republican Brotherhood?' asked John, sotto voice.

'Now, John, don't be putting words in my mouth. Besides if I told you what the police think might be going on I would have to shoot you.'

'It seems to me that the war you were worried about has only been delayed by this bigger war. The Nationalists got their Home Rule Act passed two years ago and they expect it to be put in place when this war with Germany comes to an end. On the other hand the Unionists expect it to be killed off in return for the blood sacrifice already made by so many Ulster Volunteers.'

'I fear that we will end up a divided nation,' answered Francis. 'The Canadian model of independence seems to me to offer the best of both worlds. Ireland as an independent dominion with separate legislatures in Dublin and Belfast could, I'm sure, be made to work. It's an option John Redmond's lot seem to find acceptable. But the intransigent opposition of Carson and his pals to any devolution of power back to Ireland from Westminster and the extreme language and methods used to voice that opposition will be a lesson the extremists on the Nationalist side will not fail to learn.'

'By God, but you're in cheerful mood tonight, Francis. Let's have no more politics. Tell me how is Teresa and when is the baby due?'

'Oh, she's flying. Big and round already and the baby's not due for another three months.'

'I'm glad to hear that. Please tell her that I was asking after her. Forgive me forgetting, but will this be your third or fourth?'

'Fourth,' smiled Francis and swallowed a large mouthful of his beer. He knew that John, as a single man, had little understanding of family life.

'Little Annie will be five at the end of June, Rory was three in January and Donagh is not yet two.'

'Quite the brood, my man.'

'Yes they are and its time I was getting back to them and to the books, I have a promotion exam in a month's time, which I'm worried about.' Francis stood and finished his pint.

'Francis, I'm sure that as usual, you will pass that exam with flying colours. Sure you already know more about criminal law than most of the judges in Belfast. Head Constable Maguire; there's a nice ring to that right enough.'

'Thanks, John. Flattery is always appreciated,' said Francis smiling. 'Now I must be off. Take care my friend. Will I see you at next week's rehearsals?'

'Oh yes, Your Majesty. I will be there and what's more I will have learnt all of my lines! Good night Francis. All my best to your family.'

'Good night, John.'

§

HMS Helga was anchored in the River Liffey opposite The Customs House in Dublin. Called in to support the suppression of a rebellion, her 12-pounder gun boomed repeatedly, lobbing high explosive shells over the arch of the railway bridge which crosses the river at this point. Her target was Liberty Hall, headquarters of The Irish General Workers Union and their armed militia, the Irish Citizens Army.

'What are we firing at?' asked a young gunner of his mate.

'No idea but the captain seems pleased enough so don't stop now.'

'Can you hear the army field guns banging away over there? The captain tells me that they are firing on several buildings along Sackville Street. The rebels have taken over the General Post Office, and several other buildings around the city.'

'I talked to the army messenger who met us at the mouth of the river. He told me that the shooting started three days ago on Easter Monday.'

'Why did the rebels pick on the GPO? It's hardly the centre of power in Ireland. Stupid gits.'

'Not as daft as it might seem. The GPO controls the telegraph lines connecting Ireland with Britain. So it has more than symbolic importance to the rebels.'

'Shit, this gun is getting too hot! Pour some of that water over the barrel, slowly! Good lad.'

At Dublin Castle three days earlier the duty officer reacted to reports of rebels drilling in the centre of the city. 'Just ignore them. They will play at being soldiers and go home for their tea. Besides there are no senior officers on duty. They've all gone to the races at Leopardstown.'

No sooner had the officer spoken than another messenger rushed in with the news that the rebels had occupied the

GPO and posted a notice on the door proclaiming the establishment of the Irish Republic. The duty officer decided then to send a troop of mounted Lancers down to Sackville Street to investigate.

When the occupiers of the GPO opened fire on the Lancers, three soldiers and two horses were killed. During the afternoon, two police officers were also killed and the Dublin Metropolitan Police were recalled to their barracks. At that point martial law was imposed across much of the country.

By the time the Helga had started her bombardment, many civilians had already been killed and the lives of poor inner-city families severely disrupted. One such family, the Murphys, lived in a single room at 7 Henrietta Street. Not much more than a stone's throw from the GPO.

'Seamus, you stay away from Sackville Street, you little brat.' The widowed Mrs Murphy shouted at her fourteen-year-old son. It was Wednesday afternoon and the fighting had been raging now for three days.

'A Jaysus, Ma. All the lads are down there. The Peelers have been taken off the streets and the army is too busy with the rebels to look after the shops. We'll never get a chance like this again.'

Clouds of smoke drifted across the city. There was a strong smell of cordite in the air. Mrs Murphy, torn between a God-sent opportunity to acquire some new clothes and concern for her son's safety allowed her desperate poverty to get the better of her judgement.

'All right, go on then, son. But for God's sake be careful. See if you can't get us a new coat out of Clery's. And mind out for those gurriers in the GPO. If Mr Doyle from next door wasn't in Flanders shooting at Germans he might be down there with the army shooting at those feckin eejits.'

Young Seamus Murphy darted across Sackville Street and dived through one of the large windows of Clery's department store. All of the windows to the store had been blown out by the gunfire and explosions happening around the GPO, just across the wide boulevard. If Seamus hadn't paused to look across to the GPO from where he'd been rummaging through women's coats he might have been luckier. But one of the rebels watching from a second floor window of the post office mistook Seamus for an army sniper and fired three shots at him. The first smacked off the window frame but the second shot caught Seamus full in the chest. He was dead before he landed on the pile of coats behind him.

Twenty four hours before Mrs Murphy's conversation with her son, General John Maxwell had arrived from London with instructions to 'take such measures as may in your opinion be necessary for the prompt suppression of the insurrection.' Before he'd left London he had ordered reinforcements into Dublin from Belfast and other points around the country. Reinforcements were also dispatched from several British ports. These military resources were needed in France and the government's reaction to the rebellion was fuelled by a tremendous anger at the rebel's treachery in time of war.

On the Sunday night at the end of Easter week, Francis was gathered with John Boyle and a few others in a pub in Belfast. It had been a peculiar week for Francis and his colleagues. When the trouble had flared in Dublin, police patrols in Belfast were tripled as the authorities watched for signs of trouble. But compared to the chaos being reported from Dublin, Belfast had been strangely quiet.

'I have a copy of a dispatch from Dublin Castle,' said Francis. 'It says that the insurrection ended this afternoon with the surrender of the rebels at midday. Apparently the centre of Dublin is in ruins and hundreds of people have been killed. The estimates are that there have been four hundred and fifty fatalities including one hundred and sixteen soldiers, sixteen policemen and two hundred and fifty-four civilians. In addition, there are at least two thousand five hundred wounded casualties. The dispatch includes a copy of the surrender issued by the rebel leader, a schoolteacher called Patrick Pearse. It reads:

"In order to prevent further slaughter of the civil population and in the hope of saving the lives of our followers, the members of the Provisional Government present at headquarters have decided on an unconditional surrender, and commandants or officers commanding districts will order their commands to lay down arms.

Signed, P.H. Pearse, Dublin 30th April 1916."'

'Well now what do you make of that?' asked Francis.

'Here,' said John Boyle, passing a poster around the small table for everyone to read. 'This is a copy of the Proclamation the rebels issued on Monday from the GPO.'

'I like this middle bit,' said one of the group.

"We hereby proclaim the Irish Republic as a Sovereign Independent State, and we pledge our lives and the lives of our comrades-in-arms to the cause of its freedom, of its welfare, and of its exaltation among the nations. The Irish Republic is entitled to, and hereby claims, the allegiance of every Irishman and Irishwoman."'

'Well,' said Francis, 'that's that, then. It all been cleared up. Hundreds of years of conflict and confusion and all it takes is a Dublin schoolteacher to cut through it all and sort us out. I'm not sure our Unionist brethren are going to see eye to eye with Mr Pearse.'

'It's not like you to be such a cynic, Francis. What do you think will happen to this chap Pearse and the others?'

'They will be shot, John. No question. Dublin is under martial law. The country is at war with Germany. These fellows will be charged and found guilty of treason and summarily executed.'

'That will make martyrs of them,' replied John. 'And if there are wholesale executions the public mood will shift. Right now, it seems that no one is quite sure what to make of it all. But a heavy-handed reaction from the military will turn ambivalence into sympathy and then support. You mark my words.'

§

After the excitement of Easter week and its aftermath, Francis' life turned back to relative normality. He took the Head Constable exam at the end of May and was waiting for the results when Teresa gave birth to their fourth child, Mary, in early June. Teresa, now quite confident in her mothering skills, had to balance the needs of the new baby with those of her other three children.

On the morning of Sunday 25 June the family were getting ready to go to Mass for their usual ten o'clock service. Francis, dressed in his uniform as he was due to start a shift at two o'clock, was in the kitchen dressing Donagh and watching Rory and Annie finishing their breakfast. Teresa had gone upstairs to get baby Mary out of her cot and into a bath.

Little Donagh pulled his shirt down over his short pants, wobbled a bit on legs that were not yet quite steady and said to his father, 'I'm not the baby anymore. Am I, Daddy?'

'No son. You're not. You are our little man now.'

'But, Daddy, I'm a boy. Rory is the one you call Little Man.'

Francis smiled to himself. 'Yes, son. You're right. Rory's our Little Man and so you'll have to be our Little Boy.'

Teresa appeared in the doorway clutching the baby to her chest. She looked ashen. 'Francis,' she whispered and trailed off.

Francis jumped to his feet and ushered Teresa out into the hallway. Over his shoulder he said to the children, 'Annie, keep an eye on the boys for a bit. I'm just going to help your mother.'

As Francis stepped out of the kitchen, Teresa pressed the baby to his chest and said, 'The baby's not breathing. Please God don't let her be dead.'

Francis took the baby into the front parlour and laid her on the settee. Her lips were blue and her eyes rolled to whites. He turned to Teresa and said, 'Run to the corner, love. You'll catch Doctor O'Donovan before he leaves for Mass. Ask him to come quickly and to bring his medical bag.'

But even before Teresa had left the house, Francis knew that Mary was beyond saving. He wrapped the baby in her blanket and took her back upstairs to her cot.

CHAPTER NINE

Promotion and the West

Mary Maguire's funeral took place on the 30th June 1916, the day before the 36th Ulster Division went 'over the top' at the Somme. On that first day of the Somme Offensive, over 5,500 men of the 'Thirty-Sixth' were reported killed, wounded or missing. Only one in ten of the 700 so called Shankill Boys from Belfast returned to their lines unscathed. There were no Twelfth of July celebrations in Belfast in 1916. Over the course of the war, nearly a quarter of a million Irishmen volunteered to go and fight with the British Army and over 35,000 lost their lives.

As Francis watched the tiny white coffin being lowered into its small grave his heart was broken but he locked his jaw and fixed a stony expression on his face. He wrapped a supporting arm around Teresa who had been inconsolable since Sunday morning. It was the saddest day of Francis' life and yet he would not allow himself a tear, believing that those around him needed and expected him to be strong and supportive of their grief at this terrible hour.

Teresa's parents were standing on the other side of the grave and looked as shaken as their daughter. Just two weeks before, the family had gathered for Mary's baptism and had a party afterwards at the Shanagher's house on the Falls Road.

The mourners had come to Milltown Cemetery from the funeral Mass at St Paul's Church on the Falls Road where Francis and Teresa had married six years earlier. The church was packed with family, friends, neighbours and a large number of Francis' fellow officers, including several of his Protestant colleagues. For many of them, this sad occasion was the first time that they had entered a Catholic church. A few exchanged understanding glances of a shared sense of alienation, which they suppressed because of their desire to stand with their colleague in his hour of need. Many of these officers also knew Mary's grandfather, Denis from his time on the force.

The other three children were looked after by neighbours and the only adult member of the family who was not present was Mary's uncle, the younger Denis Shanagher, who was with his regiment in the Balkans.

Back at the Shanagher house for Mary's wake, Francis began to worry about Teresa's state of mind. She had closed in on herself as her way of dealing with her grief. But Francis worried that something more than a child had been lost. Teresa was simply not herself. Her normal bright self-confident look had surrendered to an embittered scowl which twisted her face into a sneer.

When he eventually got to talk to her about how she was coping she burst into tears. 'How can God do things like this Francis? With all of the death and destruction going on in the world right now, you'd think He'd rejoice in the innocence of our beautiful baby. My mother was right when she used to say that God could be jealous. We were doing so well, weren't we? Your job, our nice house, four lovely children. Why couldn't he just leave us be?'

'Hush now, my love. You mustn't despair. We should count our blessings and accept our losses. It's the only way to survive. Otherwise how can we go on? And we have to go on, don't we? For each other and for the rest of the children. I know you are hurting badly now but it will pass, my love. I promise. There will be brighter days ahead I'm sure. Rest now and I'll see to getting the children to bed.'

Teresa surrendered to Francis' care and, at his suggestion, allowed herself to be put to bed by her mother.

As Elizabeth led Teresa up the stairs she kept a comforting arm around her shoulder and then steered her into the back bedroom were Teresa and Francis were sleeping. 'My dear, I have only small comfort to offer you. These things are sent to try us but we have to endure for the sake of those around us. There is wisdom in knowing that this too will pass. You rest now and I will take care of the children.'

§

Later that summer Francis got a message that his district inspector wanted to see him. He got on well with the DI and he rapped briskly on the office door and stuck his head around the door and said, 'You wanted to see me, Inspector.'

'Ah yes, Sergeant. Come in and sit down please. Give me a moment while I finish this paperwork. Here, take a look at this while you're waiting.'

The inspector handed a large brown envelope to Francis and returned to the paperwork he was reading when Francis interrupted.

The envelope contained a list of results for all of the police officers attached to the Musgrave barracks who had taken promotion exams. Francis ran his eye down the list searching for his own name. And there it was, he scanned across the page, Francis Joseph Maguire, Sergeant, Examined for rank of Head Constable, Passed.

A smile of satisfaction crept across his face but before it made it all the way to a grin his DI said, 'Sergeant, I'm afraid that this is very bad news indeed.'

The grin quickly disappeared from Francis' face. He looked up quickly, suddenly concerned and not understanding what his DI meant. He was relieved to find the DI smiling at him.

'Yes indeed, very bad news altogether. You see Francis now that you have secured your promotion to Head Constable we won't be able to keep you here in Belfast. You'll be sent somewhere to build your command experience and I dare say it won't be long before you'll be promoted again, to District Inspector. So it's very bad news for us but of course I'm delighted for you.' The inspector stood up and extended his hand to Francis.

'Congratulations, Francis. All the very best to you and your family. I hope you get an assignment where you will all be happy.'

'Thank you very much, Inspector. You have no indication of where I'm headed?'

'No, not yet, but your orders will come through pretty quickly. Your promotion will become effective from the first of September and you will be reassigned shortly after that. You better get your family prepared for a move.'

§

Head Constable Maguire, having served twenty years on the force in Belfast was not surprised by the news that he would be moving. He was looking forward to his new assignment but unsure of what he and his family might find in a relatively small market town in the west of Ireland. Claremorris, where Francis had been assigned, was a small rural town but it was strategically important from a security perspective as it sat on the junction of the north-south and east-west railway system in the west of Ireland and, as a consequence, it hosted both a large police and a large military barracks.

§

On a lovely warn Indian summer afternoon in late September, Francis scanned the platform at Claremorris railway station. He expected that a constable would be sent to greet the family's arrival from Belfast.

'Father, is this our new home?' Enquired little Donagh, now a self-confident two-and-a-half-year-old. Francis swept Donagh high up into the air and plonked him down on a luggage trolley.

'Yes, wee man. This is our new home. Now sit you there and don't move until I've rounded up everyone else and sorted out our luggage.'

Francis heard someone speak to his back, 'Excuse me, sir.'

He turned to find a young and fresh-faced constable offering a brisk salute while shuffling from one foot to the other. Returning the salute Francis said, 'Good afternoon, Constable. Have you been sent to collect us?'

'Yes, sir. We have brought the police tender to fetch you and your family to the barracks.'

'Very good. Thank you,' replied Francis and turned to notice that Teresa had gathered the children and found a porter to put their luggage onto a trolley. The constable offered another salute.

'Good afternoon, Ma'am. You'd be Mrs Maguire then?' he enquired.

'How do you do, Constable,' said Teresa. A hand tugged at Teresa's elbow.

'Mother', asked Annie, 'May I go to the bathroom, please?' Annie was more nervous than the young constable.

‘Can’t you wait until we get to the barracks, Annie?’

‘Right,’ said Francis, taking charge. ‘Let’s get along. Do we have everything?’ He stooped to pick up Donagh from the luggage cart.

‘Constable, would you be so kind as to show the porter here where to take the luggage? Thank you.’

‘Yes, sir. Right away. By the way, sir, the county inspector is with DI Scanlon at the barracks and they asked me to tell you to look in on them when you arrived.’

Teresa’s face was set in a grim and determined look of displeasure. Five years ago she had worked hard to get out of the barracks in Belfast and into a family home and now she found herself having to cram the family into a few spartan rooms in the police barracks in Claremorris. She was not happy but her instincts were to make the best of things and not complain.

‘Francis,’ she said, when the constables who had helped carry their luggage, had left and closed the door behind them, ‘You go and report and I will get organised here.’

‘I don’t deserve you Teresa,’ said Francis, fixing his cap on his head and pecking her on the cheek.

‘No you don’t,’ said Teresa. ‘Now get along before I get cross.’

As she watched her husband’s broad back head out of the door a small tear escaped Teresa’s eye but a smile also appeared on her lips. She felt a surge of warmth for Francis mixed with her lingering regret at Mary's absence. She turned to Annie who had been watching. 'You should be very proud of your father, Annie. He is a very good man and we are lucky to have him.'

Annie, who was only five years old, had just emerged from the bathroom and had no idea what her mother was talking about but she nodded her head firmly and said, 'Yes mother, we are all very proud of father.'

Francis asked a constable to direct him to the DI's office and when he found his way there he rapped on the door and waited.

'Come,' barked a voice from within and Francis entered the office. He was greeted by two men. The nearest to him was Charles Steadman, Mayo County Inspector and coming around the desk towards him was his new District Inspector, Charles Scanlon.

'Head Constable Maguire reporting,' said Francis.

The nearest man to him extended a hand and Francis was caught slightly off balance with his own hand travelling towards his head to offer a salute. He brought it around to accept the handshake instead.

'Head Constable, we tend to dispense with the formalities between officers if there are no constables about,' said Steadman, noticing Francis' awkwardness. 'Please take a seat and join us. We were just discussing the mood in the county now that the dust has settled on the business in Dublin.'

'Emotions are running high across Mayo,' Interjected the DI. 'The round-up of Nationalist activists which followed the Dublin insurrection at Easter, lifted quite a few Mayo men who are still amongst the many held in Frongoch prison camp in Wales.'

Francis was sitting stiffly upright. He wanted to start well with these men. He said, addressing the county inspector, 'Yes Sir. I have read your recent county reports, which I requested from Dublin Castle when I was given my orders.'

The senior man looked across at the DI before he asked, 'Have you indeed? How very enterprising. Tell me, was there anything in my reports which particularly caught your attention?'

Francis wasn't sure whether or not he was being put in his place but he decided to press on. 'Well sir, I noticed the significant increase in arrests and prosecutions for drilling and parading. That's not something we have had to contend with in Belfast, sir.'

'Strutting about like toy soldiers when there's a shortage of fighting men at the front. Really gets my goat,' said the DI. 'We should press-gang the lot of them and send them to France. They can practice their drilling over there.'

Francis said nothing but was sceptical about the value of this more confrontational policing; particularly when it is more likely to be directed at Nationalists than Unionists. He held his tongue and nodded in a non-committal manner.

The DI collected himself and stepped towards Francis with his hand extended. 'My apologies, Head Constable. I'm somewhat distracted and I've forgotten my manners. Allow me to formally welcome you to Claremorris. You come highly recommended and we are delighted to have you. This might not be Belfast, but I can assure you that there will be plenty to keep you busy and more than one challenge for you to overcome.

'The military have established a temporary barracks of wooden huts out along the Dublin Road. When full, we can have up to seven thousand soldiers in the town. As you can imagine, that has presented more than a few policing problems for us.

'Unfortunately, you and your family will have to live here at the barracks as there are not enough houses in Claremorris for you to use your housing allowance. I hope Mrs Maguire can make herself and the children comfortable. Did I notice that you have three young ones in tow?'

Francis shook the Di's hand and responded, 'Thank you, sir. Yes my wife is settling the family in as we speak. As you say, we have three children, all under five.'

'Well, very good, I hope that they all settle very quickly. We are delighted to have you in Claremorris, Mr Maguire.'

Teresa was very unhappy living in the police barracks and disliked the militaristic environment of the town. She had not really recovered from Mary's death and was deeply depressed. Having spent her whole life in the relatively large city of Belfast, she struggled to find people she could relate to in Claremorris. She found the customs and culture of the people around her very foreign and to them she came across to them as aloof and distant. A bit above herself, as more than one local remarked that winter.

Francis on the other hand slipped easily into the rural environment and readily related to both the towns-folk and the farmers in the surrounding district. His peculiar accent attracted a certain amount of curiosity but was quickly forgotten as he developed a reputation as a firm but fair policeman. His accent also helped him deal with the English squaddies billeted for training in the town. This was particularly useful when he had to address conflicts between the military and civilian populations that tended to arise from the considerable uneasiness between them.

Teresa formed a friendship with the local GP, Dr Maguire, and his family. The doctor was sympathetic to Teresa's melancholia and encouraged his wife to invite her and her family to come to Sunday lunch.

Teresa had spruced up the children and Francis was wearing his best suit on the appointed Sunday. As they walked up the path to the doctor's house, the front door opened and Mrs Maguire stepped out swinging a bucket in both hands. Catching herself mid-swing she laughed heartily. 'Well hello to the Belfast Maguires. I was about to throw this sand down the path as I'm worried that this frost will make the steps slippery. Come in, come in,' she said in a warm and friendly voice, 'We are all in the back parlour.' With that she turned and shouted, 'Doctor, our guests have arrived, come out and make them welcome.'

Francis removed his hat and was ushering the children up the steps to the front door as a commotion of barking and scampering erupted in the hall behind the doctor's wife. Dr Maguire, shouting from the depths of the house bellowed, 'Stop the dogs; don't let them run out for God's sake!'

Annie jumped behind her mother while the two little boys squealed, 'Doggies,' just as a pack dogs of varying sizes reached the porch in a flurry of tails, teeth and yelps of delight.

Francis spread his arms and hunkering down he forcibly gathered all three dogs into an embrace. 'Easy boys, easy now,' he said calmly but firmly, as his face was assaulted by licking tongues, and a clutch of dogs' tails whipped the Maguire boys' legs.

The doctor made it as far as the door and seeing that Francis had the dogs under control turned to Teresa and said, 'Mrs Maguire, how welcome you are. Please introduce me to your husband; I have been very much looking forward to meeting him.'

Lunch was served to a large gathering. The doctor's family had all come to meet the new arrivals in town. His three sons were grown men. Two were lawyers in the town and Francis was already on nodding terms with Conor Maguire. The group had agreed to dispense with formalities and call each other by their Christian names to avoid the tedium and confusion that so many 'Mr Maguires' would cause.

The older Maguire men were twins and despite being a few years their elder Francis struck up an easy friendship with Conor who worked in a local law firm with his younger brother Gerald. His twin brother was an auctioneer with a business in the town.

After lunch and despite the chill, the children were allowed to take the dogs out to the garden to play. The women retired to the kitchen and left the men discussing politics in the parlour. Francis quickly learnt that the Claremorris Maguires were committed Nationalists.

Conor was direct by nature and asked, 'So Francis, where do you stand on the Home Rule issue?'

Francis smiled, feeling the young man's passion.

'Well Conor, I was first asked that question by a Protestant clergyman back in 1896, the last time a Liberal government tried to bring forward an Irish Home Rule Bill. I've seen a good deal more of nationalism and unionism since then and, without wishing to be rude, I find little that appeals to me in either position.'

Conor was seething and, barely containing his annoyance, he responded. 'Oh come on, man. You can't just sit on the bloody fence.'

The doctor cleared his throat, 'Conor, please remember your manners.'

Francis interjected, 'Really Doctor, I'm not in the least affronted. Conor is quite right. But in truth, I don't mean to sit on the fence. Let me explain where I stand.

'If you'll forgive me for saying so, I find that Nationalists in general, but particularly those not from Ulster, do not easily understand that unionism is not just resistant to Home Rule but is absolutely convinced that Home Rule would be the death of their religious freedoms and a huge threat to their industry. I have often heard it said in Belfast that Nationalist interest in Ulster goes no further than a desire to collect taxes.'

'But,' interrupted Conor, 'there are so many protections in this legislation for Ulster and Protestantism that fearing it is quite absurd. I'm sure that, with a little time, Unionist opinion will soften and they will come around to seeing that Ireland cannot prosper without independence.'

'Well, if you will let me continue, I will try and explain,' said Francis calmly.

'Whether Protestant fears of a Dublin parliament dominated by Catholic and agrarian interests are grounded in fact or fantasy does not dilute those fears by a single jot. If we are to have any form of independence in Ireland we must first find a way to avoid dividing the country. And if we insist on the 1914 Act being implemented in full then we will descend into a civil war which will end with the country divided. I policed those monster rallies in Belfast in 1913 and, let me tell you, it would be a very grave mistake to think that Carson and his Ulster Volunteers are bluffing.'

Conor Maguire was not easily deflected. He may have only qualified as a solicitor two years before but he was a star member of the university's debating team and would rise not only to a prominent barrister but President of the Supreme Court in Ireland.

'Francis, you know as well as I do that it was the naked pursuit of power by Bonar Law and his Conservative Party which used the Home Rule debate to undermine the Liberal government. That manipulation encouraged the wholly undemocratic and armed resistance to the government by a minority group hell bent on resisting the will of the majority who wish to achieve a greater degree of self-determination.

'Furthermore if the natural right to self-determination is not the point of resisting the Kaiser then what are all those men dying for in Flanders?'

Francis was impressed with the young man's logic but he responded, 'Surely you can see, Conor, that your argument is reductive. If the whole of Ireland has a natural right to self-determination, then why should a part of Ireland not have the same right? A part which in this case has so little in common the rest of the country.'

'For a very simple reason, Francis,' responded Conor.

'Ulster is and always has been a part of Ireland, not some separate dominion. And any differences, cultural or otherwise, between Ulster today and the rest of the country are a direct consequence of Elizabethan Plantations where the natives were forcibly evicted from their lands and replaced with foreigners. If those foreigners now don't like the onward march of the nation then they can always go back where they came from!'

'Goodness me, Conor. The Ulster Plantations took place there three hundred years ago. At what point does a settler become a native?'

'So tell me then, Francis. How do you see these questions being resolved?' interjected Conor's father.

'I would describe myself as a Dominion Home Ruler. Meaning full devolution of the powers of administration and taxation should be transferred back to Ireland while at the same time Ireland remains a full member of the British Empire on precisely the same terms as Canada and Australia. That is the only way, I can see, that we can get the self-determination Conor wants without dividing the country.

'I realise that will not satisfy the extremists on either side but the British will go with it and so will the majority of ordinary people. And, most importantly, no more blood needs to be shed.'

'But,' said Conor. 'that is the sort of arrangement which the Unionists organised to resist in the first place. What makes you think that they will change their minds now? If anything, this war with Germany will harden, not soften, Unionists hearts.'

'I imagine two parliaments in Ireland,' replied Francis. 'One in Belfast and one in Dublin. The detail of how and what decisions are made where and the nature of subsidiarity would all have to be hammered in a constitutional convention. But with commitment from all sides to making it work and no opt-out option for Unionists being stirred up by the Conservatives, I believe most would see the possibilities as preferable to the alternative of more fighting, killing and ultimately the partition of the country.'

'Well, Francis, I have to say that it is refreshing to hear someone talk about this question who has clearly thought through his position. I'm not sure I share your optimism as to the possible outcomes,' said Dr Maguire. 'We have seen how well unionism can organise its opposition but the depth of feeling on the Nationalist side showed its face in Dublin at Easter. The Republican cat is well and truly out of the bag and it won't rest until we see the end of British rule in Ireland.'

Francis did not get the chance to respond as the women then re-joined the men with the children in tow and Teresa announced that it was time for them to take their leave.

The children ran ahead and Teresa slipped her arm through Francis' elbow. 'You seem very distracted,' she said, squeezing his arm.

'I don't mean to be, my dear. I was just replaying the conversation we were having about Home Rule and unionism. Dr Maguire and his sons are committed Nationalists and seem convinced that the Easter rebellion in Dublin was merely the tip of the Republican iceberg. If they are correct, then I fear that as soon as the war with Germany ends another war will start in Ireland.'

CHAPTER TEN

Politics and the descent into war

Lloyd George ousted Asquith in a political coup. He was supported in this by the Unionist wing of his own party and by Bonar Law's Conservatives. A cross-party war cabinet was formed which Bonar Law and Edward Carson were invited to join. The USA entered the war in 1917 and in 1918 her industrial might and manpower weighed the scales against Germany and her allies.

Irish Parliamentarians feared that the 1914 Home Rule Act, suspended for the duration of the war, would now never see the light of day. The threat of conscription further soured attitudes in Ireland. This swung electoral support behind Sinn Féin and republicanism. Lloyd George convened a Home Rule convention. Despite growing electoral support for independence, that issue was not allowed to be discussed and the convention was boycotted by Sinn Féin. A separate government in Belfast appealed to Ulster Unionists but not to Unionists in the rest of Ireland who were opposed to partition; the Home Rule side had many factions but was in the main also opposed to partition. The Sinn Féin boycott meant that the Independent Republican position was not represented at the convention.

Teresa did not really enjoy the run up to Christmas in the police barracks in Claremorris. She put on a brave face whenever she spoke with anyone outside the family but to Francis she was cold and withdrawn. Things came to a head on Christmas Eve. Francis had finished a shift at six o'clock in the evening and accepted an invitation from Conor Maguire to join him and some friends at the Clarence Hotel for some Christmas cheer.

One drink had become many and as usual the conversation had turned to politics. Conor was more ebullient than usual. A few days earlier the government had announced that all the Irish prisoners, held without charge since the Easter Rising, would be released in time for Christmas.

'Ah Francis, my misguided friend. Now you'll soon see just how committed the Republicans are. Redmond's Irish Parliamentary Party, and their heavies in the Ancient Order of Hibernians, will find that the whip of nationalism has slipped from their grasp. There will soon be a new, and much more formidable, political force abroad in Ireland.'

'Well now Conor, as long as it's political banners and not guns being waved around I'll be content. Now I really must be getting home. Goodnight gentlemen and happy Christmas to all.'

Francis had to push his way out of the hotel through a large crowd of British Army officers who were also enjoying some Christmas cheer. They were from the Kent Fusiliers and, Francis knew from the briefings the police received about the army garrison, that this battalion would be shipping out to France within a week. He nodded at the officers he passed and wished them merry Christmas and good luck.

After Francis had left, a ferret faced young man wearing a long overcoat slid up to Conor Maguire and nodded to him to step aside. 'Conor, you seem to be awfully friendly with that Peeler. You should be more careful with the friends you choose, you know. People are watching and not everyone approves.'

Conor rounded on the man. 'Well now, Michael, if it wasn't Christmas I'd be telling you to take a run and jump at yourself. But as it's the season of goodwill I'll just tell you to mind your manners and not be pestering me. You fellows like sneaking around in the shadows and trying to pretend that you amount to something. But you're just a bunch of scallywags. Now be off with you before I have you thrown out.'

Ferret face simply stared back at Conor without saying another word. After a few moments he smiled thinly and walked away. Conor shook his head ruefully and re-joined his friends.

'What was that about? 'asked one.

'I think some eejit must have sworn Michael Flatly into the IRB and now he thinks he's the Grand Inquisitor. If it wasn't so potentially dangerous to let fellas like him to get above themselves it would just be funny.'

It was a cold but dry evening and Francis walked at a brisk pace back to the family quarters at the barracks. All was quiet when he got to their rooms. He found Teresa sitting alone at the kitchen table. She stood as he entered and said,

'Francis, where have you been? The children were so over excited that I couldn't calm them to put them to bed. I expected you just after six. Your meal is in the oven. I ate with the children.'

At this last remark Teresa's carefully contrived calm collapsed as she tried to rush past Francis and out into the hall.

'Wait, Teresa. What's the matter? Did O'Halloran not tell you I'd be late? I passed him at the front door and asked him to pop up and let you know that I was meeting Conor Maguire for a Christmas drink.'

'Well that was mighty of you. Sending your Constable to carry messages to the little woman upstairs. Well as it happens O'Halloran didn't come up. But even if he had I would not have appreciated being abandoned on my own with the children in this awful place on Christmas Eve.' Tears began streaming down her face.

'You don't know how hard I've tried to be happy here but I'm not, I'm miserable. I miss my family. Right now they will be gathered around the piano in the parlour singing Christmas carols.'

Francis was shocked. He had been so wrapped up with his first command post, that he had not noticed just how unhappy his young wife really was. He gathered her to him and smoothed her hair which was loose down her back.

'Hush, my darling. It's all my fault. I have been so caught up in the job that I have been neglecting you. I can't bear to see you unhappy. Please trust me, I will find a way to make this right again.'

He actually had no idea what he might or might not be able to do about their situation but he spoke with such conviction and authority that Teresa simply believed him.

§

More by luck than design, Francis managed to get a new posting to take effect from 17 August 1917. He was transferred to Maryborough in Queens's County, about sixty miles south west of Dublin. Scanlon and Steadman had not been impressed when he submitted his request for a transfer but when Francis explained the difficulties Teresa was having living in the barracks and how badly she was still affected by the loss of the baby, they relented and supported his request.

Teresa's mood brightened considerably at the prospect of having her own home again and Francis hoped that she would find Maryborough more to her liking. Early in the new year and before the news of the transfer came through, Teresa had found that she was pregnant again and this news almost returned her to her old self. However she fretted more about this pregnancy than her others. She was keen to have another girl and decided that, if she did, she would call the baby Mary after her departed sister. The baby was due in early September. So when his transfer was scheduled for mid-August Francis and Teresa decided that it would be better for Teresa and the children to go to Belfast to stay with her parents, where she would be in more familiar and relaxed surroundings in the run up to the birth of her new baby. Having settled the family in Alameda Terrace, Francis went on to Maryborough to take up his new post and set up a home for his family.

When a telegram arrived with the news that Teresa had gone into labour Francis rushed to Belfast. Elizabeth greeted him at the door of the Shanagher house. 'Francis, my dear, come in, come in. Mother and child are both well and resting upstairs. Go on up to the back bedroom and I'll go and put the kettle on.'

Francis sprinted up the stairs and gently opened the bedroom door. He was delighted to find Teresa propped up in a bed cradling the new baby.

'Hello, Francis,' Teresa said, smiling. 'Come and meet your new son, Hugh.'

Francis gathered the baby in one arm and, sitting next to Teresa, put his other arm around her. 'Hello there, wee man,' said Francis. 'I hope you didn't give your mother a difficult time.' Turning to Teresa he kissed her gently on the forehead.

'Are you alright?' he asked. 'I was not happy having to be so far away when you went into labour. Your father sent me a telegram and I came as soon as I could.'

'I'm fine, just a little tired but the labour was no better or worse than with the others. I just pray to God that Hugh grows big and strong like his dad and doesn't go the way of poor wee Mary.'

'Now, Teresa, don't be worrying yourself. There is no reason to worry about that at all. Your job now is to get your strength back as quickly as you can so that you and the children can join me in Maryborough. I think you will like it a lot more that you did Claremorris. I've found us a nice house close to the barracks and there is a primary school nearby where Annie and Rory can start their schooling.'

Mrs Shanagher arrived shortly after and shooed Francis out saying that mother and baby needed to rest. Denis took Francis to a pub on the Falls Road for a celebratory drink.

'Here's to Hugh, God bless him and keep him,' said Denis raising his glass in a toast.

'Amen to that,' responded Francis.

'And may he grow up in an Ireland strong and free,' added the landlord.

'Well now, Seamus, let's keep the politics out of it, shall we?' suggested Denis.

Francis and Denis retreated to a quiet corner. Denis asked, 'Speaking of politics, the partition of the country that you have always talked about looks inevitable now. Do you think?'

'I'm afraid you are right. Lloyd George needed Unionists' support for his palace coup against Asquith, so what happens in Ulster will now be hugely influenced by the Liberal Unionists and the Conservatives. On the other hand, Sinn Féin's success in the Roscommon and Clare by-elections point to a huge shift towards a more robust attitude to nationalism in the rest of the country.'

'But,' asked Denis, 'where would partition leave Nationalists in Ulster?'

'Not in a good place I fear. But there may yet be another way forward. I've been rubbing shoulders with some Republicans in Claremorris. These are educated and considered types and they are convinced that they should emulate Carson's tactics and deploy armed force to ram home their demands not just for Home Rule but for a truly independent country.'

Denis was taken aback. 'Rubbing shoulders with Republicans! What in the name of God do you mean by that?' he demanded.

'Nothing sinister I assure you. Claremorris is a small town and a chap called Conor Maguire is a rising star in the legal profession; he and I shared the odd drink and his parents were very good to Teresa. Anyhow, Conor and his family are ardent Nationalists and have become very disillusioned with the parliamentary approach to Home Rule which, you'll have to admit, has taken us around in a huge circle for thirty or more years now.'

'This convention on Home Rule set up by Lloyd George is being boycotted by Sinn Féin because the question of independence will not even be discussed. As a result, Conor and his friends are sure that the Home Rulers and the Unionists can only succeed in dividing Ireland whereas they believe that the majority of the population across the country are ready to support demands for a truly independent Ireland.'

'Now listen to me, Francis,' responded Denis. 'It's all very well for lawyers like Carson and your new friend Conor Maguire to engage in extra-parliamentary political activity, but for God's sake man, you are a police officer.'

'Denis, I can assure you that I'm fully aware of my position and I have no intention of doing anything to jeopardise myself in any way. But the winds of change are blowing and I'd be a fool to pretend otherwise.'

Denis, far from placated by these remarks gripped Francis' wrist across the small corner table. 'Francis, I have never heard you speak in anything other than the most direct terms. Forthrightness is something I have always admired in you. This talk of "winds of change" is not like you at all. There are so many agendas at work here that you won't be able to trust anyone if you start mucking about. Be very careful, my boy, or you too will become a pawn in a very dangerous game.'

§

The family settled well in Maryborough and Teresa was much recovered from her melancholia. But the winter of 1917-18 was very harsh and heavy snowfalls brought the country to a standstill. Francis was kept busy both with regular policing activity and assisting in rescuing people and livestock stranded in one of the many snowstorms.

He was determined that the family would never again live in a police barracks. The surest way to achieve that would be to secure his next promotion to District Inspector. That rank would be senior enough to ensure that he and his family always had their own house wherever he might be posted. The step up to District Inspector involved a significant commitment of time to complete the required studies. Francis was often locked away in a back room of the house with a blanket wrapped around his shoulders to ward off the winter chill.

As the winter deepened and the new year opened, the war with Germany was brought closer to home in Ireland. German submarines sank several merchant ships off the Southwest coast and a British destroyer was sunk in Cobh harbour. These events overshadowed the Home Rule Convention which was bogged down on the issue of partition.

To the populations at large in both Ireland and Britain the convention was a minor sideshow. The real concern of the day was the Spanish flu virus rampaging across Europe and this, more than anything else, occupied people's minds in the early months of 1918. The virus was highly unusual in that it more often proved fatal to healthy adults than the young or elderly. The most vulnerable were pregnant women.

News about the spread of the virus was censored by both the Germans and the Allies so when it first appeared in Maryborough in March 1918 the local authorities were caught unaware. A British Army doctor, recently returned from the front, raised the alarm and strict quarantine measures were put in place. Francis and his officers were assigned the difficult task of keeping concerned relatives away from the isolation ward at the local hospital where the sick and dying were being cared for.

A young Constable approached Francis, 'Begging your pardon, sir,' he said hesitatingly, 'But what is it that ails these people we are guarding?'

'Constable, it is not the sick you are guarding but the healthy. The flu virus which those unfortunates in the hospital are fighting must be contained and we are therefore charged with the job of keeping visitors away.'

'And what, sir, should we do if any of the sick try to leave the hospital? I don't want to be man-handling anyone infected with the Spanish Lady.'

Francis paused before answering. He knew that extreme measures might cause a panic amongst the population and indeed amongst his constables. He put a hand on the young man's shoulder. 'I'm afraid, Constable, that the unfortunate people inside the hospital are far too ill to be thinking about walking out. So please just get on with the task of keeping healthy people out and let the doctors and nurses look after the sick inside.'

One victim of the Spanish flu was Francis' father, Roger. The flu took him suddenly and quickly. He complained of feeling ill at the end of September and died on 5 October, aged seventy-four. To contain the spread of the virus there were travel restrictions in place, so Francis travelled north to Tempo on his own to attend his father's funeral.

The small Catholic church was filled to overflowing and Francis was pleased to notice that many of their Protestant neighbours had turned out to pay their respects. Francis gave a short but emotional eulogy and expressed his regret that as his own life has been so busy that he had not been able to see much of his father in recent years.

Following the funeral, Francis' sisters asked that they sit down and discuss the future of the farm. As the oldest male heir Francis had inherited the farm. Susan and her husband Frank Murphy lived in Belfast in the Stranmillis area with their three children: Louis, Evelyn and Francis. They had no interest in the farm. Annie and her husband Pat McCaffrey had returned to Tempo from Liverpool some years earlier to look after Roger in his declining years. They were worried that Francis might want to sell the farm.

Francis assured them that he has no intention of selling the family farm and that she and Pat should consider it their home.

The Spanish flu raged across the world until the summer of 1919. It claimed the lives of an estimated forty million people, far more than were killed in The Great War. But the killing in Ireland was about to begin again in earnest.

CHAPTER ELEVEN

The West awakes

The Home Rule or Irish Parliamentary Party had dominated election results for more than thirty years. Many constituency seats were habitually uncontested and where there were contests, heavy-handed intimidation tactics were not in the least bit unusual. Against that background, and considering the humiliations they suffered in the 1917 by-elections, many Home Rulers decided to throw in the towel and not to oppose *Sinn Féin* in the UK General election in December 1918. Sinn Féin won a clear mandate to pursue independence, with 73 from a total of 105 seats.

Sinn Féin ran on an abstentionist platform and with their sweeping majority, they formed a provisional government in Dublin and issued a Declaration of Independence. The government at Westminster declared this assembly illegal. At this point few expected anything other than a war of words. But the hard men of the Irish Republican Brotherhood had different ideas.

'Good morning, Head Constable,' Francis heard as he entered the Maryborough barracks on the morning of 21 January 1919. He nodded and smiled at the desk sergeant. 'Morning, Sergeant. All quiet this morning?'

'Yes, sir. A slow night last night, thank God. A couple of our regulars sleeping it off. Oh, and a poacher who made the mistake of offering a large salmon to the DI in Bennett's Hotel last night!'

'Well, well. The fecking eejit. Isn't the Resident Magistrate sitting this morning Sergeant?' The sergeant nodded in confirmation. 'The RM doesn't much like poachers. Especially when they nick his precious salmon. I'd say your man will be getting a stretch for himself,' he said chuckling.

'Oh, you can be sure of that, sir, sure of that indeed. I almost feel sorry for the lad.'

Francis paused at the door to the inner office. 'Sergeant is the first Dáil Éireann meeting happening in Dublin today?'

'It is, sir. And it's a proud day for Ireland, I'd say.'

Francis continued on his way without responding further. *A proud day for Ireland* he mused to himself. *I wonder. I'd quite like to be there to see it, I think. Mind you with two thirds of the Sinn Féin MPs locked up in English prisons I expect they will find it difficult to make many decisions.* When Francis got to his desk there was a mountain of paperwork awaiting his attention. He set himself to that task and put politics out of his mind.

Later that morning, James Godfrey, a quarry worker, led a horse and cart along a wet road near Soloheadbeg in Tipperary. Rain poured relentlessly from a grey and unforgiving sky. Mr Godfrey was accompanied by a county council employee by the name of Patrick Flynn. Flynn was walking on the opposite side of the horse from Godfrey. The cart was laden with explosives which had been picked up from the Tipperary Military Barracks and were being taken to the quarry for blasting. The cart had a police escort which was provided by two popular local policemen, Constables James McDonnell and Patrick O'Connell. McDonnell was a Mayo man of about fifty years of age and a widower with four children. His colleague was a young unmarried man from Cork.

Suddenly, four armed and masked men jumped over a roadside fence shouting, 'Hands up!' An unknown number of other men remained in the ditches on either side of the narrow road. The constables were walking behind the cart and carrying rifles slung over their shoulders. The pouring rain made it difficult for them to see more than a few feet ahead. There would be many arguments later about just what happened next but what was not in dispute was the fact that both police officers were gunned down and the raiders made off with the cart laden with explosives. They also took the constables' rifles.

The raiders were all members of the Irish Volunteer's 3rd Tipperary Brigade. They were led by Sean Tracey and Dan Breen; both of whom went on to become notorious gunmen. Just before the raiders jumped the fence and start shooting, Tracey whispered urgently to Breen, 'Dan, you said you wanted a war and you are about to get one. But remember, to start a war you have to kill people.'

The first Dáil meeting had adjourned earlier but not before it had issued a formal Declaration of Independence and demanded the complete withdrawal of British forces from Ireland. The Dáil also appointed representatives to attend the forthcoming Peace Conference in Paris, in the hope of securing recognition of Ireland as a sovereign state.

The radio operator at the barracks in Maryborough rushed the news of the Soloheadbeg killings to Francis' office. Francis immediately ordered a general alarm and secured the arms store at the barracks. He posted extra policemen to the front and rear of the barracks with instructions to keep their eyes peeled. He set out from the barracks in a Crossley tender, with a heavily armed escort to alert and reinforce all of the patrols already out and about the town. He sent word to Teresa that he would be working a double shift but that there was nothing to worry about. Happily however, by nightfall it became clear that the Soloheadbeg incident was isolated and not part of a grander country-wide rebellion.

That evening, Francis got home rather later than expected and was relieved to find that Teresa and the children were all blissfully asleep. He sat at the kitchen table and poured himself a large Jameson which he cradled in both hands and sipped occasionally. *Well,* he thought, *Conor Maguire was exactly right with his predictions last year. The Shinners are the new men now, and they sure don't look like they are going to wait for any British government to fob them off with watery versions of Home Rule.*

But, Ulster is surely screwed now. The Unionists will be delighted with what's happening. I can hear Carson castigating the Shinners already. 'Bunch of country bumpkins who couldn't run a county fair'. What will the hard-men do now, though? That's the big question. And can the Shinners control them? Clearly not down in Tipperary by the looks of things. Francis drew his hands down his face and let out a long sigh. One thing seems certain, he thought, things are going to get a whole lot worse before they get better.

The next morning Francis worried about what he should tell Teresa about what had kept him late the night before. The implications of the Soloheadbeg shooting were clear; the Republicans might now actively target policemen. What was worse though was the statement issued by the first Dáil which demanded the immediate withdrawal of all British forces from Ireland, could easily be interpreted as giving political sanction to the murder of Irish policemen.

How to broach these issues with Teresa without panicking her? 'Good morning my dear,' said Teresa as Francis got down to the kitchen. 'What happened yesterday to keep you working so late? I heard lots of activity in the streets but didn't go out to talk to anybody.'

'A cart-load of mining explosives was stolen in Tipperary yesterday, and two police constables were shot and killed during the raid. It seems fairly clear that the attack was politically motivated.'

'Oh my God, that's awful. Those poor men. Were they married?'

'One of the men, constable McDonnell from Mayo, was a widower with four children and those kids are now orphans.'

Francis immediately regretted his lack of tact. He hadn't realised how upset he was about the murders until he'd begun to talk about them.

Francis had assumed that he would have to somehow protect Teresa from this news; instead it was she who comforted him. She could see how upset he was and went to him and embraced him gently. 'My love, it is perfectly all right to be upset. Don't bottle your feelings to protect me.'

'Teresa, you are my rock,' he said returning her embrace. 'It's just so cruel, by all accounts; those men were popular in the area. McDonnell was fifty years old and a fine and decent man. What those murderers hope to achieve by killing him is anyone's guess.'

'Come and sit down and eat some breakfast love,' said Teresa. 'I have some news that will lift your spirits.'

Francis watched Teresa expectantly as she set out his breakfast. She poured them a cup of tea and reaching for his hand she said, 'I've not been to the doctor yet which is why I've not said anything but by my own best guess I think I must be a couple of months pregnant. If I'm right we will have another baby in the summer.'

Francis was elated, 'That is the most wonderful news. And you look so well, thanks be to God.' He pulled her to him in a bear hug and kissed her gently on the lips. Young Donagh, who had wandered into the breakfast room unnoticed, said, 'Daddy, why are you squeezing Mommy?' Francis let his hug slide down and around Teresa. They both turned and smiled at the boy.

'Well, wee man. Aren't you the silent assassin creeping up on your parents like that?'

'What's an assassin?' asked Donagh. Teresa interrupted before Francis said more. 'Good morning my handsome prince and what would Your Highness like for his breakfast?' Over her shoulder she whispered, 'For goodness sake, Francis!' She raised her left eyebrow and shook her head in disbelief. Francis shrugged and reached for his uniform tunic.

'No harm done, eh?' He stooped to ruffle Donagh's hair and then reached an arm around Teresa's waist and whispered in her ear, 'To be continued,' and kissed the top of her head.

As he was about to head out the front door he stopped himself and, reaching for his key chain, stepped into the under-stairs cupboard and opened a strong box, removing his Webley revolver and a hip holster. He attached the holster to his uniform belt so it sat high up on his hip. He frowned while doing this as he did not habitually wear his side arm. But as he began his walk to the barracks he found his mood lifting as he thought about Teresa's news. By the time he reached the barracks he was smiling again.

At the main entrance he met his DI who noticed Francis' sidearm. They had talked before about whether or not officers should be armed at all times. 'Good morning, Head Constable, glad to see you in full uniform this morning,' he said smiling and nodding at the gun. 'Dublin Castle has just issued orders that all RIC personnel are to carry arms at all times.'

'It seemed a sensible thing to do today Inspector. Not that their rifles did those men much good in Tipperary yesterday. The fact that they were armed might well have been the reason they were shot in the first place.' The inspector raised an eyebrow as he moved past Francis.

'You don't really believe that, do you Francis? Those blackguards were out to kill policemen yesterday. The rifles were just a bonus for them.' The DI carried on into the street leaving Francis standing on the steps watching him walk away.

'The next person who raises an eyebrow at me is going to get the smack of a wet fish,' he muttered to himself and smiling again he entered the barracks.

Paddy Malone looked up as Francis walked into the Head Constable's office. 'Good morning, Francis. You've just missed the DI.'

'No such luck, Paddy, I met him on the steps. Anyhow, there was nothing said of consequence. You get along now, I'll take over.'

'You are looking particularly cheerful this morning. You look like the cat that got the cream,' said Paddy, as he buttoned his tunic.

‘Well, I was pretty upset earlier when I got to thinking about those poor men in Tipperary but I did get some very good news with my breakfast.’

‘Spit it out man. We could all do with some good news today.’

‘Teresa is pregnant again.’

‘Well, that is splendid news indeed. Congratulations to you both. And Teresa, she’s feeling well?’

‘Thanks Paddy, and yes she’s blooming, thanks be to God.’

‘Oh, I doubt very much that God has much of a hand in the creation of your burgeoning family, Francis.’

‘You show some respect you wee gutter snipe.’

‘Ah now, Francis. Can’t a man have a bit of a lark? Relax for goodness sake. Sure I was only pulling your leg. No offence intended. My, my, but you Ulstermen can be awful touchy betimes.’

Francis smiled at his colleague. ‘Fair enough Paddy. No offence taken.’

‘I’ll tell you what though, Francis. You’d better pass that DI exam next month. You’re going to need every penny of the pay rise to feed your brood.’

‘Yes, thanks very much Paddy. I wasn’t fretting about the exam until you said that. Now get along before I lose my patience. Let's have a pint on Friday after work. I think we are both on the day shift together.'

'Good enough, Francis. I look forward to that. Until then, my friend, keep yer back to the wall.'

§

Two months later, at a few minutes to eleven on the night of 31 March, Resident Magistrate John Charles Milling walked into the front room of his grace-and-favour house in the town of Westport in county Mayo. He crossed to the mantelpiece and opened the front of the ornamental clock sitting in the centre. He slid a key out from under the clock and carefully wound the hour hand one hour forward. He smiled to himself in satisfaction. As far as he was concerned, having the whole of the United Kingdom on Greenwich Mean Time and the innovation of daylight savings achieved by adopting British summertime were simply reassuring signs of modernity finally reaching the west of Ireland.

As the RM closed the face of the clock and returned the key to its place, his attention was drawn to a noise he heard in the street outside the house. He walked towards the front bay window but could only see his own reflection. Outside was an unyielding blackness. He paused before reaching the window, suddenly uneasy. But Milling was a former district inspector in the RIC. I'm a tough, no-nonsense person, he reminded himself.

A military man might have doused the lights, both to protect himself and to better see outside, but Milling did not think to do this. As he stepped again towards the window four gunshots shattered the darkness, the front window and John Charles Milling's chest.

CHAPTER TWELVE

Policing in Westport

Milling's murder caused outrage across the country. At Mass in Westport the following Sunday, Father Canavan read a letter from Archbishop Gilmartin of Tuam, which said, 'If the perpetrator is not insane then he is a criminal of the first order.' The archbishop went on to extort all good citizens, 'To do all in their power to bring this enemy of God, of society and of Ireland to justice.'

When the news of the killing reached Francis the next morning he was deeply shocked. He had known Jack Milling from the time when Milling was a DI in Belfast and had respected the man's commitment to fair and even-handed policing for members of both sides of Belfast's divided community.

'The Republicans were always a red rag to bull for Jack,' he said to Teresa. 'He couldn't abide them. "Blasted traitors, guttersnipes and corner boys" he would rant, every time the topic came up. I can imagine him running headlong into confrontations in recent times. He will not have adapted well to the change in the political climate.'

Milling had had several significant run-ins with the Irish Volunteers in Westport. As a former DI he worked well with the local police led by DI Short. Between them, Short and

Milling had managed to incarcerate most of the senior Volunteers and not a few IRB men, on charges ranging from conspiracy and military drilling to publishing seditious papers. There had been riots outside the courthouse in Westport on a number of occasions as prosecutions were brought against local Republicans.

Milling was under a great deal of pressure. His workload had increased considerably with the death of his friend and fellow Resident Magistrate, Charles Hinkson. He had received several death threats and had moved from his country house into the town house in Westport for better security. The Dublin authorities had actually suggested to him that he ease up on his campaign against the Volunteers. All of this had culminated in a request from Milling for a transfer out of the area. The transfer had not come in time to save his life.

'Francis, you're not suggesting that his murder was political, are you?' asked Teresa. 'That really frightens me. If RMs are to be targeted then no one is safe.'

'I can't believe that anyone in Westport would shoot Jack Milling for political reasons. I'm sure that this will prove to be a revenge killing by some lag that he sent to Sligo gaol for a stretch of hard labour. I went to Westport any number of times when we were in Claremorris and while there are strong Republican feelings about the town the police know all of the active characters well, so it would be too risky to shoot the RM even if the Volunteers had a mind to do so.'

'But Francis, as you have become rather fond of saying, times have changed.'

'Well, we're a long way from Westport now,' said Francis and moved to change the conversation.

Within months, that was a remark which Francis lived to regret. He passed his DI exams in April and was told in May that DI Short was being moved out of Westport and that he, Francis, was to be his replacement. He was instructed to take up his new post in July.

'It's quite remarkable Paddy,' Francis said to his colleague, Paddy Malone in Maryborough, 'This is the third time that I've been assigned to a new town and twice now Teresa has been due to give birth at the time of the move.'

'Poor timing indeed, Francis. And now you're going to be the boss man in Westport, a new baby will be a big distraction.'

'Oh I'm not worried about that, Paddy. Teresa is a very capable woman. She'll be grand. Besides she'll get to live in a nice house in the town and hob nob with the local gentry.'

'Meanwhile we'll do what we did with the arrival of the other babies. Teresa will go to her parents in Belfast with the rest of the children to have the new baby there. She will be well looked after by her mother and the midwife. Her sisters are a great help minding the other children.'

In early July 1919 Francis took up his post as Westport DI. Teresa and the children had travelled to Belfast a couple of weeks earlier. On the 14 July Teresa gave birth to her fifth child, Brian. Mother and child were both well when Francis paid a flying visit before dashing back to Westport.

Although he didn't tell Teresa right away, the splendid town house he had been assigned was the very same property in which the Millings were living when Jack was murdered.

'My goodness, Teresa, you are going to love Westport. We have a beautiful house in the town across the road from the Protestant Church and opposite the entrance to Lord Sligo's demesne. It's a really lovely house and we'll have a housemaid come in to help. I've already had invitations to visit a number of families which I've postponed until your arrival.'

'Francis please don't fret. I know you worry about me being dragged from pillar to post but I'll be fine, I promise. I'm very proud of your achievements and the children are excited about Westport. I've told them that they will be able to go swimming in the sea every day and they are looking forward to starting at their new schools. Everyone is excited about joining you. I hope we can do so in a week or so.'

'It's you I worry about,' continued Teresa. 'Have they arrested anyone for murdering Jack Milling?'

'No and I will be under quite a bit of pressure to find the culprit or culprits. I've reviewed the case files. There were two men seen climbing the wall behind the house just after the shooting and the house maid saw two men outside the house at about ten o'clock when she left for home. But it was a filthy night with a heavy snowfall, so I doubt very much that we will get a positive identification. Besides, people are very afraid of even talking to the police, never mind giving evidence in a court. I really don't think our investigations will get very far, four months down the road from the murder.'

'That is terrible, how can people stand aside and let such an awful crime go unpunished? Are they not outraged?'

'To be honest there is more outrage about the imposition of martial law in the county and the surcharge levied by the Council to pay the damages awarded to Mrs Milling,' replied Francis.

'Please tell me no more for now, Francis. It is too depressing and I'm very tired. Just promise me that you will be careful and stay safe. Don't give those hallions any reason to be taking pot shots at you.'

§

'District Inspector, do please come in,' the invitation issued by his new superior, the Mayo County Inspector, Charles Steadman. Francis had just arrived at the county headquarters in Castlebar for his weekly meeting with his new boss.

Steadman, who Francis had met a few years before when he first arrived in Claremorris, was a rather dour Scots Presbyterian and Francis found it difficult to warm to the man. Steadman had been particularly difficult about Francis' request for a transfer out of Claremorris and rather unsympathetic regarding Teresa's depression. A stickler for rules and protocols, Steadman also displayed a rather superior attitude to the local population having described them to Francis variously as sly, cunning, lazy and indolent.

Without preamble Steadman asked, 'No progress to report on the Milling murder investigation, I presume?'

'I have personally interviewed all of the witnesses, sir. Although, I use "witness" with some caution. Whether or not the Volunteers were involved officially, it is clear that the town assumes the perpetrators were Irish Volunteers and, for fear of their own lives, no one is prepared to put names to the people seen in and around the Milling residence on the night of the murder. There have been so many stories from around the country of people being shot as traitors and spies that people have begun to believe that just being brought in for questioning may very well put their lives at risk.'

'Inspector, are you suggesting that the RIC should drop its investigation in the face of bullying and intimidation from a handful of corner boys and village thugs? Because if so, you are not the man I've been led to believe that you are!'

Francis swallowed hard, a ball of bile having risen in his chest at Steadman's remarks. He reminded himself to stay calm before answering, 'No, sir, that is not what I meant. To put it plainly, due to a lack of support from the public, I have been unable to move this investigation forward, which I should remind you was already stalled when I arrived. The physical evidence might be traced back to the firearm in the event that we were able to recover it. But again that is a most unlikely prospect.'

'You mean the bullets extracted from Mr Milling?'

'Yes, sir. And the wall opposite the window. Two of the shots missed Mr Milling and the bullets were recovered from the plasterwork. Unfortunately there is no other physical evidence, sir.'

'You would do better Inspector to try harder to disguise that fact that you think me a fool. I don't care one jot for your opinion of me but I can assure you that my opinion of you should matter a great deal to you if you want to progress as an officer in this force. Now get out my sight and find me a murderer I can dangle in front of the press and the powers that be.'

Constable Turner was driving Francis back to Westport in the Ford Tourer. He turned and asked, 'How are you getting along with the county inspector, sir?' Turner's tone alerted Francis.

'Mind your own bloody business, Turner, and keep your eyes on the road.'

Turner was miffed by the rebuke and said little more for the remainder of the journey. Francis was still fuming when he began to ruminate to himself.

That smug, self-important bigot. What does he want us to do, drag those people in and start pulling out fingernails until someone talks. Francis suddenly slapped the back of the seat in front of him. *By God, that's exactly what that so and so wants me to do. Torture a few peasants until they talk. Well to hell with him and his ilk. I'm a policeman, not a bloody Spanish Inquisitor.*

What was it Dagg used to say about policing being at the behest of the people. Well we're losing that argument for sure. He slumped back in his seat and stared disconsolately out of the side window of the car. Eventually he sat upright and straightened his tunic. *Right, I'm a Peeler, I'm responsible for the safety and security of the people in this district and by God, that's the job I'm going to do. The gunmen, the politicians and the reactionaries can all go hang. If I can't show these people what proper policing is about, and garner their support while I'm at it, then I shouldn't be a policeman at all.* He paused for a moment. *And I shouldn't take my frustrations out on Turner.*

He sat forward and said, 'Constable Turner, forgive my brusqueness. I have rather a lot on my mind. Are your family well?'

Francis' day was not all bleak. Teresa and the children had arrived from Belfast the previous day and he was looking forward to his first family evening in some time. When he got home the house was abuzz with children scampering about excitedly. Teresa was in the kitchen, with Mary the housemaid, preparing an evening meal. On hearing the commotion being made by the children, she came out into the hall and smiling broadly said, 'Francis, you are early. What a lovely surprise. Come through to the kitchen and I'll put the kettle on. Dinner won't be ready for an hour or so.' She hugged Francis warmly and kissed him on the cheek.

When the meal was cleared and the children packed off to bed Francis and Teresa sat together in the parlour. It was a balmy evening, the bay windows were open and a gentle breeze occasionally billowed the net curtains.

'So, what do you make of Westport, my love?' Francis asked.

'It's a beautiful little town and the people I've met have been very friendly. A Mrs Meldon called this afternoon to say hello and invited us to tea. She's a charming woman whom I know you'll like. Her husband is Colonel Meldon the Resident Magistrate. No doubt you'll have met him already? Anyhow they live nearby but their family are all grown and living in England. She's going to arrange a pony and trap to take us all to the beach this week which has got the children all excited. Oh, and Father Canavan also stopped by. He said that he'd already met you.'

'Yes, he came to the barracks on my first week. I'll bet that there's not a lot that goes on in Westport that Father Canavan doesn't know about. His intelligence network will be much more efficient than ours! Anyway, I don't mean to be rude. I was very taken with the man. He seems a thoroughly decent sort.'

‘Yes, decent enough to tell me that poor old Jack Milling was shot in this very room. No doubt you were going to get around to mentioning that small matter eventually?’

‘Of course I was going to tell you. I just thought it better to let you get settled in and see how lovely the house is, before sharing the ugly news.’

‘Relax, I’m not really cross, just amused watching you squirming. I keep telling you that I’m not a delicate flower that you need to shelter from the savage winds. I’m a policeman’s daughter and a policeman’s wife. I really don’t think that you will ever shock or surprise me with how ugly the world can be. And don’t worry about Father Canavan being upset that he put his foot in something. I didn’t let on to him that it was news to me that the Millings had lived here.’

‘I’m sorry my dear. I will try very hard not to underestimate you again,’ said Francis, who was now also smiling.

§

As the year rolled on there was relatively little murder and mayhem around the country. Volunteer activity in the Westport area was inconspicuous. The police were aware, through their intelligence network that a certain amount of drilling and training was going on. They were not aware that two separate attempts by the local Volunteers at securing armaments from abroad had been hijacked by the Volunteers HQ in Dublin, and the arms sent south to West

Cork which was where the armed resistance to the British administration was at its most active.

Francis stayed true to the promise he made himself and worked hard to deliver a police service that the general citizenry could support.

Unfortunately the first opportunity which presented itself to Francis to demonstrate even-handedness, involved a public house raid in August which had political undertones and involved some gun waving.

Francis first heard Constable O'Brien's version of events. O'Brien had the annoying habit of speaking in the stilted manner of a policeman giving evidence in a court. 'I was passing Mary Gibbon's public house at about one o'clock in the morning and noticing the front door ajar, I entered the premises along with Constable McClinchy. Therein I found Mrs Gibbons standing behind the counter talking with a man I did not recognise. When I enquired of Mrs Gibbons as to why her premises was open at this hour and why a stranger was on the premises, Mrs Gibbons became very abusive and used language I would not like to repeat, sir.'

'I see, Constable. You know that we have received a complaint from Mrs Gibbons that you were behaving very aggressively and were waving your revolver in her face. At what stage did you draw your sidearm?' asked Francis.

'The stranger...'

Francis interrupted, 'You got his name, I presume?'

'Yes, sir. His name is John Flynn and he lives at Peter Street in Westport.'

Francis sighed, 'But you did not recognise him? Go on, please.'

'Well sir, Mr Flynn claimed that he was merely picking up some drink for a group of former soldiers who had bought and paid for it earlier and arranged to have it picked up when they would be passing on their way home, after attending a party in Westport.'

'These former soldiers were not present?'

'No sir. Flynn claimed that they had forgotten to pick up their drink and asked him to return to fetch it.'

'And your sidearm, Constable?'

'Ah yes, sir. Well, when I expressed some doubt as to the truth of what Mrs Gibbons was telling me she became even more abusive and the racket she was making brought her son, young Johnny Gibbons, out from a backroom. We have suspected for some time that Johnny Gibbons is a Volunteer and when he added more threats to his mother's I felt the need to draw my revolver in order to protect myself.'

'Did Constable McClinchy also draw his sidearm?'

'No, sir.'

'I take it, Constable, that no one else was armed?'

'No, sir.'

‘But you felt threatened?’

‘Yes, sir. Johnny Gibbons said that we had no right to enter the premises and that anyhow, us lot had no more than three years to go before we would be turfed out of the country.’

Francis was tiring of the conversation. ‘Right Constable. Let me have your written report along with Constable McClinchy’s by mid-afternoon. Dismissed.’

‘Yes, sir.’

Francis regretted that he was left with no choice but to summon Mrs Gibbons for a breach of the Licencing Act for having her premises open for the sale of drink at one o’clock in the morning, and John Flynn for being on the premises at that time. He also summoned Johnny Gibbons for using threatening language to Constable O’Brien.

When the case came before the magistrates, John Kelly, a local solicitor, represented the defendants. Kelly argued that Flynn had a perfect right to pick up the parcel of drink and Mrs Gibbons a perfect right to serve it to him. Kelly admitted that Johnny Gibbons had become much exercised at the presence of the police and in particular by the drawing of a gun by constable O’Brien, but that the youth had an unblemished record and it would be a shame to besmirch that over such a trivial matter.

Francis presented the facts of the case for the police and explained O’Brien’s drawing of his revolver as a natural reaction from a policeman in these troubled times, ‘when directly threatened.' Francis concluded saying that the police were happy not to press the matter and would leave a decision entirely in the hands of the court.

What Francis didn't share with the court was his impulse to kick Constable O'Brien up the backside for being an idiot.

The magistrates split their decision, fining Mrs Gibbons and Mr Flynn and binding Johnny Gibbons to the peace, one of the three magistrates, Dr Walsh, dissented but agreed to allow the majority decision to stand.

Another case, where John Kelly was defending, came up in the winter and that case haunted Francis for many years.

He was called out to a farm one mid-winter afternoon where the body of a newborn baby had been discovered. The infant's corpse was lying in an outhouse, under a feed trough, where it had been found. Francis lifted the corpse gently and cradled it in his arms. He was immediately reminded of Mary's cot death in Belfast and, to hide his emotions, he walked briskly to his car where he gently laid the corpse on the back seat.

When he returned to the cluster of policemen standing at the outhouse he said to the officer in charge of the scene, Sergeant Fahey, 'Infanticide is cruelty beyond expression. And in my experience it is usually a crime with two victims. These young girls who fall pregnant are so terrified of their families that killing their babies seems somehow the better option to them. And we call ourselves Christians; makes me sick to my stomach.'

'What happened was hardly anyone's fault but the girl's, sir.'

'Have you no heart, Sergeant?'

Embarrassed by Francis' emotions, but none the less offended by what had happened, Sergeant Fahey stopped himself disputing what had been said. 'What should we do, sir?' he asked.

Francis nodded to the cottage. 'Two girls were watching me take the baby away. They were at that window on the right. Go in and talk to them and I'll bet one is the mother and the other her pal who will have helped her hide the pregnancy. Be gentle, Sergeant, we'll have to bring charges but nothing we do will compare to what those girls will get from their families. God help them.

'I will take the baby back to Westport and get Dr O'Donovan to confirm the cause of death. Although, it looks to me as if the poor wee mite was strangled, probably to stop it crying. If the girls won't say which of them was the mother, bring them both into the barracks at Louisburgh. The midwife will be able to say which of them had a baby recently.'

As Francis climbed into the car, the young constable with the sergeant said, 'Well now isn't the DI the big softy after all Sergeant?' Sergeant Fahey, full of conflicting emotions, responded by giving the constable a clip around the ear.

'Watch your mouth young man and show some respect or you'll get the other side of me hand coming back.' Fahey stared briefly at the confused constable before walking slowly towards the farmhouse.

The post-mortem showed that Francis had been wrong about the baby being strangled and found that baby had simply died of exposure. The marks around its neck, which he took for signs of strangulation, were caused by the mother's friend pulling at the baby's head to help with the birth. When the case was eventually brought to trial in the spring, Annie Kelly was charged with abandoning her child so as to cause its death. Her lawyer pleaded on grounds of clemency that as the girl had suffered terribly already, the charge should be reduced and the case dealt with under the Probation of Offenders Act. Francis was prosecuting and said that the police would not press the case and he was happy to leave the case entirely in the hands of the magistrates. Annie Kelly was convicted and released on probation.

§

Francis had a number of exchanges with Steadman about the investigation into the murder of RM Milling and reported that his investigations had produced no evidence strong enough to support an arrest let alone a conviction. But the murder had had significant political impact and the Dublin Castle authorities were pushing for a public enquiry to be held.

Francis was sitting at his desk reviewing the files and preparing his response to a memo from the Inspector General's office, asking if he believed a public enquiry would be helpful. The RIC commanders who were in charge in Westport at the time of the murder had been transferred to other posts and he was reading their responses to the same question. In his hand was the response from the Head Constable of the time, now District Inspector Allen. Francis read, 'Still, I consider an enquiry could - even at the worst, do no harm - and the unexpected might happen, one never knows what a question will bring forth, and if one witness was caught or broken down I consider others would follow.'

And to hell with the consequences for such forced witnesses, thought Francis. *Does this fellow Allen really think that such witnesses would ever make it into a court room or if they did how long they might stay alive afterwards. No, this man was not thinking about any consequences of his recommendations. He's just fed back the response he thinks will reflect best on himself and to hell with everyone else. Well that's not my style.* Francis picked up his pen and began to write.

He reviewed the possible testimony of the six people who had already been questioned about whom or what they had seen on the night of Milling's murder. He concluded that little of additional value could possibly be learnt at a public enquiry and wrote that, 'No good will attend an enquiry, if held. The holding of an enquiry would do harm to those witnesses examined. It would place them in danger of being shot for giving information, if it were ever suspected that they told anything to the police.'

As Francis put this report into an envelope marked 'secret' to be delivered the next day by special messenger, he wondered if his would be the only dissenting voice.

The following week at his regular session with Steadman, he was somewhat surprised to hear that Steadman shared his views. 'These bloody bureaucrats know nothing about real police work. I don't want my men tied up for weeks on end going over ground we have already covered. I am disappointed that you have not managed to get a result Inspector, but I don't believe for a moment that a bunch of expensive lawyers from Dublin have any hope of doing better.'

'We need to find ways to restore confidence in the police and judiciary, if we hope to get ordinary people to come forward to support our efforts to protect the populace. A noisy public enquiry would do a lot more harm than good. We're not going to beat the Republicans by bullying hapless witnesses.'

CHAPTER THIRTEEN

Francis walked, 1920

Throughout 1920 the Irish Volunteers continued their attacks on the RIC, the provisional government called for a boycott of the judicial system and the Volunteers deployed a certain amount of intimidation to enforce that boycott. The police, powerless in the face of this activity, began to take the law into their own hands and a pattern emerged of attacks by the Volunteers followed by reprisals by the police. The British government, wishing to treat the violence in Ireland as a policing matter, recruited special constables in Britain to be sent to Ireland to reinforce the RIC. An Auxiliary police force, outside of the control of the RIC, was also established and executed a violent counter insurgency campaign. Both the special constables and the Auxiliaries were, in the main, recently demobbed soldiers and officers of the British Army.

Francis walked. He had driven out past Louisburgh to the end of the peninsula on Clew Bay. A summer's evening sun warmed his face. He walked alone. He headed to the rise above Roonagh Pier, a small fishing harbour. There was not a soul to be seen and there were no boats in the harbour. Francis was alone and he was troubled.

The Crown judicial system is collapsing under the weight of the Sinn Féin boycott. One nil for the Republicans.

The Volunteers have taken an oath of allegiance to the Dáil. That effectively makes them the official army of the provisional government. The 'Irish Republican Army'; well it has a ring to it. Two nil for the Republicans.

Republican Courts and a Republican Police Force have been established. Three nil.

Three hundred thirty-eight out of three hundred ninety-three local council elections this summer put Sinn Féin in charge. That ends any arguments about a Sinn Féin mandate to establish a republic after the general election. The people have spoken. Four nil.

By God I'm surely starting to feel like I'm on the wrong side.

Francis walked; his troubles deepening. He headed down towards the harbour.

'Dominion Home Rule' is dead. Lloyd George's 'Government of Ireland Act' will see to that. 'Home Rule all round' he calls it. Well the Ulster Unionists will embrace a new parliament in Belfast sooner than a parliament in Dublin. But this watery concoction is way too little too late for the rest of the country. Five nil.

He stood on the end of the pier looking out to the Atlantic and tried to arrange his thoughts.

And I'm now required to shove all this down the throats of the people, like it or not.

'The Restoration of Order Act' was there ever a more badly-named law?

Churchill and his bloody special militias. God save us. I should have let that loyalist mob brain him. He allowed himself a wry smile and shook his head slowly.

The Ulster Defence Association is no more than a sectarian gang.

As for the Black and Tans, no more than a rabble we're supposed to turn into special constables.

And worst of all the Auxiliaries. A law entirely onto themselves. 'Counter insurgency' makes it all sound so official. Official murder and mayhem most likely.

Francis walked.

I've got to hand it to the Shinners, their tactic of just ignoring the British Establishment in order to bring about its collapse is really working. The violence, murder and intimidation of the Volunteers is deplorable, but again, there's no denying that it is working.

Francis walked.

But now we're to have British vigilante gangs running around the country terrorising the terrorists. And I'm supposed to work with them. These blasted Black and Tans they've sent me haven't got the foggiest idea about the law. That eejit I asked the other day to tell me about his powers of arrest said he hadn't a clue. Said he'd grab the man's chin and stick him with his bayonet.

What in the name of God am I to do?

Francis walked.

I could just resign. Make the grand protest about law and order. Challenge the legality of this counter insurgency, but what good would that do? None at all, that's what. It would be a coward's act. Running away with my tail between my legs. Besides, where could we go? How would we live?

Francis walked.

I have to think about the family. Not just myself. Teresa would never forgive me if I failed her and the children.

But I can't stay on and bring terror down on the very people I'm supposed to serve.

Francis stood still and stared out to sea for a long time. Then he shrugged and walked back towards his car. His sidearm, which he was never now without, had been sticking in his ribs. He rubbed the spot ruminatively as he walked. As he climbed back into the car an idea began to take shape in his head.

CHAPTER FOURTEEN

Oaths and loyalties

The Republicans recognised that their success in undermining the police and judicial system had created a vacuum for the population at large which would have to be filled. Republican courts began to operate and Republican police were appointed, mostly from the ranks of the Volunteers, to enforce the rulings of these courts.

Francis took a train to Claremorris early the following Monday morning. He was on his way to visit Conor Maguire, the young lawyer he had befriended when stationed there. He was not in uniform as he wanted the visit to be private.

'What you are proposing will expose you to very great danger,' said Conor, when he heard what Francis had in mind.

'Any more danger than I'm already in from your pals in the IRA, Conor?' smiled Francis. 'Look, I know you must be planning one of your Republican courts to be held in Westport soon. Instead of raiding it as I'm instructed, what if I come along in uniform and observe proceedings? What I want to do is send a signal to the town that, at least my little part of, the RIC understands the people's desire for self-determination and that the police in Westport will not get in their way.'

'Well, right away I see two flaws in your plan and given time will probably think of lots more,' answered Conor. 'Firstly, some of the more suspicious-minded Republicans may assume that you are there to spy on proceedings and act accordingly and secondly, when Inspector Steadman gets wind of what you've done he'll have you up on a disciplinary charge.'

'I'll deal with Steadman; don't worry about him. And as for your hot heads I'm rather hoping that you can lay some groundwork for me and assure anyone who needs convincing that my motives are pure.'

'Besides, all kidding aside, we need a functioning court in Westport. Some of these land disputes are getting out of hand. Your Shinners have put the existing system on its uppers so we need something to fill the vacuum.'

'What strange days we live in, Francis. I never thought I'd be having a conversation with a district inspector of the Royal Irish Constabulary about running Republican courts. Next thing you be telling me is that you want to prosecute some miscreants in my court. Now that's something I'd like to see.'

'Live long enough, they say, and you'll see it all,' replied Francis. 'So you'll do it?'

'Yes I'll do it. But I'll not be tipping you off as to the court dates and location. I assume your network functions well enough yet for you to find that out for yourself. Come on, man. Let me get you back to the station before I'm accused of fraternising with the enemy.'

'You're a good man, Conor. By the way, I meant to ask, how was your stay in Sligo gaol? I was very sorry to see you prosecuted for canvassing for Sinn Féin.'

'Ah it wasn't too bad. I was amongst friends. Anyhow as the election results proved the people weren't too impressed by the British trying to supress the party just because we had the temerity to demand freedom for our own country.'

Conor stopped walking and turned saying, 'Francis, forgive my temerity but I must ask if you realise that this so called 'Restoration of Order Act,' bringing the Tans and Auxiliaries, will have precisely the opposite effect to what's intended. We've tried politics and got gaol. We win elections and get banned. We win control of County Councils and have our funds cut off. When politics and passive resistance fail there are not many options left open. I fear that violence will beget violence and the killing we've seen so far will just be the tip of the iceberg. When the real shooting starts, Francis, I sincerely hope that you'll be well out of the way.'

'It's the real shooting that I'm trying to stop, Conor. Whether the gunmen have taken oaths to the Republic or the King, murder is murder and it's my job to stop it.'

'God save you, Francis. You're either a fool or a very brave man, indeed. Why don't you just walk away, resign your job as so many others have already done?'

'I'm neither brave nor a fool, Conor, just a Peeler trying to do his job. And now more than ever doing the job properly is the most important thing I can do. Besides what else can I do?' He turned and walked into the railway station.

§

Francis noticed that Johnny Gibbons, the young man he had prosecuted for threatening Constable O'Brien, was working as a law clerk in the solicitor's office next to the police barracks. He often saw Johnny standing in a doorway, between the two buildings, taking a cigarette break. He decided to cultivate a relationship. One morning he stepped into the doorway next to Johnny with a packet of cigarettes in hand.

'Good morning, could I cadge a light for my cigarette, please?' Francis asked. 'Have one of mine,' he offered.

Gibbons looked uncomfortable but struck a match from a box he pulled from his pocket. 'No thanks, Inspector. I'll just finish this one and be getting back to work,' he said, lighting Francis' cigarette with his right hand, while at the same time indicating the lit cigarette in his left.

'Aren't you the Johnny Gibbons who I had to prosecute a while back for putting the skitters up Constable O'Brien?'

Johnny pointed to a pin on the lapel of his jacket. It was a small gold circle called a *fáinne*, indicating that the wearer spoke Irish. 'I'm Gibbons alright Inspector, but I prefer to be called by the Irish version of my name, Seán. I don't suppose you have any Irish yourself, Inspector?' he asked sneering.

'*Cúpla focal, Seán*, a couple of words. My father and sisters are fluent speakers. I joined the Gaelic League in my hometown many years ago but I was never able to get my tongue around the Gaelic vowel sounds. Besides, what Irish I do know is Ulster Gaelic, so not much use in Connaught anyhow.'

Somewhat taken aback Gibbons added, 'Well you should pick it up again Inspector. There are Gaelic League classes in Westport on a regular basis.'

'In better times maybe, Seán, maybe, but sad to say I'm not sure I'd be all that welcome in the current climate.'

'Perhaps you're right, Inspector. Anyhow, I'd best be getting back to my desk. *Slán agat,* Inspector.'

'Slán leat Seán, I'll be seeing you.' Francis turned back into the barracks, first stubbing his cigarette out on the pavement. *Useful exercise,* he thought to himself. *No doubt that young man is in the Volunteers, perhaps even in the IRB if his file is to be believed.*

And so a habit was established. Francis nurtured his relationship with Seán Gibbons and regularly stepped out of the police barracks to share a cigarette break. He and Seán became more comfortable and over a period of a few weeks Francis built an easy rapport with the young man.

§

'The Sinn Féin boycott of the police and the courts is making it near impossible for us to bring prosecutions. They have even managed to "persuade" many solicitors not to attend Crown Courts.' Francis and Teresa were discussing how difficult Francis' normal policing job was being made by the political situation.

'You mean that they are using intimidation to enforce the boycott? But, what do they expect will happen?'

'It's a clever tactic really. If they can demonstrate that the country can be managed perfectly well without British systems then more and more people will be willing to support the Republican agenda. The local election results show that it's working. Sinn Féin now control the majority of urban and rural councils. The government's response of withholding funds from those councils looks decidedly undemocratic. Unfortunately, there have been wholly wrong incidents of the police taking justice into their own hands when frustrated by their inability to bring suspects before a court. There was an incident in Tuam last month when it was reported that police officers fired shots through the windows of houses and shops after one of their colleagues was murdered in an ambush.'

'It's hard to blame the police. If the Irish Volunteers are allowed to literally get away with murder, how else do you expect them to behave?' asked Teresa.

'Teresa, really! I don't believe I'm hearing you talk like that. I expect them to behave professionally of course. Not like bloody vigilantes. If we allow ourselves to behave like the

Volunteers then we only add creditability to their position. That will lead to a downward spiral into chaos.'

'So what do you think should be done?'

'The position of the government is increasingly difficult to maintain. If the Volunteers were acting in a political vacuum then I'd come down hard on them, setting up military courts, if necessary. But, the thing is that the Irish Volunteers are effectively the military arm of the provisional government, lawfully elected by the people of Ireland. The fact the British Government chooses to regard both Sinn Féin and the Irish Volunteers as criminal organisations is sophistry. We must find a way to accommodate the Republicans and work with them, not simply try and bully them out of existence.'

'How do you work with people who are hell-bent on destroying you?'

'That is the big question, my love. And one to which, if I'm honest, I don't have the answer. But that won't stop me trying to find one, I can assure you. I thought I might start with a look in on a Republican court.'

'What? Are you mad? Do you mean that you are prepared to be seen attending a Sinn Féin court? Have you lost your reason, Francis?'

'I didn't tell you this because I knew it would upset you, but I went down to Claremorris last week to see Conor Maguire. I talked to him about the increasingly febrile political and security situation and suggested that we might keep a lid on things in West Mayo if I was seen to be willing not to interfere with the Republican courts.'

'And knowing Conor as I do I have no doubt that, just as I have, he told you that you are mad, eh?'

'As a matter of fact he did but after some discussion he accepted the logic of my plan.'

'Oh, no doubt you were very persuasive. And did he accept the logic that some trigger-happy Volunteers might see your presence as a God-given opportunity to kill a senior policeman?'

'The main reason I went to see Conor was to ask him to forewarn the Volunteers that I might attend and vouch for my intentions.'

'Well I've heard it all now! An RIC district inspector asking permission to attend an illegal assembly in his own town. You have lost your reason. Francis, I cannot stop you behaving in this fashion but please know that I disapprove in the strongest terms. I fear it will end badly for you and the family. Please forgive my vulgar language but I feel severely agitated.'

'I really don't want to agitate you further, Teresa, but I must tell you that I will always act in what I see as the family's best interest.'

§

Francis attended the Republican court held in the Westport Town Hall in July. To keep his actions official he brought along Head Constable Donlon, who Francis suspected had some sympathy with what Sinn Féin were attempting.

'Do you really think that the Shinners can just ignore the existing judiciary and carry on their own courts, Inspector?' asked Donlon as they walked across Westport to attend the court sitting.

'It's a bold move and if it is successful we could see policing and the judicial system simply fall into Republican hands by default. No doubt they'll start modestly as an alternative to district courts. But if successful why not move on to petty sessions and then the assizes. If the people trust the justice of these Republican courts then the tide will have truly turned against the establishment.'

'Well, that will be you and me out of work then, Inspector.'

'Oh I don't think so. We are some way away from the collapse of the system yet and anyhow the brave new Republic, if it ever comes, will need experienced policemen however much the Volunteers like to hate us at the moment.'

As they arrived at the hall Conlon said, 'Here we are, Inspector. How do you want to play this? I assume we're not about to conduct a raid, just the pair of us?'

'No indeed, Head Constable. You follow my lead. We're just here to observe; nothing more.'

With that Francis and Donlon entered the town hall in the centre of Westport where the first Republican court to be held in Mayo was about to commence. Rows of chairs were arranged facing a pair of tables set up in a T shape at the front. Most of the chairs were occupied. Francis spotted Seán Gibbons with the solicitor he clerked for. With them were a middle-aged couple who were clearly their clients. He nodded a greeting.

A corridor had been created down the centre of the rows of chairs. Two men were standing formally either side of the front of this corridor acting as bailiffs of the court. In the centre of the top table sat Conor Maguire, presiding. He was assisted by two other men Francis recognised as Eamon Moane and John O'Boyle.

A rumble of voices echoed around the room and several faces turned and stared at the two policemen. Conor Maguire rapped a wooden gavel on the table and called the court to order. He looked directly at Francis and there was a pause while everyone in the hall waited to see what would happen next.

Francis removed his officer's cap, stuck it under his arm and stood to attention, indicating to Donlon to follow his lead. The formality of Francis' action amounted to a salute to the court. Conor Maguire nodded almost imperceptibly to Francis and called the first case before the court.

§

Francis had one more move up his sleeve and this time he chose not to share his plan with Teresa. He'd made a study of the police files on suspected Volunteers and had settled on one name, Joe Ring, who was believed by the police to be the senior Volunteer officer in Westport.

He had met Joe Ring at the Republican court in Westport. Under the guise of the continuing investigation into the murder of Jack Milling he invited Ring to come into the barracks for a follow up interview.

As Francis entered the interview room he dismissed the constable standing inside the doorway. 'Yes, sir,' saluted the young constable as he turned to leave. Joe Ring looked up at this exchange.

'If it's a kicking you have in mind, Inspector, I wouldn't waste your energy. I told your predecessor all I know, or more correctly, the little I know, about the shooting of the RM.'

'Well now, Mr Ring, allow me to start by saying thank you for coming in to talk to me. I know that not everyone is comfortable to be seen coming or going from the police barracks these days. But then again I don't suppose anyone in Westport will doubt your Republican credentials. Will they Mr Ring?'

'Inspector, if you have something to say to me then spit it out, man.'

'Very well. I don't believe that you were involved in the killing of Jack Milling, but I do believe that he was killed because he was making life difficult for you and your friends in the Volunteers. Indeed he made no secret of his intention of ensuring that you and others spent a long stretch in gaol. But I also know that, given the fear the Volunteers have instilled in the populace, no one is ever going to tell us who pulled the trigger.'

'So, what am I doing here, Inspector?'

'I'm going to make you an offer, Mr Ring.'

CHAPTER FIFTEEN

Under pressure

As the fighting intensified the British authorities sanctioned reprisals to try and drive a wedge between the population and the Irish Volunteers. Creameries and shops were burnt and in one notorious incident a large part of Cork city was burnt down by a company of Auxiliaries in reprisal for the killing by the Volunteers of one of their colleagues. The Mayo RIC County Inspector reported in October 1920, 'That it (dread of reprisals) has seriously crippled Sinn Féin's prestige and power.'

'Francis, the report in the paper this morning says that the provisional government has called for a boycott of the RIC and that shops are not to serve the families of RIC officers.' Teresa was talking to Francis in the front parlour of their house in Westport.

'I did wonder when that would happen. I suppose we should be grateful that they haven't ordered us to be shot on sight!' responded Francis.

'How can you joke about these things, Francis? I really don't understand you sometimes.'

'My love, I'm fairly sure that what people actually do, as opposed to what the provisional government tells them to do, will turn out to be two quite different things. When you go into Duffy's store tomorrow please tell Mrs Duffy that I said hello.'

'But you've said yourself that Republican feelings run deep in this town. How can you know that I won't be embarrassed when I go to the shops tomorrow?'

'Alright, I'm sorry. Let me be serious for a moment. Things are far from easy and we are concerned about the safety of officers in the remoter police huts and stations, so we are planning on closing them and bringing the officers into the larger barracks in the towns. But here in Westport I can assure you that not only will we be served in the shops but we can safely go about our business in the town, without fear of molestation by the Volunteers.'

'How can you be so sure?'

'Quite simply because I've made a deal with the local Volunteer commander. I will ensure that Westport will see none of the thuggery and murder being practised elsewhere by the Black and Tans and the Auxiliaries and in return he will not target the RIC in Westport.'

'Holy God, Francis, you can't run this town as if it's some Wild West town and you're the sheriff laying down the law.'

'As usual my dear, you have put your finger on precisely the salient point. We have two parliaments; one elected by the people, which has been outlawed by the other, and is now regarded by most people as a foreign power. In these circumstances who exactly has the moral and practical ability to lay down any law? I joined a police force which was disciplined and respected. Now, under the colonial style leadership of General Tudor, policing has been abandoned in favour of mobster style intimidation and murder.'

'But these men are the people who murdered Jack Milling!'

'That is very probably true and I've made it clear that if I find evidence to that effect then I will make arrests. But more realistically what I want to avoid is any more murders like Jack Milling's. By either side.'

'But Francis, you have no authority over the Auxiliaries. How are you going to stop them if they choose to come into Westport?'

'Another good question, love. Happily, some niceties and protocols remain in place. If the Auxiliaries plan any operations in this area I will be informed and through some agreed channels I will ensure that any targeted person or persons are moved out of harm's way.'

Teresa shifted her again pregnant weight forward in her armchair. 'Francis, we have five children and another on the way, please God. What will happen if you are caught? Won't you lose your job and your pension? And if you do how will we eat? Where will we live?' Teresa's thoughts shifted to less mundane questions. 'If you are found out won't you be prosecuted? You might go to prison or worse.'

Collecting his thoughts Francis sat forward and reached out to take Teresa's hands in his. 'Teresa, I have come to believe that what the British are doing in this country is immoral. If I were a single man I might simply resign and take my chances. But having weighed all of the options I have decided that my moral primary responsibility is to protect the law and of course I also have a moral imperative to protect my family. By the law, I mean the natural law, the moral law, the law as supported by the majority of the people. Not emergency powers, concocted by a weak and desperate government, to cloak their repression of freedom with some semblance of respectability.

'The British public will not tolerate this violence against civilians for long and that reality will ultimately constrain the Westminster government. Meanwhile I will do what I can to keep the madness at bay, for I greatly fear the bloody mindedness of the present authorities. At the same time, I fear that the extremists on the Republican side have wound up our young men into a state where they can't wait for the killing to start in earnest.' He paused seeing that Teresa was struggling to control her breathing.

'That sounds like a speech you have been practicing, Francis. You are always so sure. So convinced of your righteousness. So confident that you know best. It is what I love about you and it is what I hate about you. Now if you'll allow me I'm going to go to bed. Please douse the lights before you come up.'

When Teresa went upstairs Francis took himself to the sideboard and poured an Irish whiskey. Turning the bottle in his hand he read, 'Jameson Special Reserve, Limited Edition'. The bottle had been a Christmas gift from a local businessman, Charles Hughes. He sniffed at the spirit appreciatively and then added a heavy dash of water from a jug. A habit he'd acquired some years earlier when he'd allow himself the occasional whiskey when on call.

He walked slowly over to the bay window; the same window through which Jack Milling had been shot. Running his hand along the window frame he found some marks left following the repairs made after the shooting. *No more,* he thought. *No more, not if I can help it.* He suddenly realised that he had not impressed on Teresa the need for complete secrecy. *She's not daft,* he thought and allowed himself a small smile as he raised the glass to his lips. He caught his movement reflected in the window and saluted himself with his glass. 'Here's to the Republic,' he said out loud.

§

One of Dublin's leading magistrates, Alan Bell, was taking a tram home following a long day at his office in Dublin Castle. He was feeling rather pleased with himself as he had scored a dramatic success, tracing and impounding one of the bank accounts which was being used by the provisional government. Sinn Féin's highly successful efforts to raise a national bond had alarmed the authorities and they'd assigned Alan Bell the task of tacking down and confiscating the funds.

As the tram came to a halt on the Rathmines road Mr Bell gathered his belongings and stepped off the tram. He was followed by two men wearing long coats and trilby hats. One of these men stepped briskly in front of Mr Bell and pointed a pistol at his chest.

'Alan Bell,' he said loudly, 'You have been found guilty of treason to the Irish People and their Republic. Your sentence is death.' With that the assassin fired. The second gunman stepped over the fallen body and fired three shots into the stricken man's head. The killers then turned and walked back down the Rathmines Road towards the city centre.

The repercussions from this murder were wide ranging and prolonged. They included a concerted effort by the authorities to eliminate those business people who had been active in their support of the bond issue. One such was Charles Hughes of Westport.

Francis got a telephone call at the Westport barracks to alert him to a planned raid by an Auxiliary patrol on Westport. The target of this raid was Mr Hughes and the caller told Francis that the plan was to arrest Mr Hughes with a view to transport him to Dublin for interrogation. The caller added that the county inspector had been asked by the Auxiliaries to ensure that the RIC would provide all necessary support to this operation. Francis knew that the reality was that the Auxiliaries would, in all likelihood, have planned to abduct and kill Hughes.

He thanked the caller for the notification and went out for a cigarette in the hope of bumping into Seán Gibbons but there was no sign of him and Francis decided that he could not risk being seen to be seeking Gibbons out. He scanned the street and noticed Father Canavan, the Catholic parish priest, coming up James Street towards him. He greeted the priest and fell into step with him as he passed.

'Good morning, Father. It's a fine day.'

'It is, Inspector. Thanks be to God.'

'Father, without wishing to compromise either of us I have very urgent information which I need someone to pass along to a third party. May I ask you if you would be willing to help me? Please keep walking and chatting in a normal manner. Who knows who might be watching us?'

To his eternal credit, Father Canavan did not break stride nor even raise an eyebrow. Without turning his head he said, 'Inspector, I have the strangest feeling that you are about to do something which is going to put us both at great risk. I know that you are an intelligent and considered person. Please tell me that you know what you are doing and have reviewed all possible alternatives.'

'Father, I do beg your pardon. I will explain myself fully to you later but right now I need you to do something which is very urgent. Please believe me when I say that if there was any other way to handle the situation I would not be involving your good self.'

The two men strolled along, each with his hands clasped behind his back. To the uninformed observer it would have appeared that the men were talking about nothing more important than the weather.

'Father, an Auxiliary squad is on its way to Westport from Castlebar. They intend to arrest anyone they believe is connected with supporting the national bond issue. Charles Hughes' name is at the top of their list. I have reason to believe that they will shoot him and I want you to get a message to him to get out of town and not return. I'm afraid that there is nothing I can do to stop these people if they find Mr Hughes.'

'Inspector may I suggest that when we reach the end of the street that you keep going and I will turn back and stroll casually to Mr Hughes' emporium.' When they reached the corner Francis turned to Father Canavan and smiled a tight tense smile.

'God bless you Father,' he said removing his uniform cap and dipping his head in salutation.

'No my son, God bless you.' The priest then raised his right hand discreetly in front of his chest and made the sign of the cross towards Francis. 'May He rescue you and keep you safe.'

With that the two men parted, walking slowly away from each other. Francis crossed the street, which allowed him to watch the priest saunter back up James Street towards Hughes' shop. *By God*, thought Francis, *I've just put my life in that man's hands, and yet it feels like the smartest thing I've ever done.*

He decided to head home for a lunchtime break. He was lingering awhile after his lunch unsure of what, if anything, he should be doing when he was startled by an urgent knocking at the front door.

When he opened the door he was confronted by one of his constables in a highly agitated state. 'Inspector, thank God you are home. Sergeant Kerrigan says you must come quickly. A patrol of Auxiliaries arrived a short while ago and they are trying to take away the lads we arrested yesterday for military drilling. The sergeant says he thinks that the Auxies will shoot those boys if you don't stop them.'

Francis had already reached for his tunic and holster before the constable finished his babble. 'Right Constable, run back ahead of me and assure Sergeant Kerrigan that I'm on my way.'

When Francis reached the barracks a few minutes later he heard loud voices from the holding cells downstairs. 'Sergeant,' said a voice he did not recognise but was unmistakably English, 'step aside or, as God is my judge, I'll shoot you on the spot.'

Francis reached the bottom of the stairs and rounded the corner to the cellblock. As he had descended the stairs he thought that he should draw his sidearm and undid the brass clasp but then he'd dismissed the idea as foolish. He did straighten his officer's cap before he came into view. One of the Auxiliary officers had heard Francis coming down the stairs and, as Francis rounded the corner into the cellblock, the Auxiliary raised his pistol and pointed it directly at Francis. He stared the man down. There was a moment of unbearable stillness as everyone waited for the next thing to happen. Nobody seemed anxious to make the first move. In his best Mancunian accent, Francis barked, 'Stand down and secure arms.'

The Auxiliary officers were unnerved and, from of force of habit, obeyed the order directed at them by someone they assumed to be an English police officer. Francis pointed at them, 'You three upstairs now, Sergeant, secure the cells.' Francis watched the sergeant lock up the cellblock and then followed the Auxiliaries up the stairs.

As he followed his temper flared. The three men were standing in the lobby when he caught up with them. 'Who's in charge here?'

Two of the Auxiliaries glanced at the third who by now had recovered his composure and was also angry, 'I am, and who the fuck are you?'

Something snapped in Francis. He grabbed the man by the lapels of his tunic and pushed violently. The Auxiliary stumbled backwards and tripped before slamming hard into the wall behind him. His colleagues made to raise their rifles but Francis was quicker freeing his sidearm. 'If one of you points a gun at me again I'll shoot. Understood?'

To the man lying in a jumble at his feet, Francis snarled, 'Get up and get out of my barracks before I do something more drastic.' For good measure he kicked the man on his backside as he scrambled to his feet.

Sergeant Kerrigan had reached the lobby just as the Auxiliaries were going out through the front door. Francis was standing watching them, his pistol clutched in his right hand, hanging by his side.

'All right, Inspector?' asked Kerrigan as he nodded at the gun.

'Yes Sergeant, thank you.' Francis slowly returned the gun to his holster and turned to the sergeant. 'Post two men at the front door, armed with rifles, and barricade the rear entrance. No one comes in or out without my specific say so.'

'Right away, Inspector.'

Francis went to his office and closed the door behind him. He sat down heavily and wiped his hands across his face and then stared blankly at the wall in front of him for some time. Eventually he picked up a pen and started writing an Incident Report.

When he'd finished, he picked a blank sheet of paper and began working on a resignation letter. As he was about to sign his letter he'd paused, stared again at the wall for a long time, and then slowly crumpled the letter into a ball and threw it into the waste paper basket under his desk.

CHAPTER SIXTEEN

Dammed if you do, dammed if you don't

RIC discipline was not rigorously enforced. Support from their senior officers, including the Chief of Police, General Tudor, encouraged reprisals. Mark Sturgis, Under Secretary at Dublin Castle, noted in his dairy in December 1920, 'These men have undoubtedly been influenced by what they have taken to be the passive approval of their officers, from Tudor on downwards, to believe that they will never be punished for anything.'

A parting shot from the Auxiliaries' leader about how they would deal with the Fenians out in the countryside had worried Francis.

He'd dispatched Sergeant Kerrigan to the Hughes' homestead in Lankhill to forestall any action there by the Auxiliaries. Francis expected that once they'd been foiled in the town, they would pursue Mr Hughes out into the country. As the sergeant later reported, he arrived just in time to prevent the shooting of Charles Hughes' nephew who shared his uncle's name. The Auxiliaries were lining young Charles up against the wall of the family farmhouse when the sergeant arrived. 'He's not the one ye want at all.' He'd told them. 'This lad's a good gossoon and no bother to us.' Luckily for the younger Charles Hughes, the Auxiliaries believed the sergeant and quit the farm without shooting anyone.

‘Well done, Sergeant,’ responded Francis to this report. ‘Now I think we both need a drink. What say you to a dram over at the hotel?’

I’d say I’m your man, Inspector.’ Drained of adrenalin the two men quit the police barracks and walked over the bridge to the hotel. They passed Father Canavan as they reached the bottom of James Street.

‘Good evening officers,’ said the priest. ‘A grand quiet evening is it not?’

‘It is to be sure, thanks be to God,’ replied Francis.

‘God needs a little help now and again, Inspector. And we are lucky that we have those amongst us who are men enough to give it when called.’

Francis tipped his cap to the priest and said, ‘Indeed so, Father. Good evening to you now,’ and walked on towards the hotel.

His sergeant looking puzzled asked, ‘What was that all about, Inspector?’

‘I have no idea, Sergeant, but maybe Father Canavan has somehow heard about your heroics out at Lankhill already. Either way I’d not lose any sleep over it. Here we are, let’s go in and get that drink.’

§

'District Inspector, I've had a very difficult conversation with Captain Robinson, of the Auxiliaries. He says that the RIC obstructed his men on their raid in Westport last week. What have you to say about that?' Francis was in Castlebar for his mid-November briefing with County Inspector Steadman. He was sitting across from Steadman at the county inspector's desk. The desk was a rather fine partner's desk, made of a rich mahogany with a baize insert covering most of the surface. Steadman was perched on a high-backed swivel chair. Both the desk and the chair were Steadman's personal property. The chair Francis occupied was standard government issue; wooden and uncomfortable.

'Sir, if you care to describe preventing murder as obstruction, then I'd have to say, "Guilty as charged."'

'Look here, Maguire, you'll not be so bloody cocky if I put you on a charge of insubordination, so don't try and be clever with me. This is not a game, this is a war.' Steadman was being deliberately rude in not using Francis' rank but Francis choose to ignore the slight and tried to stay calm.

'With all due respect, sir, we are not operating in a military zone. If and until such time as martial law is imposed in Mayo, it remains the job of the RIC to keep the peace. If we are to stand aside and permit Crown forces to commit murder then I want that in writing from General Tudor. But we both know that I will never get such written orders.'

Steadman was furious, but did not immediately respond, so Francis pressed on, 'I have no intention of ever allowing, never mind instructing, anyone under my command to break the law. As it says quite plainly in the constable's handbook, we get our authority to police the people from the people. If we abuse that authority it will evaporate and we become powerless. We will be dragged down into a mire of killing and reprisal which will destroy us all.'

Steadman did not explode as Francis feared he might. Instead he said coldly, 'Inspector, you have unfurled your colours and now we all know where you stand. Very instructive. You are dismissed.'

'Good day, sir,' said Francis and turned to the door. As he began to pull the door behind him Steadman said, 'Watch your back, Inspector, these are dangerous times.'

Francis turned and stared at Steadman and struggling to control his rising temper he said slowly, 'County Inspector, I know that I'm a policeman, but I have no idea who or what you are.'

'What in hell does that mean, Maguire?'

Francis said no more as he closed the door slowly and firmly. He was shaking with rage as he walked to his car. His anger swept over him, first at Steadman and then at himself for allowing Steadman to provoke him. *By God, Francis, you've done it now. No going back. Why did I allow that fool to provoke me? He's an idiot and a bigot. This won't end well.* Francis unconsciously fingered his sidearm as he climbed into the waiting car.

'Everything alright, District Inspector?' asked his driver, holding the door open.

'Yes, yes, fine Constable, thank you. Let's get back to Westport, post haste.'

§

A month later, in December 1920, the family were all in Belfast where Teresa had gone to have her newest baby, a boy they named Frank. Denis again took Francis out for a celebratory drink. Francis' old friend John Boyle joined them at the pub on the Falls Road.

'What a year we have had Francis. I never thought I'd live to see the day when the sectarianism we always feared in this city would be unleashed so destructively. If you are Catholic you are assumed to be a Nationalist and either way a target for the hatred of the Loyalist mob. Did you know that over six hundred homes and businesses were destroyed in the rioting?'

'I've read the reports, John, but I didn't realise things had become so bad.'

'Bad, you have no idea. Back in July thousands of men descended as a mob on the shipyards and expelled all of the Catholics and even attacked any Protestants who didn't support them. There were terrible beatings meted out and by the end of it, twenty-two people were dead. Lots of men jumped into the river in fear of their lives.'

'What did the police or army do?'

'Even if they were willing there was not much that could have been done against such a large mob. Of course many of the rioters were ex-service men with nothing but time on their hands and as we've seen before neither the army nor the RIC are willing to challenge the loyalists with live rounds, which is what would have been needed to stop them.'

Denis shifted uneasily, although he'd retired from the police some years earlier, he'd retained his natural loyalty to the force that a lifetime of service had instilled. He looked around the pub from the vantage of their secluded corner. They were in the same corner which he and Francis had occupied when they argued about Francis' friendship with Conor Maguire. Francis remembered his father-in-law's anxiety back then and promised himself not to burden Denis with tales of recent events.

The pub's other customers were a mixed bunch of office clerks and labourers, most of whom Denis knew on sight. There were a couple of burly and rough looking characters at the bar who seemed to Denis to be taking an unhealthy interest in his conversation with Francis and John.

The tiled floor of the pub was covered in sawdust to absorb spilt beer and the dirt carried in from the street. The air above the drinkers was heavy with cigarette smoke. A gentle burble of conversation and laughter rose from the crowd and was absorbed by the cloud of smoke which appeared to be suspended from the ceiling of the pub. The two men whom Denis had noticed at the bar seemed curiously detached from the hubbub around them. Denis excused himself and walked slowly across to them. Francis had his back to the bar so didn't notice where Denis was headed. To attract Francis' attention John nodded at Denis' back. As Francis turned he saw Denis reach the bar but he could not hear what was being said.

One of the men leant forward so that his face was right up against Denis', the other man began to stand up from his bar stool. Before Francis had time to react, the bartender reached over the bar and held this second man by the arm, leaning forward, he whispered into the man's ear. This man then reached out and put a hand on his friend's shoulder restraining him and eased him back onto his barstool. Denis nodded to the bartender and walked back to re-join his table.

'What was that all about, Denis?'

'I noticed those two taking too much interest in our conversation so I simply suggested that they mind their own business. The chap who got in my face said that he knows that you are an RIC district inspector and didn't want you fouling the air with your stink of treachery.'

'Should we leave?'

'Good God no! The bartender has known me for forty years or more and he's what you might call "well-connected" in the Nationalist community. He put those lads straight, so there's no need to concern yourselves. Are ye ready for another pint, boys?'

'Jesus Christ,' exhaled John, 'We're not safe on the streets and now we're not safe in our own local. When and how will this all end?'

'Not soon, John, and not well. Come on, Denis, let's buy a bottle of Jameson and take it back to your house, shall we?' asked Francis.

'Ay right,' responded Denis. 'You're probably wise. This place is a dump anyhow, let's go.'

As they stood to leave Francis noticed the bartender nod to three men at the far end of the bar. These men picked up their drinks and joined the pair Denis had challenged. He overheard the bartender offer to buy a pint on the house and ask the pair if they knew any of the others. Francis smiled inwardly thinking, *It's good to have friends watching your back.* He waved goodnight to the bartender and followed the others out into the street.

Back in the safety and comfort of the Shanagher front parlour the three men relaxed and their conversation naturally returned to the political situation.

'Things seem quiet enough over in Westport, Francis. You've had none of the excitement we've seen here. Are the Volunteers active at all?' asked John.

'Mayo has more than its fair share of Volunteers. We know the senior people and keep tabs on their movements. So far, I suppose we have been lucky. We've seen no shooting since Jack Milling's murder. We did have a bit of excitement last month when the town was raided by a squad of Auxiliaries. They were looking for some local notables who have been active in support of the Sinn Féin bond issue. But we were able to make sure no one was hurt.'

John started to ask how Francis managed to do that but Denis cut across John's question and, fixing Francis with a direct and stern look, said, 'Francis is playing two sides against the middle, are you not, Francis?'

The three men were huddled around a small coal fire burning in the grate. The warm glow from the fire cast a flickering red light onto their faces. John sat back startled by Denis' question. Francis leant forward and put his glass down on the hearthstone and rubbed his hands together over the fire, warming up after the walk back from the pub through the cold and damp winter's evening. After a moment he reached down to retrieve his glass and sipped appreciatively. He settled back in his armchair and stuck his feet out towards the fire. Everyone in the room knew that he was buying time. He himself was not sure what he wanted to say next.

'Is there a man anywhere on this island who would not appreciate a warm fire and a decent whiskey on a night like this?' he asked almost wistfully. 'We are not all so different from each other, are we? British, Irish, Unionist or Nationalist, we all like a good dram of whiskey and a warm fire, do we not?' Francis had been looking into his glass as he spoke; he looked up and smiled gently at his father-in-law. John, who was shaking his head slowly from side to side, opened his mouth to speak but then changed his mind and closed it again.

Denis was not as taken aback as Francis expected. Looking worried and concerned he said, 'You might well be right, Francis, and while there is much which divides us we have more in common than many like to admit. But I suspect that your problem might be that one of the things on which all sides might agree is that they'd all gladly shoot you!'

John had taken to staring into the burning coals. Francis put his now empty glass on the hearthstone and sat back in the armchair, its high back covered with a lace antimacassar protected him from the cold air coming off the window behind him. The room projected a deceiving impression of normality.

'Denis, you once said to me a long time ago that you thought I was a good policeman and would make a good officer one day. I've never forgotten that compliment. District Inspector Dagg, the man who first persuaded me to become a policeman, said something similar to me when I enlisted. All I'm trying to do now is to live up to those expectations. I know that trying to keep the peace when there are bullets flying might seem a futile exercise but I don't hold with murder whether it's revolutionary or extra-judicial.'

'Francis, I don't doubt that you have thought about what you are doing,' interrupted Denis but, before he could continue, John also cut in.

'Hang on a minute, just what is it that you are doing, Francis? What does Denis mean when he says that you're playing two sides against the middle?'

Francis shifted around in his seat so that he was looking directly at John. 'The powers that be clearly want a "gloves off" response from the police to the violence being perpetrated by the Volunteers but I'm afraid that ignores what happens afterwards. No doubt we could crush this rebellion by burning out the civilian population and shooting all suspects on sight but the politicians seem to have no concerns about how to win back public support once we've taken precisely the sort of action which is bound to drive even the most moderate people to the extremes.

'Look what happened in Balbriggan a few weeks back in response to the killing of two policemen. The RIC and the Tans burnt down half of the town including the textile factory which was the only employer in the town. There will be no meaningful investigation and certainly no prosecutions following that atrocity.'

'Francis, all very tragic I'm sure, but you still have not answered my question. Just what is it that you have done or are you doing?'

Denis stood and fetched the whiskey bottle and a jug of water from the sideboard. He poured each of the men a large measure and added a dash of water to his own and John's glass and a heavy dose to Francis', knowing his habit of adding too much water to his whiskey. He sat back down and turned again to Francis, 'Well, Francis, why don't you tell all? It will do you good to talk and if you can't talk to us who can you talk to?'

And so Francis finally unburdened himself to his friend and his father-in-law. He told them how he started out as a so called 'Dominion Home Ruler' but now with the country about to be partitioned and his Ulster already on its way to becoming a second class dominion, he had turned to republicanism as the only way forward. He talked about his difficulties with County Inspector Steadman, his opposition to official reprisals and intimidation, and how he had saved Charles Hughes from being murdered.

'That's not all,' he finished. 'Since the business with Charles Hughes I have been regularly supplying the Volunteers with information about army manoeuvres and Tan patrols. And, so far so good, I have managed to keep the two sides apart.'

'Jesus Francis,' said John. 'No wonder Denis says that all sides might want to shoot you! Are you mad or what? It sounds like one of those penny Western novels with you as the isolated Sherriff standing on the moral high ground.'

Francis laughed. 'That's almost exactly what Teresa said.'

'She knows?'

'Some of it but I've spared her the details.' Francis paused and then said, 'Look, what I'm doing is not as mad as you all seem to think. There is mounting pressure on the government to abandon their heavy-handed approach and call an end to these reprisals. The mainland press is hostile and even the king has voiced his displeasure. Something has to give and soon. Without wishing to be cliché it is none the less true that the darkest hour is just before the dawn.'

'Well you may not wish to sound cliché but that is exactly what you are doing. Look Francis, I know how the RIC works and in the current climate it is not just scaremongering to suggest that you might be shot for what you are doing. You can't control the bigger picture here. The lines are drawn and you have to choose which side you will stand on.'

'You may well be right, Denis. But my conscience will not allow me support reprisals nor can I condone murder by the Volunteers. It may also be true that this violence has been inevitable ever since the Ulster Volunteers armed themselves. But regardless of the who, the whys, or the wherefores of how we got to this point, I simply must do what I can to minimise the mayhem in my own district.'

'What happens when the local Volunteer commander comes under pressure to become more active? How do you know that he will not use you for his own ends until his unit feels strong enough to take the offensive?'

'That is a very fair question and I suspect that what you say is in all likelihood what will happen sooner or later. Perhaps I'm being naive but I'm buying time in the hope that a broader settlement will emerge before I lose control of what happens in Westport.'

Denis looked sad and worried. 'And what about your family; my daughter and my grandchildren? What will become of them if your grand scheme comes crashing down around your ears? The very least that will happen to you is that you will be dismissed from the force and stripped of your pension rights. How will you support your family then Francis?'

'If the worse comes to the worst, we will go and live on the farm in Tempo. We'll not be homeless and we'll not starve.'

'That farm is not big enough to support you all and besides Teresa knows nothing about farming or country life, nor do your children.'

'I'm not suggesting that the farm is a perfect solution but simply that we would have a place to go if that becomes necessary. Longer term, once the killing stops, there will be opportunities in whatever new administration emerges.'

'Does Teresa know that is your plan?'

'No, she does not. And I'd appreciate it very much if neither of you discuss any of this with her. I'd rather deal with each day as it comes than have her fretting about what might or might not happen.'

'Francis, you may be very clever but you know nothing of women in general, or my daughter in particular, if you honestly believe that she is not fretting about the future.'

CHAPTER SEVENTEEN

Shooting in Westport

In the face of continuous harassment from the police and under pressure from their Dublin HQ, to spread the fighting wider around the country, the Volunteers formed Flying Columns in which small bands of dedicated and typically young men, took to the countryside and disrupted the authority's effectiveness by cutting their means of communications and ambushing police and army patrols when and where they could.

Thomas Heavey and three of his fellow Volunteers walked out of the hills and strolled casually into Westport just after dark on a Friday evening late in January 1921. They were in search of some action. The Westport brigade had yet to engage with the enemy as a unit and young Thomas and his friends were bored tramping about the hillsides and fed up being cold and hungry.

'So, Thomas, what's our plan?' asked young Jack McDonagh.

'We'll have a look about, right casual like. Play it cool, lads, and if an opportunity presents itself, well, we'll take it and finally have ourselves a pop at the enemy.'

The group sauntered through the town and stopped at the Glendinning Monument on the Octagon. From there they could see down James Street to the South Mall and the stone bridge over the Carrowbeg River. They could also look along Shop Street and observe the front of the RIC barracks.

The few locals who noticed the group gave them a wide berth. There were no comings or goings from the police barracks and the group started to bicker about what to do next. The boys were hungry so one of the trio, Mick Staunton, suggested that they stop into his family's home, in the town, for their dinner. Mrs Staunton greeted the boys enthusiastically. 'Come in, come in lads, sit ye down and I'll fry up those pork chops I got from the butchers this morning.'

There followed a rather bizarre conversation where everyone pretended that it was entirely normal for these lads to be living rough on the hillsides of Mayo and popping in for their dinner as though visiting from a distant town where they had found employment. The talk was of hurling, football, of the quality of the pork chops and the recent improvement in the weather. No one mentioned what the boys were actually doing nor of the raids made by the authorities on their homes as part of the efforts to track them down.

After they had been fed and watered the young men took their leave and Mrs Staunton somehow remained stoic and waved them away from her front door. They made their way back up to the Octagon at the top of James Street. After a brief debate about what they should do, Thomas convinced them to take a few shots at the police barracks. They took up positions around the base of the monument, checked the revolvers they were carrying and fired a few volleys at the barracks. They were disappointed when they got little or no response from the police. After waiting a while they decided to slip away into the night and headed back out to the countryside to re-join their column.

The front of the barracks had been fortified some weeks before Heavey's raid and the bullets fired by Thomas and his friends skipped harmlessly off the shutters covering the windows. Francis was in his office clearing up some paperwork and heard the desk sergeant call for the constables billeted in the station to muster arms and prepare to defend the barracks. Francis swore to himself. 'What in the name of God is going on?' He fastened his tunic and strapped on his side arm. 'Damn, damn, damn,' he muttered as he descended to the front office.

There was a confused melee as the sergeant issued rifles to each constable from the store. When he saw the DI on the stairs the Sergeant shouted, 'The Shinners are attacking, sir!'

'I had guessed as much for myself, Sergeant, thank you,' said Francis sardonically. 'Who's upstairs at the front and have you secured the rear entrance?'

'O'Malley is at the front checking what if anything he can see through the observation slits in the shutters and we are boarding up the rear right now, Inspector.'

A constable across the lobby, with his rifle stuck through the shutter shouted, 'Permission to fire, sir,' and loosed off two rounds into the night.

'Hold your fire,' shouted Francis over the din. 'What are you shooting at, Ryan? Can you see anything?'

'No, sir, I just want to make sure that no one is sneaking up on the front door with a bomb, sir.'

'Very good, Ryan but I don't want anyone shot in error. Are the gas street lamps burning? Can you see any movement in the street?'

'Yes, sir, the street lights are working but there's nothing moving out there.'

'Right, everyone hold your fire. We don't want to be shooting innocent civilians. I'll go up and join O'Malley and check if we can see what is going on. Stay calm and be alert.'

As he climbed back up the stairs Francis was fuming. *I can't believe Joe Ring has ordered this attack. I'll bet some bloody hot heads have become bored tramping about the hillsides and thought it would be a good idea to take a few pot shots at the barracks.*

'O'Malley, I'm coming up,' shouted Francis. He didn't want the constable shooting at him when he went through the door. 'What can you see out there?'

'Nothing, sir, not a thing and no more shots have been fired since those first volleys a few minutes ago. The shots had to have been fired from the Octagon as there is nowhere else with protective cover and a line of sight on the barracks.'

O'Malley was very nervous and was clutching his rifle rather too tightly.

'All right, O'Malley, relax. I'm sure that we are not about to face a full-scale attack. Take a few deep breaths and you'll be fine. Keep your eyes peeled and shout if you see any movement.'

'I'll bloody well swing Joe Ring for this,' muttered Francis to himself as he headed back down to the front office. 'Sergeant, let's put a patrol out on the streets. I'll lead. We'll slip out the back door and approach the Octagon from three directions.'

§

Francis made a point of connecting with Seán Gibbons the next day. 'Seán, get word to Joe Ring that I want to see him and soon. Some idiots were taking pot shots at the barracks last night. Castlebar had to be alerted and it was all I could do to stop a full scale search of the area.'

'Did you see who it was, Inspector?'

'Of course not. They'd cleared off sharpish after their bold and daring attack. I put patrols out into the town but I knew we would find nothing.'

'I'm not sure how long it will take to get a message to Joe or if he'll be willing to come into town.

'Don't muck me about, Seán. We both know your communications are very efficient. As for Joe coming into town, I don't want him to do that. I'll meet him at a place of his choosing in the countryside.'

'Fair enough, Inspector. No offence intended. I'll do want I can.'

§

What Francis did not know was that his own annoyance was as nothing compared to the rage the news of the attack provoked in Joe Ring. Earlier that morning when the Volunteers returned to the barn where they were billeting, they found the three lads sound asleep. It wasn't long before the boys began to almost fear for their lives as they experienced the tirade of abuse poured on their heads by Joe Ring. When Ring had found, the night before, that the three young men were missing he guessed that they would attempt an attack on the RIC in Westport. This, he'd surmised, would provoke the dispatch of reinforcements from Castlebar. So he'd force marched the column to an ambush spot on the Castlebar – Westport Road, where they'd all spent a long and very miserable night waiting for the reinforcements which never came.

A speedy court-martial was held and the resulting sentence was the expulsion of the three young men from the column. When tempers cooled this was reduced to a 'caution.'

Seán Gibbons reported a sanitised version of this story to Francis later the same evening and brought a message about how Francis could meet Joe Ring the following night.

As he set out for this meeting Francis decided not to wear his uniform or take his sidearm, worried that the Volunteers might not be able to resist confiscating them. He also reasoned that a sidearm would be of no help to him if the Volunteers decided to shoot him.

His instructions were to drive unaccompanied out of Westport towards Aghagower and stop at the junction in the boreen just before Kinlooey Lough. The lough sits in a lonely isolated spot surrounded by rolling countryside. When Francis switched off the car's engine he found himself in complete silence and darkness. He sat awhile in the car but after a few minutes, when his eyes adjusted to the darkness, he decided to get out and stretch his legs. Not a single farmhouse light was visible and the night completely still. Francis walked back in the direction from which he had come and then stopped after just a few yards for want of any light to guide him.

Fishing in his jacket pocket Francis produced a packet of cigarettes and a box of matches. Cupping his hands around a match he lit up and drew hard on a cigarette, he then dropped his head back onto his shoulders and expelled a smoky breath slowly towards the night sky.

He felt the chill night air seeping into his bones and stamped his feet hard on the roadway, an old beat policeman's trick, to keep his feet warm. He could hardly see ten yards in any direction. The almost total darkness was occasionally relieved with a slight break in the cloud cover. He was feeling very exposed. *What in the name of God am I doing?*

I'm a bloody sitting duck standing here. Where in hell's name is Joe Ring?

A sharp scream from the other side of the hedgerow behind him startled Francis. As he spun around to confront whoever was there he realised that the noise was the mating bark of a fox. He had almost dropped his cigarette in fright and nervously brought it to his lips to draw on the comfort of the warm smoke. A low soft voice chuckled at him out of the darkness, 'Jaysus, Inspector, you're mighty nervous this evening. You nearly jumped out of your skin just now. You need to relax or you'll give yourself a heart attack.'

'You can hardly blame me for being jumpy, Mr Ring. As you'll no doubt know, some of your lot were taking pot-shots at me two nights ago in Westport. And I've been standing out here in the cold and dark for nearly an hour waiting for you to show up. So please don't try my patience any further or expect me to see anything funny in my situation.'

'District Inspector, in case you had not noticed there's a war on and quite frankly my friend, as far as every Volunteer in the country is concerned, you are on the wrong side. So it's hardly a great surprise that some of them might have had a go at shooting you. Besides, as I understand things, a few rounds were fired at the police barracks and not at any actual police officers. So don't you think that you might be overreacting a wee bit?'

Francis flicked his cigarette butt into the hedgerow and turned to walk back towards his car, 'Come on, Ring, let's sit in my car and get out of the blasted cold.' As the two men settled into the front seats of the car Francis shifted his weight so that his back was pressed against the door and he was facing Ring. He turned the ignition key and a pale glow from the instrument lights meant that he could just make out Ring's features across the three feet of space which separated him from the IRA commander.

'Do I have to call you District Inspector? It seems a bit peculiar in the circumstances.'

'Francis is my Christian name but why don't you call me Frank.'

'Right so, Frank it is. First, Frank, let me say I'm very sorry for what happened in Westport. Those lads set that operation up in direct contradiction to their orders. Suffice it to say that they have been court martialled and disciplined. You will appreciate that for your safety we have kept your support for the cause a closely guarded secret. I can't very well issue an order which says "Don't attack the police in Westport as the officer in charge is on our side."'

'Let me be quite clear with you, Mr Ring.'

'Joe, please.'

'All right then, Joe. You must realise that my intention is to avoid murder, not to support it. I don't approve of the violence being perpetrated by either side. The Unionist's threat of violence has been sufficient to cause the partition of the country and Republican violence and British reprisals will tear what's left of it to shreds. How will we make peace on these islands after we've been killing each other like dogs? How long will that take, Joe? Answer me that.'

'Frank, I'm not the thinker you are. I see things simply in terms of our fight for freedom from British imperialism. Every generation of Irishmen has risen up against British oppression. Our generation has, at last, a very real chance of success. Our children will not thank us if we fail. The division, death and destruction which will be caused along the way is a price we will have to pay.'

The fox which had startled Francis earlier screamed again in the darkness and was answered by the chattering of several foxes. The two men smiled at the interruption.

'Life at some levels carries on regardless, Frank, eh? Anyhow, whether you agree with our methods or not is beside the point. You have shown yourself ready to support us and, as far as we are concerned, that is all that matters. But we need you to do something rather specific, Frank.' Joe paused when he said this and a heavy silence hung in the atmosphere.

'And what might that be, Joe?'

'Every time a rebellion has been foiled in Ireland the authorities have succeeded because we have been let down by our own people informing on the rebels. As you will well be aware there are spies and traitors amongst us now and they are causing us severe trouble. We want you to find out who the local informers are, Frank. Find out and tell us so we can put a stop to them.'

Francis exploded, he shouted, 'So you can drag them out of their beds, tar and feather them, after you've tortured them, and then shoot them in some desolate bog? If you think that I'll be party to that sort of thing you have greatly mistaken me, Joe. Now get the hell out of my car.'

'Calm down. I know there have been atrocities around the country and no doubt the odd personal score has been settled in the name of the shooting of spies. But, trust me, that is not our way here in Mayo. If you identify informers, we will simply put the frighteners on them with a late night visit and a few well-chosen words. If the Tan murder squads are denied information then they won't be as free with their killing, will they?'

Francis did not reply. He shifted around in his seat and gripped the steering wheel hard in both hands. Staring into the darkness through the car's windscreen he experienced an overwhelming sense of vertigo. He was falling and he knew it. A panic rose in his chest which he suppressed through the sheer force of his will.

Eventually he felt calm enough to speak again, 'Joe, it's time I got back. I will think about what you ask and send word via young Seán. Good night and God bless. Please go now.'

Neither man was certain of his position. Both were taking considerable risks just talking to each other. Francis was feeling both annoyed and naive about the situation in which he had found himself.

Joe climbed out of the car without speaking. He was holding the door open and standing looking back in. ‘Goodnight Frank. May God keep you in the palm of his hand but never close his fist.’ With that he was gone and Francis was once again alone in the dark.

CHAPTER EIGHTEEN

Suspicion

Cardinal Logue, Catholic Primate of All Ireland was a Nationalist, but he along with the rest of his hierarchy consistently condemned the Irish Volunteers. In one pastoral letter he wrote: 'Holy Ireland, the land of St Patrick, shall never be regenerated by deeds of blood or raised up by the hand of the midnight assassin.'

Francis woke the next morning with a clear head. He had decided what he would and would not do and more importantly he had an exact understanding of where his personal lines must be drawn. He had become a supporter of 'The Cause', as Joe Ring put it.

He reflected to himself that the violence, or at least the threat of it, started with the belligerence of the Ulster Volunteers back in 1914. He was sure that the coming partition of the country had been caused by a combination of that belligerence and the failure of Nationalists to take unionism seriously. He had also accepted that his hopes for an Independent Dominion solution along Canadian lines were at best naive.

As he lathered his face he thought about the stupidity of the government in believing that the use of reprisals could subdue the population. In fact, he was sure that the violence and intimidation which was being perpetrated by the authorities was driving previously moderate opinion into the Sinn Féin camp. He wondered if he was slowly coming to accept Conor Maguire's logic that when all peaceful means of protest have been suppressed the only option left is armed insurrection.

Francis wiped the remaining soap from his face with a damp cloth and looked at himself hard in the mirror. He decided that he looked a bit grim, and then he thought, *All of this is grim but none of it means that I will be party to murder by either side.*

As he put on his uniform he reviewed his decision to continue to warn the Volunteers of threats to their safety and convinced himself again that it is the right thing to do. But under no circumstances was he going to deliver the names of any individual informers. *Joe Ring is a man of his word but, as has been demonstrated this week, he is not in complete control of the actions of his men.*

Heading down to the kitchen where Teresa was preparing his breakfast, Francis remembered that there was an anonymous letter on his desk exposing Seán Gibbons as a member of the Volunteers. He smiled to himself, deciding to show Seán the letter when he got to the barracks.

As Francis entered the kitchen Teresa noticed the smile. 'You're looking cheerful this morning, my dear. It's good to see you smiling; you have been so distracted of late. What's cheered you up?'

‘Nothing and everything, my love. Some difficult issues I have been wrestling with have fallen into place for me. That’s all.’

‘Do I want to know what they might be?’

‘Probably not,’ he said smiling. Taking Teresa into his arms he hugged her closely to his chest and kissed her lightly on her forehead. ‘I’m beginning to see some light at the end of this very dark tunnel and I have a plan to steer us towards it. Now I must eat my breakfast and get on or I’ll be late.’

After finishing his breakfast and planting a less than chaste kiss on Teresa’s lips, Francis said, ‘If I can, I’ll pop home for lunch. But only expect me if you see me.’ He then strode out of the house and headed towards the police barracks.

When Francis got there he was greatly annoyed to find that the front desk was not manned. He stomped upstairs to his office, knowing that the noise he was making would alert the desk sergeant to his arrival. Swinging the door to his office open Francis was brought up short by the sight of County Inspector Steadman sitting behind his desk and reading his correspondence.

‘Good morning, District Inspector, how are you this morning? I thought I’d pop down to see how you were all getting on. Please come in and take your seat.’ Steadman stood and ostentatiously gestured to the seat he had vacated. He kept the letter he was reading in his hand.

‘It is heartening, is it not, to find that there are members of the public so sickened by the murderous Fenians that they are prepared to help the police by writing letters such as this one?' Steadman handed over the letter he had been reading. As Francis feared, it was the letter exposing Seán Gibbons.

He glanced casually at the letter and said, 'County Inspector, what a surprise. Have you been offered any hospitality?'

'Yes, thank you. Your desk sergeant is making a pot of tea. I anticipated your arrival and asked him to bring two cups.'

This veil of civility was unnerving Francis who, despite his best efforts to constrain himself, couldn't help asking, 'Was there something in particular you wanted to talk about, County Inspector?'

'Well in truth, nothing and everything.' Francis smiled inwardly remembering that he used a similar expression with Teresa earlier. Steadman continued, 'I have been reviewing our last conversation in my head again and again, and I find that I remain greatly disturbed by your overall attitude. You simply do not appear to realise the importance which attaches to our ability, as a force, to contain and subdue this spate of violence. The government have given the RIC a vote of confidence in leaving us in charge of matters but we are perilously close to losing that confidence and finding ourselves side-lined by the army.'

'Professional soldiers and their officers might be a little less inclined to treat the general population as the enemy, sir.'

'You see, Francis, that is precisely the sort of remark which worries me.'

Holy God, thought Francis, *he's playing with me. The man is even stupider than my worst fears.* 'Sir, my feelings about how this crisis is being handled and my expectations that it will all end badly are hardly unique. Even the king has felt moved to voice his concerns about the violence being perpetrated by the authorities.'

'We are officers sworn to do our duty. You have clear instructions, Inspector, but you chose to ignore them. It is not your place to quote the king at me but to do as you are ordered. It is one thing to have differences of opinion on tactics. But quite another to be openly sympathetic to these rebels. For example, Inspector, can you tell me please what action you have taken since receiving that letter you are holding in your hand?'

'The individual named in this letter is known to us, sir. We have suspected him of being a supporter of the Republican cause but have no evidence to use against him. Francis tossed the letter onto his desk. 'That letter is of precisely zero use to us. We can't make arrests based on anonymous accusations and, as we do not know who wrote the letter, we can't go and question them regarding what evidence they may or may not have.'

'So in other words, District Inspector, you have done precisely nothing. Am I correct?'

Francis knew that he was being painted into a corner but he was not sure how to divert the conversation. 'Sir,' he tried. 'since my arrival in Westport we have managed to keep a very tight lid on Sinn Féin and the Irish Volunteers. There has been no Nationalist related violence in the district since I took charge. You will remember that my predecessor had to face several riots, considerable public disorder and, of course, the murder of the Resident Magistrate, while he was in charge.'

'Your predecessor and Mr Milling between them effectively decapitated Sinn Féin in this district. Now I get reports of open defiance of judicial authority by a Republican court, which you yourself actually attended.' Francis started at this last remark.

'Oh yes, Inspector, you didn't think I knew about that did you? You are not the only policeman to whom the people of this town write letters. You think you are being very clever playing two sides against the middle, don't you? Well there's lots which you don't know. Like for instance that some of your colleagues have taken to referring to you as the "Sinn Féin DI". I need men I can trust, District Inspector, and it is increasingly obvious to me that I can't trust you. I will be making my reports to that effect and we shall see what the Castle thinks of your behaviour.' Steadman stood to leave. He picked up his baton and fixed his cap firmly on his head. 'Good day to you,' he said as he firmly closed the door to Francis' office behind him.

Francis slumped back into his chair. *Damn, damn, damn,* he swore to himself. *I'm done for.*

He decided to go for a walk. First making sure he had his cigarettes and matches in his pocket. He was about to set out when there was a knock on his office door. The desk sergeant appeared with a tray laden with a pot of tea and the necessary accoutrements. When he found Francis alone he said, 'Will ye not be wanting the tea, Inspector?'

'No sergeant, the County Inspector needed to hurry back to Castlebar but thank you anyway.' The sergeant turned back out of the office door muttering to himself. Francis ignored the man and remembering the informer's letter, he picked it up, folded it carefully and put it in his tunic pocket before heading out into the street.

His mind was racing as he tried to figure out how he might possibly keep his job and his career and then he began to fear that even his life might be in real danger. He loitered outside the barracks, smoking and hoping to catch Seán Gibbons on his way into the lawyer's office next door. As he paced he began to focus on the avenues open to him. After a while a calm descended on him and Francis was surprised at how collected he felt, as though part of him always expected that he would eventually end up in just such a plight. He had also concluded that his only hope for survival was to get support from the highest authority he could reach before Steadman queered the pitch. *But who has that access and would they be willing to help?* He found that his feet were taking him towards the rectory and Father Canavan.

The housekeeper failed to hide her surprise when she opened the front door and found Francis standing there with his officer's cap tucked under his arm. 'Good morning, Mrs Doyle. Is Father Canavan at home, by any chance?'

'Good morning, Inspector. The Father is in his study but he doesn't normally accept callers at this hour.'

'If you'll let him know that I'm here and need to see him on some urgent police business I'm sure Father Canavan won't mind being interrupted.' Mrs Doyle was unimpressed at this attempted trampling on her authority but under Francis' unrelenting glare she yielded and admitted him. Instructing him to wait, Mrs Doyle bustled along the corridor to a room at the back of the house.

Francis was shown into the priest's study and as he entered Father Canavan stood up from behind his desk and crossed the floor quickly with his hands extended in greeting. 'Inspector Maguire, come in, come in,' he said, grasping Francis by the hand and elbow. 'Please take a seat over here by the window. Mrs Doyle, would you mind putting on the kettle and making us a pot of tea please? Thank you very much.'

The priest sat opposite Francis, a small table separating their knees. The priest's face was full of concern but his breathing was calm. He looked steadily at Francis and waited for him to speak. The man's demeanour helped Francis relax and he sat forward, rested his elbows on his knees and clasped his hands together in an unconscious mimic of someone praying.

'I'm in grave trouble, Father, and I need your help.'

The priest's hands were folded together resting on his round stomach. He opened them, palms up as though accepting a parcel. 'Please Francis, tell me what ails you and be assured that where I can help you I will of course do so, God willing.'

An hour later Francis was driving south as fast as possible to the home of Dr Thomas Gilmartin, Archbishop of Tuam. The drive was arduous, covering forty miles of lonely country roads around the foot of the desolate Partry Mountains. The police touring car was all too easily recognisable for any Irish Volunteer flying column lying in opportunistic ambush but Francis was oblivious to the possibilities of danger. The car's suspension creaked and jolted over the uneven surface of the bog road. The brakes were tested to their limits on the sharp bends and at one point Francis narrowly avoided hitting a cow as she waddled across the narrow road. He was carrying a letter to the archbishop from Father Canavan.

As the archbishop had consistently spoken out against violence from all quarters, Francis was optimistic about getting his support. Following a night of extreme police violence in Tuam, provoked by the killing of two policemen, the archbishop had said, in a widely reported sermon, that he hoped God's justice would strike the first man, whether policeman, civilian or solider who fired a criminal shot.

He was greeted by the archbishop's secretary, Father O'Brien, a young and keen administrator devoted to his archbishop, and to his own advancement. He was somewhat officious and standoffish, suggesting that Francis leave the letter with him and that he would present it in due course to the archbishop. Francis insisted that he see the archbishop immediately on a matter of life and death and that the contents of the letter were strictly for the archbishop's eyes only.

O'Brien relented, never before having witnessed a demand for an immediate audience from a senior police officer. He agreed to take Father Canavan's letter directly to the archbishop. Francis was shown into a library where he kicked his heels for some time before the door opened and Dr Gilmartin let himself into the room closing the door quietly behind him. 'District Inspector Maguire, I presume?'

'Your Grace,' replied Francis, 'Thank you very much for interrupting your day to see me.'

'Please Inspector, take a seat,' said the bishop, as he did so himself. 'Father Canavan writes that you are a man of principle who deserves our support.'

CHAPTER NINETEEN

Banishment

The violence perpetrated by the security forces stemmed originally from a very real frustration that the police were being asked to carry the fight to the Volunteers without any support from the public who, because they were frightened, intimidated or sympathetic could or would not support the police. But official reprisals were now part and parcel of British policy in Ireland.

Cardinal Logue now found himself condemning the actions of the authorities, '...these acts of power cannot fail to create exasperation, recklessness, despair and general disorder.'

Following his meeting with the archbishop Francis had to face the return drive to Westport made more hazardous by the fact that the winter darkness had fallen before he set off. When he got back to Westport he returned the police car to the compound at the rear of the barracks and instead of entering the building he slipped out onto the street through the arched entrance.

There was a cold January wind blowing in off the sea and Francis stepped into the doorway of Shanleys Drapers to light a cigarette. By chance Seán Gibbons walked past with another man just as Francis extinguished his match. From the shadows of the doorway Francis hailed Gibbons in not much more than a whisper, 'Seán!'

Gibbons was briefly startled but then recognised Francis by the light reflecting off the buttons on his tunic. He stepped into the doorway and, picking up Francis' furtiveness, he hissed, 'By God, Inspector, you put the heart across me then. What in Hell's name are ye doing lurking in doorways at this time of night?'

'Seán, get word to Joe Ring as soon as you can. I'm going to be sacked. The Unionists have got me. Apparently they are calling me the "Sinn Féin DI".'

When Francis reached his home a short while later he was still too agitated to hide his concerns from Teresa. Happily the children were all asleep in their beds and Mary, the housekeeper, had left for the night.

'Francis, you look so drawn. Take the seat by the fire while I warm some food for you. What has happened?'

'I'm not sure where to start, love. It has been a very long day and I'm afraid that I may be in quite a bit of trouble.'

Teresa was torn between her concern for her husband and her anger that what she feared most about his recent behaviour looked like it was arriving at her door. Francis realised that his remarks had frightened her and he added. 'Don't worry, my love, I will tell you everything in a moment but first be assured that we are all perfectly safe and some very important people are looking out for us as we speak. Let me go up and change out of my uniform, then I'll pour us a couple of whiskeys when I get done eating.'

After his supper Francis recounted the main events of his day including his drive to Tuam and meeting with the archbishop. Despite her increasing anxiety, she remained stoic in the face of each new revelation. She even managed what Francis mistook for a joke about his being called the Sinn Féin DI. 'I take it that your new rank is not a promotion then?'

'It's not really a laughing matter, Teresa.'

'I assure you I'm not laughing. Not even remotely amused. I warned you that what you were doing would be the ruination of us. And now look where we are. What will become of us, Francis?'

As she asked this question Teresa's stoicism deserted her and she collapsed in a heap onto an armchair sobbing, 'Will you be prosecuted?'

'Of course not. Steadman has no grounds to fire me let alone bring a prosecution. All he knows for sure is that I don't approve of the policy of sanctioned reprisals and that I observed a Republican court without intervening. Neither is an unusual position and many if not most of my colleagues feel just as I do.'

He knew that he was understating the seriousness of his position. He could well become a target of a reprisal squad, if such an idea were promoted by Steadman or someone further up the chain of command. He knew how easy it would be to pin his murder on the Volunteers. But he was nevertheless regretting sharing as much as he had with

Teresa and wanted to give her a feeling that all was not lost, although he didn't really believe that himself.

'But you told me that you have been passing information on to the Volunteers. What if that is found out?'

'Only you, me and my Volunteer contacts know about that so there is no need to worry on that score.'

Annoyed by Francis' apparent flippancy about what he was doing, Teresa asked, 'How can you support these murderers Francis? I despise them and all they do. Murdering policemen, shooting people who dare stand up against them, intimidating shopkeepers, tarring and feathering girls for stepping out with a solider. They are nothing but thugs and bullyboys. And what have they achieved? They've brought chaos and destruction down on our heads. The country will surely be divided and Ulster isolated and all for what? What can this killing possibly achieve that politics would not?'

Teresa subsided. She had never before spoken so strongly to Francis about her attitude to the conflict.

Francis crossed the room to her side. He was taken aback by the strength of her feelings, but he needed to get her to see his point of view. He took her hand in his and rubbed his thumb across the back of her hand. 'What you say might well have been true back when those constables were murdered in Tipperary. But things have changed and we both know it. The British government has consistently ignored the views expressed at the ballot box in support of Nationalist parties. They caved into Unionist extremism and have responded to

Nationalist extremism with unprecedented violence of their own.

'Think about those bodies found last month. Three young men tortured and shot and not even the hint of a proper investigation. One of them apparently burned to death. There have been too many such killings, conveniently blamed on internecine fights amongst Republicans, which look to me much more like extra judicial killings by members of the security forces. Or look at the chaos in Balbriggan. Those were policemen running riot and shooting up the place, not Volunteers.

'This violence is at best being ignored by the powers that be but in reality it is being actively encouraged, and I'm just not prepared to be a party to it.

'But look, now is not the time for you and me to have this argument. We need to consider how we will cope with whatever happens next.'

'All right,' responded Teresa calming herself. 'So what do you think is most likely to happen?'

Francis decided to offer his best-case scenario, 'When the authorities receive Steadman's complaints about me they will also get support for me from the archbishop. My guess is that they will decide to move me elsewhere and replace me here with a hardliner.'

'And what if you are wrong? What if they fire you? We will be thrown out of our home and where will we go, what will we live on?'

'Worst case scenario, we could go and live on the farm in Tempo until things return to some sort of normality.'

'The farm! You are joking aren't you? How could we all live in that little cottage? And what would your sister and her husband have to say about that? The neighbours will be delighted to have the Sinn Féin DI living next to them!'

'Now Teresa, you are overreacting. And now you are worrying about the attitudes of people you have not even met. Really, this conversation is getting silly.'

'How dare you patronise me, Francis. You have put the safety and security of this family at risk. You, who have worked so hard to get to your position, have risked it all for what? To keep some murderers from getting what they are due. And now you have the nerve to say I'm being silly.'

The strain Francis had been under all day, beginning from the moment he'd found Steadman sitting at his desk that morning, was taking its toll. 'My love I'm very tired and don't want to argue with you anymore. I suggest that we wait and see what comes next before fretting about this or that option. I'm going to go up to bed. Will you come?'

'All right Francis,' she said with a heavy sigh. 'Go up without me. I'll clear up in the kitchen and follow you up.'

Francis stood and leaning over Teresa he kissed her on the top of her head, 'I love you, my dear, and I promise I will do my best to fix things as well as I can.'

When Teresa heard Francis' tread on the staircase she let out the sob she had been supressing and heavy tears rolled down her face.

§

Two weeks later Francis was back in Castlebar meeting Steadman again. He had not heard anything since his meeting with the archbishop when Dr Gilmartin had promised to write to General Talbot, Chief Constable of the RIC and to the Home Secretary.

Steadman was in a foul mood and greeted Francis with barely disguised contempt. 'I don't like you District Inspector and I don't give a damn whether or not you like me. So let's get this over with shall we.'

'County Inspector,' responded Francis in as civil a manner as he could muster.

'I recommended to the Castle that you be dismissed from the Constabulary and shorn of your pension rights. It seems, however, that you have friends in high places who have suggested that we should be able to find a way to address your concerns about how the RIC conducts itself and the lack of training in police procedures which can hamper our new Auxiliary colleagues. That, as far as I'm concerned, is the bad news. The good news is that I have been given the authority to relieve you of your command responsibilities with immediate effect.'

Francis was stunned. He had come to this meeting prepared for the worst but he was now unsure of just what Steadman was saying and what it meant for his future. He said nothing but fixed Steadman with a steady glare in an attempt to hide his rising anxiety.

'Your orders are to present yourself at the training camp in Gormanstown next Tuesday the first of February. You will be responsible for the training of incoming special constables in police legal procedures. This is a temporary assignment and will last until the brass decide what to do with you. There is no billet there for your family so they will have to stay here in Westport. I'm afraid that they will have to vacate the house and move into the police barracks as your replacement will need that accommodation.'

Francis was thunder struck. At once outraged that his family are to be so shoddily treated while at the same time relieved on hearing that he would after all survive. Steadman was still talking but Francis had stopped listening. He was thinking about how he would break this news to Teresa. The following Tuesday was only four days away. He noticed that Steadman had stopped talking and was apparently waiting for an answer to a question he had asked.

'I'm sorry County Inspector. I didn't hear your question,' he said standing and retrieving his cap from the sideboard. He turned to look at Steadman and raised an eyebrow as if to ask the man to repeat himself.

Instead Steadman simply shrugged and said, 'District Inspector, you are dismissed. Good day to you.'

During the drive back to Westport Francis had the time to ruefully acknowledge that someone in the RIC hierarchy had a twisted sense of humour. He wondered if it was General Tudor himself. What better Machiavellian response could there be to the archbishop's concerns about the Black and Tans' lack of professionalism and Steadman's desire to be rid of Francis? *Let's put the Sinn Féin DI in charge of training the Tans! Quite brilliant really,* admitted Francis.

The drive back was interminable but when his driver pulled into the barracks courtyard Francis wished that they were still driving. He knew that he had to go straight to Teresa and break the news to her. She would hate that he was leaving her on her own with the family and especially resent having to move out of their splendid town house and into the police barracks.

As he turned the key in the front door to their house, Francis decided to be economical with the truth. He knew that there was cowardice in this, but reasoned that telling Teresa the whole truth would do little to alleviate her distress and besides he didn't want the next three days to be full of argument and recrimination as he had no idea how long they might be separated. Hanging his cap on the hall stand he formulated a way to explain his version of events in the best possible light.

Teresa emerged from the kitchen wearing an apron and drying her hands on a dishcloth. ‘Hello love, I didn’t expect you at this hour. What has happened?’ Francis embraced her warmly.

‘It seems that the archbishop has come up trumps. A rather unexpected solution has been developed, some of which will be uncomfortable for a while but it is mostly good news. Let’s get a cup of tea and I will tell all.’ He guided her back into the kitchen and while she filled the kettle he pulled a seat up to the kitchen table.

She brought a pot of tea to follow the milk, sugar, cups and saucers which she had set out while waiting for the kettle to come to the boil. Francis fussed with the teacups, pouring tea and adding milk and sugar to both cups. Teresa watched and waited, at once anxious to hear the news and at the same time dreading what she was about to hear. Eventually he sipped from his cup, replaced it on the saucer and slowed his breathing to calm himself.

‘Right,’ he began, ‘First the good news. You know how much concern has been expressed about the behaviour of the special police officers, the so-called Black and Tans. Many people from the king on down have been urging the government to take steps to restore discipline across the force.’ Teresa nodded, encouraging him to get to the point.

'Well,' he continued, 'I have been told that I'm to be responsible for the training of the next contingent of special constables.'

'Oh Francis. That's marvellous news. You are not going to be fired?'

'No. But the task removes me from direct policing responsibility which is how the authorities are punishing me. And of course the training and more particularly the outcomes of the training will be closely monitored by the top brass and the government.'

Teresa's face clouded over as the implications of this news began to dawn on her. 'The training camp is in Gormanstown in County Meath isn't it? You said that you thought we might have to move. Will we have to do so right away?'

'No, not right away. All of this is only temporary. The influx of special constables won't continue indefinitely. And besides, the reality is that there are no available family quarters in Gormanstown.'

'So you will be going away on your own, leaving us here?'

Francis was all too aware that they were getting to the nub of the matter and knew to that he could not delay the bad news very much longer. 'Yes, you'll stay here in Westport, so there won't be too much disruption and the children can stay in school. But I'm afraid to say that we will have to move out of this house as it will be assigned to my replacement.'

'Move out! Where to?'

'The safest place will be the police barracks.'

'Oh no. Please not the barracks. You know how much I hate living in a barracks. I thought we had put all of that behind us. And safest, are you serious? The one place in town most likely to be attacked by the Volunteers is the barracks!'

Francis tried to take Teresa's hand but she stood up from the table and went to the window which looked out onto the back garden. She gathered herself and turned back to him. 'When will all of this happen?'

'This weekend, I'm afraid.'

Teresa was crestfallen. 'This weekend! That is only a couple of days away. Oh, God!' She sank back into her chair, 'Why so sudden? How long have you known?'

'The county inspector gave me my orders this morning in Castlebar. I came straight home to tell you the news. I know it is very sudden but I have to follow my orders. I will be taking the train to Dublin and then on to Balbriggan on Monday morning. We will get you and the children settled into the barracks by Sunday.'

Teresa looked up slowly. It had dawned on her that they were both caught in a spiral of events, over which neither of them had much, if any, control. She realised that bickering with Francis about their circumstances was not only pointless, it was coming between them. She was discovering a strength she did not know she possessed. Unbidden, her mind had begun to apply itself to the practicalities. She allowed Francis to take her hand and at that moment she began to take charge of her marriage and her husband. 'I have no doubt that there is more to this unseemly haste than you are telling me, but I have no wish to hear any more. I know that you have tried to behave honourably throughout and you know that as your wife I will do whatever is needed to support you.' She covered their clasped hands with her free hand and rubbed his hand reassuringly. 'How long do you think you will be away?'

Francis was bowled over by this sudden transformation in her. His heart swelled with love for this amazing woman. He swallowed hard to control his emotions. 'At this stage I really don't know. These are very unusual times and there are no protocols or procedures for a situation like this. I expect it will be no more than a couple of months, three at most. And I should be able to get back to Westport occasionally.'

'Whatever happens, Francis, know that I love you. Don't worry about me or the children. We will be fine and there are plenty of good people here in Westport who will look out for us if need be.'

Francis was overwhelmed with gratitude for Teresa's support and her fortitude. He tried to express his feelings when she leant forward and kissed him lightly on the lips and brushed her hand down the side of his face. She shook her head slightly and smiling the gentlest smile Francis had ever seen telling him, without words, that words were not needed.

For an hour or more after that they simply sat holding each other by the hand. Neither spoke nor felt the need to speak. They had grown as individuals and as a couple. Neither would ever be entirely dependent on the other again and as a consequence they would remain entwined together in an unbreakable bond for the rest of their lives.

§

When Francis arrived in Balbriggan he was aghast at the sheer scale of destruction the town had suffered. He knew, of course, that the prior September a large contingent of police had descended on Balbriggan, burning and shooting, following an ambush which resulted in the deaths of two policemen. But he was not prepared for the level of damage they had wrought. Most of the houses on the main street were in ruins, as was the large hosiery factory which had been the town's principal employer.

To have suspected that sanctioned reprisals would lead to ill-discipline and ultimately chaos was one thing, but he was shocked to see the reality of the policy. A prosperous town not twenty miles from Dublin ruined, not by the Volunteers but by the police. *How can we get back to any sense of normality,* he wondered. He was feeling ashamed of his uniform when the police tender, which had been sent from the training camp at Gormanstown to collect him, pulled up in front of the station.

A young Englishman in a Black and Tan uniform saluted him and offered to carry his suitcase. When Francis remarked on the destruction the policeman said, 'I wasn't here myself when all of this kicked off, District Inspector. It must have been quite a show.'

'Quite a show? Do you have any idea of what you are talking about, Constable? This was not the scene of a military battle, this was mayhem perpetrated by police officers. The RIC will never regain its role as protector of the peace when it is allowed to become one of the main agents of chaos. This was not "quite a show" it was the moment the police became the enemy of the people. We will never again be able to walk the streets of this town and expect the trust and respect of the citizenry.'

'Inspector, I did not mean to speak out of turn. I arrived in Gormanstown in November and everyone who has talked to me about what happened here has said that a bloody good lesson was taught to the rebels.' Nothing more was said during the short drive to the training camp.

'District Inspector, do come in. Welcome to Gormanstown.' Francis was being greeted by, Geoff Smithers, the camp commandant. 'Will you join me in a whiskey?' Smithers was already pouring generous measures into two crystal glasses he had fetched from the sideboard.

The walls of the office still bore some of the paraphernalia from when the camp was an RAF training camp. Photographs of elegantly moustachioed young men standing next to their aeroplanes sat alongside pictures of the king and a silkscreen print of the famous RAF roundel. Smithers noticed Francis scanning the walls and said, 'Yes, yes, I know. Not quite the Phoenix Park Depot is it? I keep meaning to get this place sorted out but there never seems to be the time. Anyhow, never mind. Please take a seat.'

'Tell me, District Inspector, are you really the Shinner I'm told you are?'

The commandant's directness appealed to Francis who decided that he was going to like the man. What could be worse than Steadman? He decided to match his new superior's directness.

'No, sir,' he replied. 'I'm an old-fashioned law and order policeman who objects to murder and mayhem. But somehow that's enough to have earned me the title of the Sinn Féin DI.'

Smithers roared with laughter, 'Sinn Féin DI! Well that's a good one.' Suddenly serious, he added, 'Look Inspector, quite frankly I don't give a damn about your politics. We have a job to do and every bugger in Ireland and England is watching to see how well we do it. So, whatever you do, don't screw up here. Understood?'

'Very clearly, Commandant.' Francis raised his glass in salute, '*Slainte!*'

'You are a bloody Shinner,' laughed Smithers, draining his glass. 'Come on, we have work to do!'

CHAPTER TWENTY

Gormanstown

Towards the end of April 1921 the police gazette was reporting on the successes that the security forces were having in subduing the activities of the Volunteers around the country. By this time the Volunteers, having taken an oath of allegiance, were operating with the official sanction of the Dáil and were renamed The Irish Republican Army. The Dáil had also made a formal declaration of war against Britain.

Francis quickly found that, contrary to popular belief as promoted in the Republican press, the men he was working with and training at the Gormanstown camp were not the sweepings off the streets of Britain, nor were they the filth of British prisons. Nearly all were veterans of the Great War, fallen on hard times, who had joined the Irish police in search of a decent living. As Englishmen they were naturally loyal to the Crown and they despised the people they perceived to be Republican terrorists. As former soldiers they were accustomed to discipline and Francis was convinced that if properly led they would behave responsibly.

Many of these men bore the physical and emotional scars of war. One young man was particularly withdrawn. Constable Henry Jones was from Newport in Wales. He joined the Welsh Guards in 1916, when still a teenager, and was gassed in France in 1918. He was demobilised in 1919. Like many similar veterans he had found it very hard to get regular work since he'd left the army. He carried out his training and fitness exercises without complaint and indeed with some diligence but he did not mix easily with the other men. There was a distant joylessness about young Henry which disturbed Francis. He worried about how Henry might cope with the stress of a guerrilla war.

As with any group of young men, particularly those hardened by war, there were more than a few rough types who exhibited a distain for discipline and a recklessness which suggested that they believed that they have nothing left to lose. These men were typically hard drinkers and Francis' most difficult moment at Gormanstown came when he encountered a group of these scallywags, as the commandant called them, attempting to break into the camp store. He was a bit surprised to find Henry Jones was one of the thieves. When he confronted the group the ring-leader, a brawny bruiser from Liverpool, by the name of Keane, turned on Francis, 'Why don't you just turn around and walk away and no one will be any wiser.'

'Sir!'

'What's that?'

'When you address me, Keane, you call me "Sir!"' As Francis said this, he stepped in close to the man and challenged him with a hard stare. Keane did not notice that the others had stepped back. One turned to the man next to him and muttered, 'Let's scarper before this kicks off.'

'Good idea,' nodded his mate and the group Keane expected to back him melted into the darkness.

Keane did not notice this had happened as his eyes were fixed on Francis. He then pushed his luck and sticking his face in Francis' said, 'And you can kiss my arse, sir.'

A single hard blow to Keane's solar plexus dropped the man to his knees. Breathing hard he surreptitiously reached into his right boot-top and drew out a short handled blade. Francis was reaching for the man's collar to pull him back to his feet.

As Keane pulled one foot in front to help himself stand, he slipped the hand holding the knife behind his back. Just as he was about to bring the knife up in an arching blow, Henry Jones kicked Keane from behind knocking him sideways and followed up by stamping on Keane's wrist forcing him to drop the weapon. Keane screamed in pain and swore at Jones. 'You've broken my wrist you little Welsh bastard. I'll do you for this.' Jones kicked Keane hard in the face, knocking him unconscious.

'Sorry about that, sir,' he said to Francis, 'I'm obviously Welsh. I'm also small and as it happens I have no idea who my parents are so, strictly speaking, Keane there was entirely correct. But I'll not have the likes of him calling me a "little Welsh bastard".'

'Constable Jones,' smiled Francis, happy to find support in unexpected places. 'I'm obliged to you for your assistance. You remember the talk I gave yesterday on the use of reasonable force. I'd say you got that situation just about right. I see your other friends have slipped away. Go and get some help to throw Keane in a cell. I will wait here in case he comes round. We'll ship him home to Liverpool after he spends a wee while resting in an Irish prison.'

§

Early one Tuesday morning just two months into his time at Gormanstown, Francis got a message that Smithers wanted to see him. 'Ah, Inspector Maguire, come in, come in. I have news which I think will please you. Sit down, may I offer you a cup of tea?'

'No thank you, sir.' Francis raised a single eyebrow indicating his desire to hear the news.

'Of course. Didn't mean to stall. It's just that you are being returned to a command position with immediate effect.'

Francis was so surprised that having just sat down he immediately stood up again, which caused Smithers to smile ruefully. Francis sat again. 'That is wonderful news Commandant. Do you know where I'm to be posted and at what rank?'

'As from the first of April you will be the district inspector for the district of Raphoe in County Donegal.'

'That's not far from where I grew up in Fermanagh. Although I can't say I know the area. I've not noticed many reports of Volunteer violence in that district lately?'

'Raphoe is closer to Londonderry than Donegal town and has a fairly even mix of Unionist and Nationalist people amongst the population. Quite what the mood is in the town these days I can't say. But if partition comes, Raphoe will be on the Nationalist side of the border, which will not be popular with the Unionists in town.'

Francis was still struggling to absorb the unexpected news of his reprieve and while naturally pleased he was also somewhat sceptical about his superiors' motives. 'Do you know why the brass have had a change of heart about me?'

'To be honest, I did wonder at that myself and while I was not given any reasons for your new orders I expect that the bottom line is that there is a critical shortage of experienced senior officers. So I doubt there are any Machiavellian machinations here. They are sending you back to a command position because they can't afford to do without you. But while Raphoe is not the Republican hot spot that Westport is you'll have Ulster Volunteers as well as Irish Volunteers to deal with. But I forget that you are an Ulsterman. None of the divisions and factions in Ulster will surprise you.'

'No sir, indeed not. Although as you said, quite what the likely partition of Ulster will mean for Donegal remains to be seen.'

§

Back in Westport the family had settled into as normal a routine as was possible. The four boys were sharing a bedroom over the front of the police barracks while Teresa,

Annie and baby Francis, shared a back bedroom along the corridor. A third room with a field kitchen had also been allocated to the family. Teresa found the overcrowded barracks very uncomfortable but it was an adventure for the boys.

Francis travelled to Donegal via Westport having written earlier with the news about his new assignment. He and Teresa agreed that despite her discomfort it would be better for the children to stay on in school in Westport. As he sat in the train taking him to Donegal he reviewed the conversation he'd had with Teresa.

'Realistically it will take a couple of weeks to sort out accommodation and schools in Raphoe which means it would be the end of April before the children get to their new school and there will only be the month of May left before the school closes for the summer. Why don't I stay here with the children until then?'

'Are you sure Teresa? I know how little you like barracks life?'

'Yes I dislike living in the barracks but we have good friends and neighbours here and they have been very kind. I have lost count of the number of times I've been told by people how sorry they were to see you moved out of Westport after such a relatively short time here.'

'So we'll stay, and you get up to Raphoe and focus on the job. You need to re-establish yourself and rebuild your reputation. It will be easier to do that, if you don't have to worry about us for a couple of months.'

'I never expected that you'd be back from Gormanstown so soon anyway. So I have been working on the assumption that I'd have to put up with living in the Westport barracks until the summer. So truly, this arrangement is just as I expected things would be but with the added good news of knowing that there is a fixed date by which it will end and we will all be together again.'

Francis smiled inwardly. *I'm a lucky man with a brave and wonderful wife. And she is quite right, I do have a chance to re-establish myself. This mayhem can't go on for much longer. Surely there will be moves to find a way to bring peace sooner rather than later. But meanwhile I'll steer clear of contact with the Volunteers but I'll have nothing to do with reprisals either.*

§

Teresa wrote daily to Francis and in early May reported on an ambush at Tourmakeady on the Westport to Derrypark road where four RIC officers were killed. Francis had not yet seen any police reports on the ambush and some of the detail in Teresa's letter shocked him greatly. Not least because two of the men who were killed had worked for Francis when he was Head Constable at Claremorris and he knew their families. He sent condolence letters and made a telephone call to Sergeant Goulden at Ballinrobe, from where the attacked convoy had been dispatched.

'District Inspector, good to hear from you. How are things in Donegal?' asked the sergeant when Francis got through.

'Very well, Sergeant. But I gather things are not so good there. Please let the men know that my thoughts are with them. I have written to the families of the men who were killed but I confess that I was at a bit of a loss as to just what to say. All of this killing is so senseless.'

'Senseless is not the word for it, Inspector. Did you see Constable Flynn's report, sir?'

'No, Sergeant. I've seen no official reports. I only know what I have read in the papers and what my wife writes to me.'

'Here's what we know, sir. Constable O'Regan was driving the Ford with Sergeant Regan sitting next to him. I was going to go with the patrol myself but at the last minute, Head Constable Frawley offered to go in my place as he knew I was busy with some paperwork. So I guess I'm lucky to be alive.'

'Lucky indeed, Sergeant, but can you tell me how the men were killed?'

'Poor O'Regan was killed by the first shot and the Ford crashed into a gatepost throwing the others into the road. Shots fired from the other side of the road killed Constable Oakes and the same volley wounded Sergeant Regan and Constable Flynn. At that point the Volunteers rushed the car and when they found Sergeant Regan lying wounded on the ground one of the gurriers turned him over and said "Regan, you gave me a ticket for not having a light on my bicycle," and then he shot the poor defenceless fellow dead on the spot.'

'What happened to Flynn?'

'Flynn played dead and they left him alone, clever chap. We have a team going through every summons ever issued by Sergeant Regan in the hope of identifying the murderers.' Francis heard someone in the barracks interrupting Goulden.

'Oh. I'm sorry, sir, I'm being called to the front desk. I have to go. You take care of yourself. I'll tell Mrs Maguire we talked when I see her next. Goodbye, sir.' Goulden rang off leaving Francis sitting at a desk in Raphoe holding his head in his hands.

'Holy Mary, Mother of God, pray for us,' he whispered, drawing his hands across his face. *I have failed utterly. This is just what I was trying to avoid. Four men dead, and known to the killers it seems. Are there no depths to which we won't sink?*

§

A couple of weeks later some noise in the street outside the police barracks woke young Donagh. He peered out between a break in the curtains. The blue gaslight over the front door brightened the otherwise dark street just enough for him to see what was happening. He was perched on the top of a set of bunk beds pushed up against the wall by the window overlooking the street to the front. His brother Hugh was asleep below him and Brian and Rory were in bunk beds across the room. There was a fireplace in one corner but the grate was missing and the flue blocked with an old potato sack. Donagh was not sure what woke him.

As he watched, a lorry reversed up to the doorway of the barracks. Donagh didn't recognise the uniformed men in the lorry who began dropping bundles onto the roadside. After a minute or two he realised that the bundles were in fact men, dressed in rough farm-hand clothes. He then noticed that the men being dropped onto the roadway were not moving. The first bundle was close to the steps of the barracks where it had been unceremoniously dumped and was quickly followed by three more which lay crumpled on the ground between the back of the lorry and the steps of the barracks.

The front door to the station beneath the boy's window flew open. Sergeant Kerrigan appeared and began shouting at the men in the lorry. Three more of his father's men appeared in the street and milled about in a confused and disorganised way, which frightened Donagh more than the bundles in the street. He had never seen his father's men behaving like this. Head Constable Donlon shouted at his men to go and get the police lorry from the rear yard. More light played across the wet road from the opened front door and the boy could better see the bodies lying in the road. He noticed that the second man was missing a shoe. When he realised that the men were dead he was bewildered. He had never seen a dead person before but his fright was offset by a macabre fascination.

At that point Donagh was surprised to see his mother appear in the street. The light from the entrance hall cast her shadow across the ground below him where it reached the rear tailgate of the lorry.

‘Head Constable,’ he heard his mother ask, ‘What has happened?’ Donlon did not immediately respond. He was busy instructing his men who were lifting the bodies off the street and onto the back of the police lorry.

‘Careful you clumsy oafs, there’s no need to treat these boys with disrespect. O‘Dwyer, run and fetch Father Canavan.’ He turned to Teresa, ‘Mrs Maguire, please go back inside.’

O’Dwyer had not moved and was saying something Donlon could not hear.

‘O‘Dwyer, what are you muttering about?’

‘Well, Head Constable, the priest won’t come out for these bastards; hasn’t the archbishop excommunicated the bloody lot of them? May they rot in hell.’

Teresa did not go back indoors as asked, instead she stumbled further out into the street. Donlon had turned away from her and did not notice what was happening behind him. As Teresa approached the dead bodies lying in the back of the police lorry her eyes adjusted to the moonlight. She halted suddenly, drawing a sharp intake of breath. A small barely audible cry escaped her lips and she shuddered as the horror unfolded itself to her disbelieving eyes. ‘O my God, Francis,’ she whispered, lips trembling, ‘What have they done?’

CHAPTER TWENTY ONE

Raphoe

Reports about reprisals against the civil population in Ireland did not play well in the British press and the government faced growing pressure to change tactics. The political climate had significantly evolved since 1914 and the Government of Ireland Act 1920 paved the way for the partition of the country. Few welcomed this prospect.

Francis spent April and May in Raphoe on his own while the family stayed on in Mayo. The relatively even balance of Unionist and Nationalist opinion in Raphoe created a strange atmosphere where both communities were anxious about the future of the town, albeit with opposing views as to the preferred settlement.

In policing terms, there was as much concern about keeping the armed sections of both communities apart, as there was about the safety of security personnel. Francis got this briefing from his new county inspector. He was again challenged about his sympathy for Sinn Féin and warned to keep his nose clean and to do his job.

'Stay out of politics, Inspector Maguire, and you and I will get along just fine,' was the clear and unambiguous conclusion to his first meeting with the county inspector.

He visited Annie and Tom in Tempo a couple of times and found the town as divided as Raphoe. Annie, who had never taken any interest in politics, was incensed by what had been happening around her.

'The raid on the Tempo barracks was an outrage. The sergeant who was killed was a popular man and I'm sure that no local lads would have been involved in such a cowardly act. But on the other hand some of the things which have been done by the police and the auxiliaries, especially in Derry, have staggered belief.'

'Well, Annie, I'm afraid that such are the times we live in.'

'Shooting up towns and burning creameries is hardly going to endear the police to the public.'

'I'm not defending the policy I'm merely trying to understand why a previously disciplined force has descended into chaos. I have actively opposed reprisals and stood in the way more than once. My own position has not been without difficulty.'

'I'm not attacking you, Francis, but even you must see that the police will never be trusted again.'

'Much as it depresses me to say so, I'm afraid that you are right. But, for better or worse, I've decided that I can be of more use staying on and trying to change things than I can by walking away. And, of course, I'm not alone in the force. Many of my colleagues feel exactly as I do.'

Once he had arranged accommodation and schools, Francis travelled to Westport to gather his family. Teresa and the three older boys were waiting at the railway station and, as he stepped down from the train, Francis was engulfed by his children. The little boys competed for attention as the family walked towards the barracks. Teresa was shocked when young Donagh began to tell his father about the bodies he saw being thrown into the street outside the barracks.

'And then, Dada, Head Constable Donlon came out and shouted at the English policemen,' said Donagh in a gabbled rush.

Teresa leaned into Francis and whispered, 'I had no idea he'd seen anything. He never said a word about it until now.'

'Well, wee man, let that be a lesson to you not to be up in the middle of the night looking out of the window, instead of being asleep in your bed.' Francis scooped up Donagh and carried him on his shoulders, much to the consternation of Hugh who was struggling to keep up.

'It's not fair, Dada. Donagh is older than me and can walk faster. I want a carry.'

'Now, Hugh, what am I always saying about "I want"?'

'I want, never gets,' pouted Hugh.

'That's right, Hugh. Now here,' Francis said putting Donagh back down. 'You boys run along to the barracks so that Mamma and I can have a little chat.' The boys scampered up the street and Teresa hugged Francis by the arm as they walked along.

'It is so good to have you back, Francis. Things have not been good while you have been away. And that awful night two weeks ago will stay with me for a very long time. Raphoe is hardly Belfast but it will still be good to be back in Ulster.'

'You know, my love, the killing of those boys and, more significantly, the disrespectful way their bodies were dumped outside the police barracks will, I hope, be the beginning of the end. The government is coming under pressure to come up with better solutions.'

'Oh, Francis, you should have been here the next morning when the Marquess showed up at the barracks. He was in a foul mood. I could hear him downstairs berating the DI and demanding an explanation for such disgraceful behaviour.'

Francis interrupted her. 'A while back one of the local Volunteers told me that the IRA in Dublin have instructed the Westport Company not to harass the Marquess in any way as he can be an unofficial conduit to the British government.'

'Someone needs to tell the local security forces about that,' said Teresa. 'There was a really funny moment last week. The Marquess was in town when the funeral for one of the Tans killed in an ambush passed through. The Marquess was wearing his farm clothing, including a cloth cap. Looking, so I was told, for all the world like one of the local peasant farmers. Anyhow, as the funeral passed by, one of the soldiers escorting the funeral kicked the Marquess in the pants because he didn't remove his cap. You can imagine the amusement of the rest of the crowd when the Marquess rounded on the man in his best Queen's English.'

'Anyway, enough about Westport, what's the mood in Raphoe? Are people nervous now that partition looks inevitable?'

'As you can imagine, partition is not a popular outcome with anyone there, Unionist or Nationalist. Everyone seems to be hoping that it will be temporary, and that the Ulster Unionists will decide to merge in some way with the new parliament in Dublin. I can't see that happening myself and it's only people who don't understand the mind-set of your typical Ulster Unionist that do. Unfortunately, that seems to include all politicians in London and Dublin.'

§

The bad news of the unexpected death of Teresa's mother reached her just before she and the children were due to join Francis in Raphoe. Elizabeth Shanagher was sixty-three years old when she caught a flu in early April. Her flu had developed unexpectedly into a pneumonia which quickly proved fatal.

The Shanagher family gathered at St Paul's Church on the Falls Road for the funeral. Francis and Teresa travelled separately to Belfast. Much to young Annie's annoyance, Teresa left the children with the Meldons in Westport. Annie felt that at eleven years old she was old enough to attend her grandmother's funeral.

'Annie, I need you to stay with your brothers and help Mrs Meldon look after them. I will only be gone for a couple of days and when I get back we will be packing up to go to

Raphoe to join your father. So please be a good girl and do as I ask without any fuss.'

All of Teresa's brothers and sisters were in Belfast for the funeral including May, who had lived up to expectations and become a nun some years before.

'I confess John, I find Belfast a depressing place.' Said Francis to John Boyle at the wake following the funeral.

'Recently I'm inclined to agree. But for many like me, this is our home and we'll not be bullied out of it by Unionist thugs. Having said that, I have no criticism for people who decide that life would be better elsewhere. Make no mistake the Unionist bully boys are in charge from the top on down and the likes of James Craig will waste no time building a Unionist hegemony at the expense of the Catholic population in Ulster. Whatever grand expressions of harmony and mutual respect Carson might make.'

'I've not heard you so angry about this before, John.'

'Partition will be a disaster for the Nationalist community in Ulster and your Sinn Féin friends in Dublin should bear that in mind.'

'The Shinners don't believe partition will come, or if it does, that it will stick.'

'If that's so then they have never been at an Ulster Volunteer force rally. The Unionists would rather sup with the devil than sit in a Dublin parliament with a Catholic majority. They are convinced that they'd be squeezed dry with taxes and forced to accept Catholic dogma, irrespective of their own religious beliefs.'

'I know that you are entirely right, John. I've said as much many times myself. But my "Sinn Féin friends", as you call them, are not listening.'

After Elizabeth's funeral the family were relieved to hear that Denis planned on moving out of the Falls Road to a safer suburb, taking his two unmarried daughters with him. 'It's something Elizabeth and I had been considering and now I don't think I want to live in this house anymore without her,' was how Denis explained his decision to his family.

Kathleen and Getta, Teresa's sisters and, both still young women, promised the others that they would look after their father allowing their brothers and sisters to return to their own lives and families.

§

Once reunited, the Maguire family settled quickly into life in Raphoe and Teresa made friends with a Mrs Long who went out of her way to make them welcome. There was little political violence but as normal police work had become next to impossible, Francis decided to keep his head down and began to anticipate the future.

There was one shooting incident in late June when Francis was leading a routine patrol near Castlefinn where they had set up a checkpoint. A car with a single occupant drove through without stopping. One of the police officers manning the checkpoint called for the car to stop and opened fire on the vehicle when it accelerated away. Francis called for the officer to cease firing and subsequently resisted a suggestion from the local British army commander to organise a general roundup of suspected Volunteers in the area.

During one of his trips to report to the county inspector, Francis met his counterpart from Letterkenny, DI Pat Walsh. Walsh was an avuncular man and long serving police officer. Like Francis he had risen through the ranks rather than joining the force as a commissioned officer. He invited Francis to join him for a pint before they returned home.

'So, Mr Maguire, is it true that they call you the "Sinn Féin DI" in Westport?' Walsh asked with a teasing gleam in his eye.

'Yes, District Inspector, it's true.'

'Pat, please, and if I may I'll call you Francis. And don't worry, my sympathies lie in a similar direction.'

'Don't get me wrong, Pat. It was the Unionists who put that badge on me. But I'm not a fan of mayhem and murder, whoever is doing the shooting. All I did was prevent murder. But whether it's Auxies who fancy a bit of summary execution, or Volunteers shooting up passing police vehicles, I despise the lot of them.'

'A reasonable man can't argue with that position. But tell me Francis, where do you stand politically speaking? What would be your solution to this morass?'

'I have long described myself as a "Dominion Home Ruler". But to keep the Unionists on board we would have to have separate parliaments in Dublin and Belfast. That has always seemed to me to be the only way to keep the country united. I worked in Belfast during the Loyalists' monster rallies and saw the depth of resistance to a Dublin parliament. If the 1914 Home Rule Act had gone ahead, I believe that the Irish Volunteers would be fighting the Ulster Volunteers as we speak. Indeed it may yet come to that.'

'What about yourself, Pat, where do you stand?'

'In truth I'm probably more the Sinn Féin DI than you are. I think the British government were and are spineless in their attitude to Ulster unionism. They should have faced them down in 1913-14 and prevented their arming. General Wilson should have been court martialled for instigating a mutiny of senior officers. Instead they bloody well promoted the man.'

'In short, my view is that the Unionists taught the Republicans the true value of armed resistance and I for one am glad they learnt the lesson well.'

Francis smiled, 'I wish I had your certainty that an independent Ireland was both achievable and worth the bloodshed. And make no mistake, Pat, it's not the British that are the obstacle to Irish self-government, it's the Irish. If we could agree on a vision for the future of the country, getting the British establishment on board would be the easy part! Let me get you a pint?'

'Now you are just being mischievous. And yes, please, another pint will be very welcome.'

Pat Walsh and Francis developed an easy acquaintance. Their shared views on policing standards and philosophies combining with differing views on the political conflict. Francis was none the less surprised when Pat admitted to him that the description of a Volunteer wanted in connection with an attempted attack on a police patrol near Letterkenny exactly fit a man he knew well, a doctor in the town. 'But I have no intention of arresting him,' said Pat. 'Instead I'm going to warn him that his cards are marked and to keep a low profile for a while.'

'Why would you do that, Pat?'

'We are in the dying days of this British administration. One way or another their time is up in this country and high time as far as I'm concerned. When the shooting stops there will be a new administration to be formed and I want to be part of the future, not the past.'

Pat Walsh was proved right rather more quickly than even he could have anticipated when Sinn Féin swept the board in a general election in May to elect members to a new devolved parliament in Dublin. 'Look at this general election for goodness sake. Lloyd George thinks that allowing direct elections to a devolved parliament in Dublin will somehow bring a political solution to the conflict. The only problem with that idea is that no one takes it in any way seriously. The devolved powers are an insult to democracy and the voters know it. They have dismissed this panacea with scorn.'

'I take it that you are not impressed then, Pat?' asked Francis sarcastically.

'The whole thing is a joke which has only served to demonstrate just how far removed the British have become from what's happening on the ground in Ireland. British policy in Ireland lies in tatters. And the only political party with any representation is Sinn Féin.'

'Other than the Ulster Unionists, you mean!'

'Oh, without question the Unionists are busily building their wee fiefdom in Belfast and the Shinners are equally hell-bent on ignoring the Belfast parliament. Imagining, somehow, that it will evaporate in the face of their convictions. But the British have only themselves to blame.'

'Pat, you may very well be right about everything you say. But my thoughts are with the families of the fifteen policemen who were killed in the two days following the election. What have your Shinners got to say to those widows?'

'Casualties of war, Francis. No more and no less. Irishmen like you and me, doing the job like you and me but they were unlucky and we have made our own luck.'

'By the way, did you hear that the loyal Unionists are to be rewarded by King George who is going to open the Unionist parliament in Belfast next month? No doubt there'll be words of conciliation, which James Craig and his henchmen will nod sagely at while planning to build a Protestant citadel in Belfast.'

'You have family in Belfast don't you, Francis? God help them. The Unionists opposed Home Rule because they feared a legislature dominated by Catholic dogma. Now they've got their own legislature and let's wait and see just how accommodating it is of dissenting voices and opinions. I for one am not optimistic and forecast bigotry and exclusion. Meanwhile it will be business as usual for the Volunteers and they'll keep pushing now that they can see that Lloyd George has played all his cards. Sooner or later he will have to start talking to the Shinners.'

CHAPTER TWENTY TWO

Truce and treaty

An agreed truce ended the violence in July 1921 and in December 1922 a peace settlement was agreed in London between the British government and the Sinn Féin negotiating team. While this was ratified by both the Dublin and London parliaments in January 1923 and by a subsequent general election in the Irish Free State, as it was called, many Republicans, including Eamon De Valera, believed that too much had been conceded to the British.

This dispute over the Anglo-Irish Treaty split both the IRA and Sinn Féin. There were sporadic outbreaks of violence and De Valera expressed the feelings of the dissidents when, after the general election victory for the pro-Treaty side, he declared that, "The majority have no right to do a great wrong". In Northern Ireland the Unionists, while unhappy with the agreement, moved rapidly to consolidate their position. A parliament was formed in Belfast and opened by King George, who made a conciliatory speech expressing his desire to see Ireland reunited in friendship. Pogroms against Catholics in Northern Ireland persuaded many to leave for England, the South or further afield.

During the truce Francis got a letter from Joe Ring in Westport inviting him to come and meet himself and one Michael Staines. Staines, a revolutionary turned politician, was also originally from Westport, although Francis had not met him.

Staines had been charged by Sinn Féin with oversight of the truce in Mayo and Galway and had recruited Ring to help him. The situation was febrile. The Volunteers fully expected hostilities to reopen at any moment and were training accordingly. The security forces, on the other hand, were sure that the end game was in play and generally followed orders to keep a low profile and not harass the Volunteers.

The three men met in a hotel in Westport. As Francis crossed the street to enter the hotel he thought he'd caught a glimpse of Seán Gibbons but as he was running late for his meeting he didn't stop to chat.

His meeting with Ring and Staines was cordial and the pair asked a number of questions about how best to deal with their counterparts on the British side of the truce. They also talked about investigation techniques and how Francis would recommend that they handle any incidents that may arise.

'I suppose, Mr Staines, that you can be one hundred per cent confident that if there were any "incidents", as you call them, that there is no way they would have official sanction from within the Volunteers?'

'You quickly put your finger on the central issue, Mr Maguire. Feelings are running high and we are worried that some individual or group might use the cover of the truce to take revenge for one issue or another. On the broader stage, what both sides will want is plausible deniability so that a flare up here or there doesn't reignite the whole country.'

'Conspiracy is not really my field, Mr Staines. But I will say that it is always easier to nail down a single culprit rather than a large group. So whatever the origins of any incident you can be sure that if it comes from the authority's side there will be no hesitation to hang individuals out to dry. There'll be no closing of ranks around any miscreants at this stage of the process.'

'That is what I'd hoped you would say, Inspector. Joe spoke very highly of how you handled yourself here in Westport and how you stopped the British assassination squads.'

'I tried to be agnostic on the subject of whose assassination squads I stopped, Mr Staines. Whether their colours were red, blue, or green, they were all assassins to me and I tried to stop them committing murder. When the dead are finally counted, how many of them will have been Irish? We've been awfully busy killing each other in order to persuade the British to withdraw from Ireland.'

Joe Ring was smiling broadly. Francis turned on him. 'You find that amusing, Joe?'

'Not in the least, Frank. I assure you. I was smiling just now because I agree with you. Shooting British soldiers always seemed more sensible to me than shooting Irish policemen!'

Staines was looking uncomfortable, 'Gents, if we may, I'd like to return to the matters in hand. Who knows, between us we might be able to make a small contribution to the work of keeping the guns silent.'

The three men returned to their conversation about keeping the truce working in Mayo and Galway. During the course of the conversation, Francis had the decided impression that Staines was assessing him and had contrived the meeting primarily for that purpose.

When they finished talking Staines and Ring took their leave as they were returning to Galway, where the two sides had set up liaison offices.

As Francis headed back to Raphoe he mused to himself, *Curious conversation. I wonder what Staines really wanted and if he got it?*

§

The papers reported continuously on the progress of the peace talks, which went on far longer than expected, but as Christmas approached speculation was increasing that a deal was at hand.

Francis and Pat had many debates about the most likely shape of whatever agreement might eventually be reached. 'Whatever happens, Francis, I think we can safely assume that the RIC will be disbanded and the likes of you and I will be put out to pasture.'

'I agree. It's hard to see how we could continue after all that has happened these past couple of years. But any new police force will need experienced officers. Surely any willing to serve a new administration will be welcomed.'

‘I’d like to think so, Francis, but the reprisals carried out by the RIC around the country will have left a lot of bitterness amongst ordinary people who were unwittingly dragged into the conflict, not to mention the likely hostility we’d face from former Volunteers.’

When the terms of the Anglo-Irish Treaty were announced in December, Francis, like many others either side of the proposed border, was particularly unhappy about the partition of the country. But he decided to lend his support as he suspected that the Treaty represented the best outcome that could be achieved, given the overall circumstances in which it was negotiated. ‘Mind you,’ he said to Teresa one day, ‘I can’t believe that I will have to cross what amounts to an international border to go and visit my sisters in Tempo or Belfast.’

As anticipated the Treaty included an agreement to disband the RIC and replace it with separate police forces in Northern Ireland and the Irish Free State. Francis got a letter from the depot telling him that he would be one of the last to be demobilised. His last day with the RIC would be 17 June 1922. His demobilisation notice included the good news that he was to be awarded an annual pension of four hundred and three pounds, payable monthly and commencing in July 1922.

‘It’s not exactly a king’s ransom, Pat, but we will be comfortable, I’m sure. As I’ve stayed on to the bitter end they have added twelve years to my service record so, effectively, I’m retiring early on full pension. But I’m only forty-eight years old Pat. I'm too young to sit about doing nothing. Besides, there is so much to be done. A new police force needs to be built. Surely the new government must look to the likes of you and me to help with that. Many of our Unionist colleagues seem sure that they will be able to join the Royal Ulster Constabulary. I'm not so keen on that option. The sectarianism evident across Ulster, especially in Belfast, very much puts me off seeking any role in Northern Ireland.'

'Well, Francis, if you'll let me get a word in, I have some news which will please you.'

Francis hadn't noticed the wry smile of amusement on Pat's face which his spiel had produced. 'Stop sitting there like the cat that got the cream man, and tell me your news for God's sake.'

'I received a letter this week from none other than one Mr Michael Collins, Chairman of the provisional government. He has invited me to join a committee being formed next month in Dublin to plan the establishment of the new police force.'

'That's bloody marvellous news, Pat. Good man yourself. Now I'm no committee man but whatever I can do to help just shout. Who else will be on this committee?'

'I've not seen the full list yet but Collins says that a number of former RIC men, who proved themselves supporters of the Republican cause during the Tan war, will be invited. A politician by the name of Michael Staines will be the chairman.'

'Staines is it? I met him in Westport during the truce. I got a call from the Westport IRA commandant, a chap called Joe Ring, asking me to go down there and meet Staines. I liked him. Very charming fellow and sharp as a tack. I had the decided feeling that I was being assessed in some way.'

'Well, if you know the chairman, and I'm going to be involved, it won't be long before you'll get dragged in yourself, Francis.'

The committee Pat referred to met in Dublin in February 1922 and quickly formed a number of subcommittees to address the core elements required to build the new police force. As Pat Walsh predicted Francis got a letter from Staines inviting him to go to Dublin to meet Michael Collins with a view to taking on responsibility for the training of the new police force.

§

Teresa and Francis agreed that he should go to Dublin and explore the opportunity extended by Michael Staines. The family would stay in Raphoe until the political situation settled down and his own future was clearer. When Francis got to Dublin in March, he found that he had landed in a highly volatile environment.

His meeting with Michael Collins lasted but a few minutes. Collins greeted Francis warmly and looking him up and down said, 'District Inspector, you're a big fella aren't you? Would have made a fine target for one of those Mayo sharp shooters!' Laughing at his own joke he invited Francis to take a seat.

'Mr Maguire, we need to move fast to put a new police force in place but at the same time we mustn't make a buggers' muddle of it. Michael Staines and Joe Ring tell me that they want your help. You also have Pat Walsh's endorsement so please consider this interview a formality.'

'That is very kind of you, Mr Collins. I told Michael Staines that I'm more than willing to help in any way I can.'

The two men talked for a few minutes; Francis about his views on civil policing and Collins on his efforts to avoid a complete split within the IRA and Sin Féin.

'If we cannot hold the pro- and anti-treaty sides together somehow, I'm afraid that we will see the shooting start again; only this time we would be shooting at each other and that is something which I very much want to avoid.'

'Well, Mr Collins, until the Tans arrived, is that not what we were doing anyway?'

'Inspector, I'm not going to fight that fight again! We killed agents of the Crown. Their nationality was never an issue for me. And you can't say that we didn't succeed. But look, we need to put all of that behind us and move on. Staines and Ring say they want you and there is no doubt that your skills and experience are needed. I'm more than happy to have arguments about how we do things going forward but I won't be asked to justify the Tan war. So let's move on, shall we?'

Francis demurred saying, 'Forgive me, Mr Collins. I appreciate your candour as you no doubt will appreciate that we will simply have to agree to disagree on these issues.'

Collins smiled ruefully, 'I can see that you are your own man, Mr Maguire, I think you will be a great addition to the team being put together to build our new police force. But we need to move quickly. Can you start right away?'

'I'll need to dash back to Raphoe to see to my family but I can be back in a couple of days.'

'Fair enough. I'll send Michael Staines a memo telling him to expect you.'

As Francis stood up to take his leave he couldn't resist returning Collin's banter. 'If, as you clearly fear Mr Collins, the shooting starts again, please be careful out there. As big as you are it would take a poor shot to miss you.'

CHAPTER TWENTY THREE

A new force

The new administration in Dublin were working to avoid a civil war with those opposed to the Anglo-Irish Treaty. At the same time they had to quickly put in place replacement mechanisms for the maintenance of law and order. A new police force was needed and needed quickly.

'We both know it makes no sense for us all to go to Dublin at this stage. Let's see how things develop before we uproot the children again.' In this fashion Teresa again encouraged Francis to pursue his career while she kept the family on an even keel. 'But promise to come back to Raphoe as often as possible. We will all miss you terribly.'

'My love, I remember saying to you many years ago that I don't deserve you. You are the best wife any man could wish for.'

'And I remember saying that you were right; you don't deserve me. Now take me to bed before I change my mind.'

Francis got back to Dublin a couple of days later, late in March 1922. He was greeted warmly by Michael Staines and Pat Walsh. 'We have men pouring in every day wanting to join the new police force. We need to move fast. The government has accepted the recommendations of the organising committee. We have good teams working on recruiting and conditions of service, I'd like you to focus on training.'

'The force is to be called the Civic Guard and I'm Commissioner. You will report to Pat here who is Assistant Commissioner. If willing, you are to be in charge of police training.'

'Training? I will happily do that for a while. Just so long as we are agreed that once things are put in place and working properly, I will return to active policing. I don't want to spend the rest of my days in the Depot.'

Pat Walsh was smiling at the other two men. He said to Staines, 'I told you he is a proper policeman and won't want to be a desk jockey or a classroom theorist.'

'Francis, we are under huge pressure to get a functioning police force up and running immediately. The only practical way to do that is to bring in experienced RIC officers like you. However, many of the rank and file who have signed up have been fighting with the Volunteers against the RIC and they won't take kindly to taking orders from men they consider to be the enemy. So, hence this subterfuge of bringing you in under cover of being an instructor. Later, once things have settled down we will put you back in a command post. You have my word on that.'

'Commissioner, I told Mr Collins that I am willing to do whatever I can to help. If being a police instructor is what is needed then that's what I'll do. But I'll hold you to your word to get me back to proper policing again.'

Staines stood and extended a hand to Francis. 'Welcome aboard, Francis. Let's organise some lunch and get started on the work. I notice that you haven't asked about terms and conditions.'

'No sir. I assume that we will continue to be under-paid?' responded Francis.

Staines was too much the politician to rise to that bait. 'We have recommended pay grades in line with the RIC terms and conditions. I will confirm the details as soon as I am able to do so. Your job title will be "Legal Instructor".'

'Now if all of that is satisfactory I want to go and get someone to join us whom you know.' Staines left the room and returned accompanied by Joe Ring.

'Frank, it is a pleasure to see you again. You are looking well.'

'Well I declare to God, if it isn't Joe Ring. Don't tell me that they have persuaded you to become a policeman?' Francis walked across the room and shook Joe by the hand.

'We have quite a few Mayo men with us, Frank, and they are not all former IRA men either. One of the first people to join the new police force was none other than your Sergeant Kerrigan from Westport.'

'Well well, and here we all are playing for the same team. The Home Team!' laughed Francis. 'Oh, and please, Joe, call me Francis.'

§

Francis found that the new recruits were housed at the Royal Dublin Society's premises in Ballsbridge but the accommodation was totally unsuitable for their purpose and there was little or no training taking place. Happily within weeks they moved about thirty miles south west of Dublin to the former British Army camp on the Curragh in County Kildare. Later in the year the Civic Guards took over another former British Army camp to the North of Dublin at Collinstown.

Pat Walsh was briefing Francis on some troubling developments. 'You know that you and I are part of a handful of former RIC officers invited to join the Civic Guards in senior roles? Well each of us has in some way demonstrated our support for the Republican cause. However, the rank and file down in the Curragh, who are nearly all ex-Volunteers, have been unimpressed with the number of senior roles going to former RIC men. We are getting reports of a mutiny. The buggers are talking about going on strike!'

When Staines visited the Curragh camp to investigate he brought Joe Ring and Francis with him. 'I want men at my back I can trust absolutely. I honestly don't know what to expect. My fear is that some anti-Treaty elements have infiltrated the Curragh camp and are stirring up dissent.' When they got there Staines called all of the recruits out on parade and challenged them to show their loyalty by joining him and abandoning their strike. He was surprised when only a small number did so and most of those were Mayo men like Joe Ring. The camp was heavily armed and emotions were running high.

Staines and his senior officers left the camp quietly and unobtrusively. When Michael Collins got a similar reception in Kildare a week later alarm bells started to ring.

Staines suspended all of the Kildare recruits and cut off their pay and supplies. Worried that the arms at the camp might fall into anti-Treaty hands he sent Joe Ring back to the Curragh to move the rifles to safer storage in Dublin.

§

'Did you hear what De Valera said in Thurles last week?' As Pat asked Francis this question he picked up a copy of a newspaper and read. "If the Treaty were accepted, [by the electorate] the fight for freedom would still go on, and the Irish people, instead of fighting foreign soldiers, will have to fight the Irish soldiers of an Irish government set up by Irishmen. The IRA will have to wade through the blood of the soldiers of the Irish government, and perhaps through that of some members of the Irish government to get their freedom". This is incredible stuff. The man is a menace. How does he expect that the romantic young men who formed the IRA flying columns and the young women who supported them, are going to react to this kind of invective? It's like throwing petrol on a fire. Simply outrageous!'

'Why doesn't the government issue a warrant for Dev's arrest?' asked Francis.

'Collins is still trying to find a way to avoid out and out conflict. He worries that any move to silence dissenting voices could light an explosive fuse.'

In mid-April Francis was running a seminar on police procedures at the Curragh camp when a messenger interrupted.

'Sorry to barge in, Inspector, but I have important news. A large party of anti-Treaty IRA men, led by Rory O'Connor, have taken control of the Four Courts in Dublin. The army has been put on alert. But for the moment Mick Collins has decided to take no direct action.'

When the messenger left Francis allowed a discussion on the implications of these developments. Wrapping it up to get back to their work he said, 'We are on a slippery slope now, gentlemen, and no mistake.'

At the general election the country voted to support the Treaty. British pressure built on Collins to do something about the activities of the anti-Treaty militants. During one of his visits to Raphoe Francis was talking to Teresa about the rising temperature.

'Depressing as it is, I'm afraid that the shooting is about to start again and this time the conflict will be entirely our own.'

As Teresa responded her face drained of colour. 'When the truce was announced I so hoped that life might return to some degree of normality. Will we be in any danger?'

'Other than protection duties the police are wisely being kept out of any direct confrontation with the Irregulars. That role is left to the National Army. So if civil war does come I will be spared any direct involvement, thank God.'

'The Irregulars?' asked Teresa.

'Language as ever is important so the government has named the anti-Treaty forces the "Irregulars" and the pro-Treaty forces the "National Army". The split in the IRA now has its own labels.'

§

Staines invited Francis to a briefing at Dublin Castle.

'I have decided that my position following the Kildare mutiny is untenable. The government has accepted my resignation and I'm to be replaced as Commissioner by Eoin O'Duffy. Do you know him?'

'I can't say that I've ever had the pleasure.'

'To be quite honest he was not the cabinet's first choice but as head of the National Army he has demonstrated an inspirational capacity for leadership which belies his relative youth. I'm sure that he will do a fine job.'

'Pat Walsh has also resigned and Joe Ring has decided that he is more of a solider than a policeman and has joined the National Army to support the fight against the Irregulars. Happily, O'Duffy has insisted that Pat Walsh is retained as a special advisor and I'm sure it won't be long before he is reinstated as Assistant Commissioner.'

'Should I resign?'

'No. There is no call for that and besides what you are doing is far too important for the long term. I have talked about you with O'Duffy. He wants to meet you as soon as possible and meanwhile asks that you just keep your head down and get on with your job.'

Following a commission of enquiry into the causes of the police mutiny, a debate ensued on the question of whether or not the police should be armed. Francis discussed this issue with the officers he was training and the consensus was that they would prefer not to be armed.

'I see an opportunity here to make a big statement about our commitment to a return to being a civil police force,' said Francis when he discussed this issue with Pat Walsh. 'When I joined the RIC we were well on our way to being just that and I seldom carried a gun until I was ordered to do so after the 1916 Rising.'

'I agree with you, Francis, but I want you to wear your gun tomorrow and your best uniform, please.'

'What's happening?'

'We're forming a small parade of police officers to go to Dublin Castle with Mick Collins and Michael Staines to take the formal handover from the RIC. I thought you might like to be there.'

'Like to be there. I'd love it. Thank you Pat.'

Francis felt a pang of regret as the remaining RIC personnel at Dublin Castle handed over the premises and marched off with little or no ceremony. *And so,* he reflected, *I've just seen the RIC pass into history with hardly anyone there with me to watch.*

As the new force evolved from its starting point of replicating much of the structure and administrative rules of the RIC, decisions such as not arming the new police force set the Civic Guard firmly on the road to being a conventional civil police force. Even at the height of the Civil War the Irregulars did not, by and large, target the police beyond a low level of harassment and nuisance making.

Michael Staines left no doubt about his desire to see the development of a true civil police force when, giving instructions to the first batch of officers being sent out around the country he said, 'The Civic Guard will succeed not by force of arms, or numbers, but on their moral authority as servants of the people.'

CHAPTER TWENTY FOUR

Chief superintendent

Ireland was plunged into a civil war in June 1922 when the National Army, led by Michael Collins, attacked the Four Courts building in Dublin, which had been occupied by anti-Treaty forces for some weeks. A bitter and internecine conflict continued until 24 May 1923, when Frank Aitken, the new anti-Treaty commander, ordered the anti-Treat forces to, 'Dump their arms.' By then, both Arthur Griffith and Michael Collins were dead. De Valera supported this decision and issued a statement to the Irregulars saying, 'Further sacrifice on your part would now be in vain and the continuance of the struggle in arms unwise in the national interest. Military victory must be allowed to rest for the moment with those who have destroyed the Republic.'

As the Civil War escalated and the conflict became increasingly violent and bitter, Francis was very glad to be isolated from the strife in his role as police Instructor. The quality of accommodation and training facilities for the trainers and the new recruits increased significantly once the British vacated the Depot in the Phoenix Park. The Civic Guard immediately took possession and, like the RIC before them, used the Depot as their national training centre.

Before that happened Francis spent Christmas day 1922 at the Collinstown camp with the senior staff, including the camp adjutant, Joe Murray. The group traded stories of adventures and misadventures from the Tan war. Joe, who had been an IRA officer in Donegal, told a long story about the difficult time he had had investigating allegations made against an estate worker that fingered this individual as an informer.

Joe's story ended with him recounting that the car which was due to pick him up arrived very late and the driver was shaken after running through a police cordon and being fired on for his troubles. Joe recounted that he'd seen bullet holes in the side window of the car which seemed to confirm the driver's story. Francis queried some of Joe's details about times, dates and locations and then began laughing.

'My God, Joe, were you in charge of the IRA party on that day? I was district inspector in Raphoe and in charge of the police and military patrol. You can thank me that you were not all pulled in.'

In February 1923, Commissioner O'Duffy secured the government's permission to establish an Officer Cadet Corps. This decision was not taken lightly as there was general consensus that the new police force should promote purely on the basis of capability and experience and not rely on a privileged commissioned officer class such as that which had defined the senior ranks of the RIC.

When asking Francis to take charge of the training of these cadet officers, O'Duffy explained his logic. 'I'm all for a meritorious system of promotion. But I have to be realistic. The fact that our force is made up almost entirely of men with little or no police experience means that we simply don't have enough experienced men to fill all of the command positions.'

'The Officer Corps will be based at the Phoenix Park Depot and at the nearby McKee barracks. We have found you a house on the North Circular Road which is convenient to both. I'm sure that you will be pleased to be reunited with your family and be able to house them in some comfort. It can't have been easy for you or them to have been separated for so long during these difficult times.'

'Commissioner, I'm flattered but I must say that I did not join the police to become an Administrator, regardless of the importance of the job. I'm a policeman and policing is what I want to do.'

'Pat Walsh told me that he and Michael Staines made a commitment that you would return to an active command role once the training centre had been properly established. I won't renege on that promise but I do need you to take on this important job. Recognising both the significance of the role and to reward your commitment, I have been given the government's permission to promote you to Chief Superintendent, with immediate effect. You will report directly to me for the duration of this assignment. Given that we are planning on two cadet training groups, each running for six months, the whole assignment will take twelve to eighteen months to complete depending on how long the selection and planning takes. After that, you have my word that we will find a command position for you.'

'Commissioner, how can I possibly refuse such a generous offer? Of course I'll take the job, and gladly. And you have my word that we will turnout an Officer Corps of which you will be proud.'

Teresa swelled with pride when Francis brought the news of his promotion home to Raphoe. 'Chief Superintendent! How magnificent! Congratulations love. I'm tremendously proud of you Francis.'

'The news gets better, my love.'

'What could be better?'

'The job comes with a big house in the centre of Dublin, walking distance from where I will be working. We will all be back together again at last!'

Teresa threw her arms around Francis and danced him around the room. His heart leapt in his chest. He had not seen Teresa this happy in some time and he could scarcely remember when they'd last danced.

'Steady on girl,' he laughed. 'You will frighten the children.'

Sure enough the noise they were making attracted several of the children up the stairs from the kitchen. Teresa made them all stand upright in a straight line across the room. 'Now children, I want you all to stand to attention and give your father a proper salute.'

There was much confusion, giddy excitement and general milling about. 'What's this all about Mother?' asked Annie, who felt that she had better set about re-establishing some semblance of order in the house.

'Come on now everybody, attention!' said Teresa loudly, 'Annie, boys, I'm very proud to introduce, Chief Superintendent, Francis Maguire.'

Annie squealed in delight, the older boys clapped their hands and executed a crisp salute. Hugh asked in wonder, 'What's a Chief Superintendent, Mummy?'

§

In March 1923, Francis took up his new role training the Officer Cadet Corps and the family moved to Dublin, to the promised house on the North Circular Road. They were all delighted to be back together again. The older boys were accepted into Belvedere College, the Jesuit school for boys, in the centre of the city.

The family were blessedly isolated, almost cocooned, from the worst excesses of the Civil War and lived as close to a normal family life as circumstances would allow.

One afternoon, towards the end of May, the household was empty except for Brian who was ill in bed with measles, and Teresa, who was taking care of him. They were startled by repetitive gunfire, the racing of car engines and blowing of horns in the street outside the house. Teresa found Brian staring out of his bedroom window. 'Come away Brian, it's dangerous to stand there.'

'What's happening, Mummy?'

'The war is over, Brian. And the people are celebrating.'

§

At the end of July 1923 the Civic Guard was renamed *'An Garda Síochána'*, 'Guardians of the Peace.' By early 1924 both groups of Officer Cadets had completed their training. At a passing out ceremony the Cadets presented Francis with a splendid commemorative silver platter as a gesture of their gratitude.

Pat Walsh asked Francis to come and see him.

'Francis, you have done a wonderful job. And we are all very grateful. Well done. We promised to assign you to a command post. O'Duffy specifically asked that I follow that up as soon as the first Officer Corps graduated. We are sending you to take charge of County Limerick. This will be no cushy assignment, Francis. The recent violent history of Limerick city and the depth of Republican feeling there means that this is a difficult posting and, quite frankly, I'm very glad to have a man of your experience to put in charge. Of course Limerick is also a tragically poor city with associated social ills. So recognising the scale of the policing task involved here, we have allowed you one of the largest contingents of police officers in the country. And of course whatever happens, we will do whatever we can to support you, Francis.'

Francis enthused about the opportunity to Teresa. 'My love, I have a feeling that we are heading into what I hope will prove to be the happiest years of our lives. We will have a large house on the edge of Limerick city. Apparently it needs some repairs but once those are finished we'll make it a really comfortable home. With my salary as Chief Superintendent and my RIC pension we will be very well off. Annie will be able to join convent as a novice as she wishes and the boys can attend the local Jesuit school.'

After what proved to be Teresa's final pregnancy a baby girl was stillborn in January 1925. Teresa had never fully accepted the loss of Mary all those years ago in Belfast. They had also named this child Mary. Teresa's grief wounded her deeply and her sadness at the loss of another baby was profound. But she was older and more robust and did not allow the loss of this precious child to cast her into the deep depression which had afflicted her after the earlier baby's death.

§

As Pat Walsh had said, Limerick was a poor city and had seen more than its fair share of trouble in both the Tan and civil wars. But when the government announced the largest engineering project of the time in the whole of Europe, a tremendous optimism took hold in the city. The project was to build the world's largest hydroelectric power station on the Shannon River, up-stream from the city. The contract was awarded to the German engineering firm Siemens, and while most of the technical and managerial jobs would go to Germans, thousands of labourers would be required and that was the one thing that the country was not short of.

The ambitions for the project were large with the expectation that the whole of the country would be electrified once the power station came online.

However, the mood quickly turned sour. The work was hard, dirty and dangerous and the labourers were angered when they found that they were to be paid agricultural rather than industrial labourers' rates. Strikes followed which were sometimes violent. The company pleaded inability to pay, as the contract terms with the Irish government set the pay rates in the first place. This 'passing of the buck' led to violent protests and rioting.

A monster rally was called by the Trade Union and Francis drafted in virtually every able-bodied policeman from the surrounding counties to help maintain the peace. He paced about his office worried about what might happen when the meeting broke up. He was conscious that the strong show of force by the police, intended to deter any riots, may have just the opposite effect and add fuel to an already inflamed situation.

To hell with this, he decided. He put on his best uniform and despite the advice of his colleagues, he walked alone to the hall where the union rally was taking place. When he spotted Francis, the speaker at the podium stopped in mid flow. Francis briskly walked the full length of the hall, through the hostile crowd. Many of the strikers were armed with pickaxe handles or iron bars. The speaker turned to the chairman who stood up and met Francis at the foot of the stage. A low murmuring broke out as the men to the sides asked what was going on and why the speaker had stopped. A few shouts rang around the hall. Francis was granted permission to address the gathering and clambered up onto the stage. As he did so he removed his officer's cap.

'Men,' he called out. 'I am Chief Superintendent Francis Maguire of *An Garda Síochána*.' A wave seemed to course through the crowd. Several men shouted insults. Many waved their weapons in defiance. Francis did not flinch.

'I'm not here to threaten anyone but neither am I here to negotiate.' The crowd quietened. Some hushed the others to let the man speak. 'Nor am I here to tell you that your grievances are unfounded and in any event, it is beyond my power to address those grievances.'

'So why are you here?' shouted a voice from the middle of the crowd. That shout drew jeering from many others.

'I will tell you why I'm here. I'm here because if you go out on those streets armed and angry, as you are, we all know that the night will end in mayhem. That mayhem will no doubt lead to the destruction of homes and businesses, battered heads and broken limbs and possibly,' Francis paused, 'some people will die tonight.'

'Most of the destruction will fall on people who have done you no wrong. My police officers will be forced to stop you and some of them will no doubt get hurt. Those officers are people just like you; Irishmen, former farm labourers for the most part, seeking a better life for themselves and their families. Just like you.'

'And what will you achieve? Nothing. In fact, you will harden public opinion against you. That in turn will harden the government's position and set your objectives backwards not forwards.'

'Withdraw your labour if you wish; something, of course, that you are perfectly entitled to do. Demonstrate peaceably and do no harm and you will make your point and stake your claims more loudly than if you allow yourselves to be dismissed as a bunch of trouble-makers.'

'We fought hard to win control of our own country. Then we fought each other over how the country should be defined. Let us fight each other no more. Use your heads not your hearts. Allow these union men behind me to do your talking. I'm asking each and every one of you directly. Do not cause any trouble tonight and please let us all go home and sleep peacefully in our beds. Thank you.'

Francis turned and acknowledged the committeemen, fixed his cap under his arm, and walked slowly through the hall. He made eye contact with as many individuals as he could. He nodded as he did so and several of the men unconsciously nodded back at him. One or two simply glared, their anger undiminished.

The next morning Francis got a telephone call from Commissioner O'Duffy, 'Francis, that was the bravest and possibly most dangerous thing you could have done. You are lucky that they didn't start their riot by beating you to a pulp. But it worked, you magnificent man. Those people listened to you and there was, I gather, no trouble at all after the meeting?'

'One or two drunks had to be detained overnight but otherwise we had a quiet night. Thanks be to God.'

'God had little to do with it, my friend. What did you say that was so persuasive? Did you threaten them with the Riot Act?'

'No, sir. I issued no threats. I simply appealed to their reason and goodwill. And they listened. They already knew that we were prepared to deal with them if we had to. As they walked to the meeting they had to pass the largest number of policemen they will have ever seen in one place.'

'Francis, we are again in your debt. Well done. I'm putting you up for a commendation. But do me a favour and leave off the heroics for a while!'

'Yes, sir. I will do. Thank you, sir.'

Francis sat back in his office chair and lit a cigarette. After taking a long drag he allowed himself a small smile of satisfaction and slowly blew a stream of smoke towards the ceiling.

CHAPTER TWENTY FIVE

A flag draped coffin

Ireland in 1926 was emerging from the revolutionary period and beginning to shape its own future. A national radio broadcaster was launched but the shadow of repressive conservatism was thrown across the land when the government bowed to pressure and formed an advisory committee on Evil Literature.

'You are overdoing it. You need to take better care of yourself.'

'I'm absolutely fine, my love. Never felt better. But I promise we will have a little holiday in the summer. Maybe go up to Westport?'

'That would be lovely. Let's do some planning later. I'd better go down and rescue your sergeant. Would you like another cup of tea before you go?'

Teresa and Francis were talking in their bedroom while he finished dressing for his day's work. His driver, Garda Jim Connelly, was down in the kitchen keeping an eye on the children and waiting for his Chief Super. A large radio set was tuned into a broadcast from Radio Éireann, the new national broadcaster. As Teresa entered she smiled at Connelly and said, 'Nothing on the wireless corrupting your morals this morning I hope, Sergeant?'

'No fear of that, Mrs Maguire. Aren't the censors doing a grand job of keeping the airways clear of all evil?'

A work crew was just arriving outside. They were there to finish the job of restoring the house, which had been damaged during the War of Independence. Francis heard their lorry and leaned out of the bedroom window to greet the crew, 'Good morning, gentlemen. It's good to see you.'

'Good morning, Chief,' responded the foreman.

'Another week or so should see the job finished?' Asked Francis.

'Indeed so. God willing.'

Francis tipped his forehead in a mock salute and straightened up to finish fastening his tunic. As he did so he felt a pain in his side which he instinctively rubbed with is right hand. He decided it was a touch of indigestion and acknowledged to himself that perhaps Teresa was right and he was overdoing things. Picking up his cap he followed Teresa downstairs.

'Right, Sergeant, let's get going. I want to get out to the barracks at Bruff and surprise those lazy so-and-sos before their breakfast.'

'Dada,' cried young Frank, 'Can I come with you today?'

Francis looked to Teresa for a decision and she nodded her approval. 'The rest of the boys will be going out to school shortly so why not take him along. You know how much he loves going.'

'Right then, wee man. You'd better hop to it and get your shoes on.' Frank bolted for the door and his father shouted after him, 'And put your big coat on, it might be cold in the car.'

Francis turned to Teresa, 'If we have time, I'll stop by the convent and see if I'm allowed to visit Annie. Have you anything you'd like me to take to her?'

'No love, not that I can quickly put my hand on, anyway. If you see her tell her that we'll all come out next Saturday.'

Francis liked to turn up unannounced at the district police stations early in the morning and conduct surprise inspections. When Jim Connelly drew the car up outside the station in Bruff, Francis asked him to stay in the car with Frank while he went into the station.

The front door was unlocked and he let himself in. 'Hello!' he shouted, but got no response. He lifted the drop-down counter top and let himself into the rear office. 'Hello!' Still no response, then he heard shuffling in one of bedrooms upstairs. He bounded up the stairs two at a time. Garda Eamon Rice got the fright of his life when he emerged from his bedroom only to run headlong into his Chief Superintendent.

'What in the name of God is the meaning of this?' demanded Francis. He was about to barge into the other bedrooms when he suddenly doubled over as a spasm of pain kicked him in his side. Francis staggered back against the wall and a sweat broke out on his forehead.

'Chief, are you all right?' asked Rice.

'No Guard, I'm not. I have a fearful pain in my right side. Help me down the stairs please. Jim Connelly is waiting outside in the car. I'll have him take me to the doctor.'

'Chief Superintendent, your appendix is severely swollen and may have already burst. It needs to come out and I want to get you to a surgeon as quickly as possible. The best man is in St Vincent's hospital in Dublin. I'd call for an ambulance but to be honest your police driver can probably get you there faster than anyone else. Go now please and don't hesitate. I will take young Frank home to his mother and explain what is happening. Be assured, you will be fine but waste no time please.'

The next morning Francis woke in a hospital bed in Dublin and was delighted to find Teresa sitting beside his bed.

'Good morning, my love.' He managed in a whisper.

Teresa sprang to her feet and picked up a damp cloth which she used to pat his brow. 'Well you gave us all one hell of a fright. How are you feeling?'

'My side feels like someone has kicked six bells out of me but other than that I'm fine, I think. What happened? I don't remember much between leaving the doctor's in Limerick and waking up here just now.'

'Your appendix burst. Apparently it probably burst when you collapsed in Bruff. In all likelihood Jim Connelly saved your life driving up here like a lunatic. I came up on the train yesterday evening. The boys are being looked after by the neighbours.'

A doctor appeared in the doorway. 'Ah, Superintendent Maguire, glad to see that you have woken up. How are you feeling?' As he asked this question the doctor lifted Francis' wrist and measured his heart rate.

'As I was just telling my wife, Doctor, I think I'm fine other than feeling like I've had a good kicking.'

'When you got here yesterday we removed your appendix and all we could to make sure that no infectious material was left behind. But appendicitis is not to be taken lightly and we want to keep you here for at least a week to monitor any post-operative infections. They may lead to sepsis which can be fatal.'

Two weeks later Teresa was again sitting beside Francis' hospital bed. She was holding his hand and silently weeping. Earlier that day Francis had lapsed into a coma resulting from the sepsis the doctor had worried about. Francis never regained consciousness.

§

A seven-man Honour Guard fired a third volley of shots over the grave of Chief Superintendent Francis Maguire, completing the formal twenty-one-gun salute. A green white and orange tri-colour flag, proud symbol of the newly created Irish Free State, was draped over the coffin. A force of 120 uniformed army and police officers made a crisp salute and stood stiffly to attention, not wishing to let themselves down in the face of the more rigidly disciplined Honour Guard. A quiet sob was heard here and there and broad tears ran down several faces. As the flag was removed and the coffin lowered into its grave a priest splashed holy water onto the coffin lid. The Sergeant-at-Arms signalled the soldiers and together four of them folded the flag with crisp military precision. With great ceremony they passed the folded flag back to the sergeant who then marched around the grave and presented the flag to Garda Commissioner, Eoin O'Duffy. He in turn stepped towards Teresa and dipping his head in a formal salute said, 'The nation of Ireland will be forever grateful, Mrs Maguire. Your husband has been taken from us before his time and his parting is a great loss to us all. May he rest in peace.'

Commissioner O'Duffy took a deliberate and slow step back from Teresa and turned to march back to the head of the column of soldiers and Gardaí which had escorted Francis' funeral cortege to Glasnevin cemetery an hour earlier.

This was the same cemetery which, four years earlier, at the height of the civil war, received the remains of Michael Collins. Unlike that occasion Francis' funeral procession did not attract the Dublin throng. So, despite the full formalities of a state funeral, there was no public outpouring of grief at the passing of this relatively unknown police commander.

On O'Duffy's signal the Gardaí Depot band struck up a lachrymose funeral march and the column moved slowly away leaving the family and the other mourners behind. The escort reversed the route it had marched from St Vincent's hospital in the centre of Dublin. Francis had died there a few days earlier following a prolonged illness arising from his appendicitis.

As the mourners began to file out of the cemetery Teresa, supported by her eldest children, Annie, Rory and Donagh, began walking toward the funeral car. A stocky figure stopped in front of Teresa. 'Mrs Maguire, you don't know me, but your husband was a man for whom I had the highest regard. There are many people alive today who owe their lives to his actions and the curious thing is that they may never know it.'

'How very kind of you to say so. I didn't catch your name' responded Teresa to the vaguely familiar man standing in a diffident manner in front of her.

'I beg your pardon, Mrs Maguire, my name is Seán Gibbons and in truth I've not met your late husband for a number of years but when we "worked" together I was Adjutant of the Westport division of the IRA.'

Catching the confusion on Teresa's face Gibbons stopped himself. 'I do beg your pardon, Mrs Maguire. I should not have spoken, especially today. I assumed that Mr Maguire had spoken of me? Or at least told you of his...' Gibbons trailed off into silence in the face of Teresa's storming look.

She stiffened and through tight lips in a voice barely above a whisper she said, 'Mr Gibbons, your condolences are appreciated but I'm sure you are making a mistake about knowing my husband. He despised men like you.' With that Teresa gathered her family and, brushing past Gibbons, made for the funeral car.

Covering his embarrassment Gibbons fixed the hat he'd been clutching behind his back onto his head and stared numbly at the departing backs of the Maguire family.

'What's up, Seán?' said a voice at his elbow. Gibbons turned to find the speaker was Michael Staines. Staines was with another man Gibbons did not recognise.

'My God Michael,' said Gibbons. 'She didn't know.'

'Or maybe, Seán, she'd prefer not to be reminded. These past few years have many strange tales to tell and which of us knew what about whom and when we knew it, will never be fully clear and perhaps that is just as well. I beg your pardon, gentlemen. I forget my manners; you don't know each other do you? Seán, this is Assistant Commissioner Pat Walsh. Pat, this is Seán Gibbons from Westport, where he was adjutant of the West Mayo battalion during our recent unpleasantness.'

'Michael, you were always the grand man for the understatement,' said Gibbons with a smile and turning to Walsh extended a hand and said, 'Pleased to meet you, Commissioner Walsh. Did you know Chief Superintendent Maguire well?'

‘I was very pleased to call Francis my friend although in truth I did not know him all that long. What, may I ask, is it that Mrs Maguire does not know?’

Staines interrupted. ‘My goodness, Pat, ever the policeman eh?’ His humour served to break the slight tension which resulted from Walsh’s question. ‘Shall we pick this conversation up again at the wake gentlemen?’ He added and made to move away from the graveside.

‘And aren’t you the smooth politician, Michael?’ retorted Walsh. ‘You’ve come a long way since you clambered out onto the roof of the GPO in 1916 waving the tri-colour.’ This was added with a sly grin.

Gibbons looking uneasy said, ‘I’m not sure that I’d be welcome after that exchange with Mrs Maguire.’

‘But you must come, Seán,’ insisted Staines, ‘Pat, tell this fellow that you’ll arrest him if he refuses.’ Gibbons demurred with a nod and the three men walked towards the waiting car. Staines turned to the others and said, ‘Between us we might even manage to piece together the story of Francis Maguire.’

‘Possibly,’ responded Pat Walsh. ‘But we’ll need some people from Tempo and Belfast to fill in the blanks. I never really heard Francis speak much about his early years although he was fond of expounding his views on the failures of Irish nationalism.’

‘Oh indeed,’ said Staines. ‘Francis pinned my ears back more than once on how partition of the country was the inevitable consequence of the failure of Republicans to understand and address the depth of northern unionism. “Ulster,” he used to say, “might as well be on the dark side of the moon for all the understanding there is of it in the rest of Ireland.” But let’s stick to the man himself. Tell me, where did he pick up that peculiar accent of his?’

§

Francis’ wake was winding down so that just a small group of men remained in the officers’ mess in McKee barracks. Michael Staines, Eoin O’Duffy, Pat Walsh and Seán Gibbons were there. As were John McCormick and John Boyle who had joined the group when Gibbons had gone in search of people who could fill the group in on the years Francis spent in Tempo and Belfast.

‘What an extraordinary story. I’m so pleased to have finally heard the whole thing,’ said Staines. ‘Seán, do you really believe that Mrs Maguire knew nothing at all about the support Francis lent to the Volunteers and the risks he took doing so?’

‘Judging by her reaction at the graveside this morning I’d have to say that she had little or no idea what Francis was doing. Or if she did she clearly didn’t approve,’ answered Seán.

‘What do you think was his turning point? I mean when did he decide to turn against the RIC?’

'We may never know the answer to that question but it would be my guess that it was when the British started to undermine their own judicial system with sanctioned reprisals against innocent civilians. And most especially when the government effectively ordered the RIC to shoot first and ask questions later.'

'That makes some sense, but why didn't he just walk away at that point?'

Pat Walsh spoke first. 'Not all of us thought that walking away was the best option. Francis was a policeman through and through. He was also a highly moral man. Walking away, especially when he thought he could do something to prevent the mess getting worse, was simply not his style. Besides, he had a wife and six children to support. Mrs Maguire is no country girl and Francis was no farmer. So I hardly think taking them all back to the family farm in Tempo was ever seriously considered.'

'Ah yes, the farm,' says Staines. 'What happened to that I wonder?'

'As it happens he talked to me about that once,' said Walsh. 'When his father died in 1918 Francis inherited the farm. His sister Annie was living on the farm with her husband. They were here earlier did you not meet them?' Michael shook his head.

'Anyhow, Francis had no interest in the farm and told me he thought that his sister and her husband should have it as they had looked after his father. I gathered from her today that she and her husband intend to stay on the farm.'

'One other loose end if I may, gentlemen. How did Francis get on with the big fella?' asked Gibbons.

'As far as I know he only met Mick Collins the once when Mick wanted to meet the RIC men we were putting in senior roles. I wasn't at that meeting myself but immediately afterwards I got a note from Mick telling me to go ahead so they must have got along fine,' said Staines. 'What do you think Pat?'

'I'd have guessed that the pair would get along well. They were both essentially first-class administrators and would have appreciated each other's efficiency. Francis did tell me that he couldn't resist having a go at Collins about the Volunteers' killing of policemen. I laughed about it with him at the time. There he was at what amounted to a vitally important job interview and Francis starts laying down the law to Mick Collins.'

John Boyle had been silent for much of the evening only speaking when asked direct questions about Francis' time in Belfast. Following this exchange he sat forward and said, 'If Francis tore a strip off Collins I'm not in the least bit surprised. The Volunteers killed a lot of RIC men who were personally well known to Francis. But that alone would not have been the reason for his having a go. Francis would never have accepted that any of the violence committed by either side was necessary or productive in the first place.'

'I overheard what Teresa said to you, Seán, and I know exactly what she meant. Francis was first and foremost a policeman. Just as she said he would have despised any and all murderers whatever their supposed cause or righteousness.' Boyle subsided. 'I have no wish to cause offence, gentlemen. I know that each of you had your own motives for whatever you did or didn't do, just as Francis had his, and I know that he respected each of you for that.'

Staines, ever the politician, sought to smooth things over when he added, 'You know, gentlemen, we were the lucky ones. We all lost friends and relatives to violence over the past few years and yet we survived. There were people in Francis' life who should be here this evening, Joe Ring and Mick Collins for example. Francis Maguire was a survivor but his luck ran out and his premature death is a loss to us all.' Staines raised his glass in salute, a gesture followed by the others. 'May he rest in peace,' offered Staines who was echoed by the group as they all drained their glasses.

Seán Gibbons acknowledged John's remarks with a gentle nod of his head and then stood to take his leave. 'Gentlemen, it is high time I was on my way.' He fixed his hat on his head and folded his coat over his arm. As he turned towards the door he stopped and said, 'For the brief time I knew him I can say without a flicker of doubt that, in so far as he possibly could, Francis Maguire always thought and acted as an honourable Irishman. What more could anyone ask of him?'

AFTERWORD

Growing up in Ireland in the sixties and seventies, I was scarcely aware of the significance of my grandfather's role in the formation of *An Garda Síochána.* As boys we used to do battle in our parents' house with his dress swords and revolvers which our grandmother thought were safely hidden in a trunk in our attic.

My grandfather's involvement with the Irish Volunteers was never once spoken about and we were unaware of it until I researched the witness statements at the Military Museum in Dublin. Finding the first reference to him in those statements was the 'Gotcha' moment which inspired the writing of this book.

Equally, I was unaware of the 'otherness' my widowed grandmother suffered as she struggled to care for her children in a Dublin where many people, with long memories, could not reconcile themselves to Teresa's Belfast connections or to the fact that both her father and husband had at one time been officers in the Royal Irish Constabulary.

The legacy of the Irish War of Independence and the subsequent Civil War created an embittered silence, where a mutter or a sideways glance was all that was required to remind you that your *bona-fides* as a loyal Republican would always be in question. Happily, we grandchildren lived in a world where small-minded nationalism was always trumped by an aspiring and forward-looking faith in a Republic, proud to take her place on the world stage.

Author's note

The possibility that a pact existed between Joe Ring and DI Francis Maguire is based on circumstantial evidence and the attack by Thomas Heavey and his friends occurred in May not January 1921. Otherwise little in this book is invention.

Some readers may be curious about what happened to his family after Francis' death.

Teresa moved, with the children, to Sandymount in Dublin to be close to some of her relatives, including her brother Denis. Frank, spent his school years in Belfast with his aunties, as Teresa found it difficult to look after all of the children on her own. The older boys, including my father Donagh, returned to Belvedere College in Dublin to complete their secondary education. Annie became a nun, with the Faithful Companions of Jesus (FCJs), and ultimately became a school principal in Switzerland. Rory was ordained a Jesuit priest and spent most of his life on missions in Africa and China. Donagh trained as an accountant and married my mother, Winnie Kelly, in Dublin in 1949. Teresa lived with Donagh and Winnie in Sandymount, until her death in 1968. Brian raised a family in Clontarf, Dublin, and Frank, the youngest, raised a family in London where he lived to the ripe old age of ninety-one.

Acknowledgements

I have relied heavily on the genealogical research undertaken by my uncle, Frank Maguire. His patient work on our family's history inspired this book.

I'm deeply indebted to the writings of so many historians and academics from around the world that it would be impractical to list them all here. For readers interested in expanding their knowledge of the period I have included a list of the works I personally found most accessible and informative.

I want to specifically acknowledge the help of Captain Donal Buckley, a local historian in Westport, and Ivor Hamrock at the Mayo County library in Castlebar. Also, Jim Herlihy for his data on the RIC and Sgt Paul Maher at the Garda Museum in Dublin Castle. The staff at the Belfast Telegraph archive in Belfast, The National Library of Ireland, the Irish National Archive and at the Bureau of Military History in Dublin are all due my thanks.

But most of all I have drawn on the many witness statements available at the Military Museum in Dublin and now online at http://www.bureauofmilitaryhistory.ie/bmhsearch/browse.jsp. Specifically, I have relied on the statements by Joe Murray, Michael Staines, Tomas Heavey and most especially Seán Gibbons. The valediction to Francis Maguire which closes his story is directly lifted from the witness statement made by Seán Gibbons.

A special thanks to The Brighton and Hove Hatchery and in particular The Novel Writers Group, who supported, critiqued and encouraged. You know who you are!

And, finally, I must thank my long ago departed father, Donagh Maguire, who shared with me his boyhood memories of terrible days in Westport.

Any errors are my own.

Timeline of modern Irish History

1609 Flight of the Irish Earls and the effective completion of the English conquest of Ireland.

1610-1640 Plantation of Ulster. Mass settlement of primarily Scottish Protestants in Ulster on land confiscated from rebellious Irish Earls.

1649/50 Cromwell crushes rebellion in Ireland.

1690 The Battle of the Boyne. William III of Orange defeats James II to claim thrones of England and Ireland.

1798 Failed Protestant-led Republican revolution in Ireland.

1801 Act of Union closes Irish parliament and transfers legislative power to London.

1840s The Great Famine. Population of Ireland falls by one-third.

1886 and 1893 Home Rule Acts fail to pass in Westminster. Land reform begins the end of landlordism in Ireland.

1910-1911 Liberal government with support of Irish MPs and King George V pass the 1911 Parliament Act which breaks the power of the House of Lords.

1912 Ulster Volunteers formed to block Home Rule. National Volunteers formed to safeguard home rule.

1914 Government of Ireland Act passed and immediately suspended due to outbreak of war with Germany. National Volunteers split on issue of joining British army.

1916 Irish Republican Brotherhood stages an insurrection in Dublin. Irish Republic declared. Insurrection is violently suppressed by the British Army and the leaders are shot.

1918 Irish Parliamentary Party swept aside by a landslide vote in favour of Sinn Féin in general election.

1919 Sinn Féin MPs refuse to take their seats in Westminster and set up a rival parliament in Dublin called Dáil Éireann. The Irish War of Independence starts.

1920 Black and Tans and Auxiliaries formed to support beleaguered Royal Irish Constabulary.

1921 Truce is called. Negotiations lead to a peace treaty. The Treaty terms are rejected by Republican extremists.

1922 Ireland is partitioned. Irish Free State established. Civil war follows.

1923 Civil war ends when the anti-Treaty forces decide to pursue their aims through parliamentary channels

.

ULSTER COVENANT

Ulster's Solemn League and Covenant.

Being convinced in our consciences that Home Rule would be disastrous to the material well-being of Ulster as well as of the whole of Ireland, subversive of our civil and religious freedom, destructive of our citizenship and perilous to the unity of the Empire, we, whose names are underwritten, men of Ulster, loyal subjects of His Gracious Majesty King George V., humbly relying on the God whom our fathers in days of stress and trial confidently trusted, do hereby pledge ourselves in solemn Covenant throughout this our time of threatened calamity to stand by one another in defending for ourselves and our children our cherished position of equal citizenship in the United Kingdom and in using all means which may be found necessary to defeat the present conspiracy to set up a Home Rule Parliament in Ireland. ¶ And in the event of such a Parliament being forced upon us we further solemnly and mutually pledge ourselves to refuse to recognise its authority. ¶ In sure confidence that God will defend the right we hereto subscribe our names. ¶ And further, we individually declare that we have not already signed this Covenant.

The above was signed by me at ____________________
"Ulster Day," Saturday, 28th September, 1912.

____

God Save the King.

PROCLAIMATION OF THE IRISH REPUBLIC

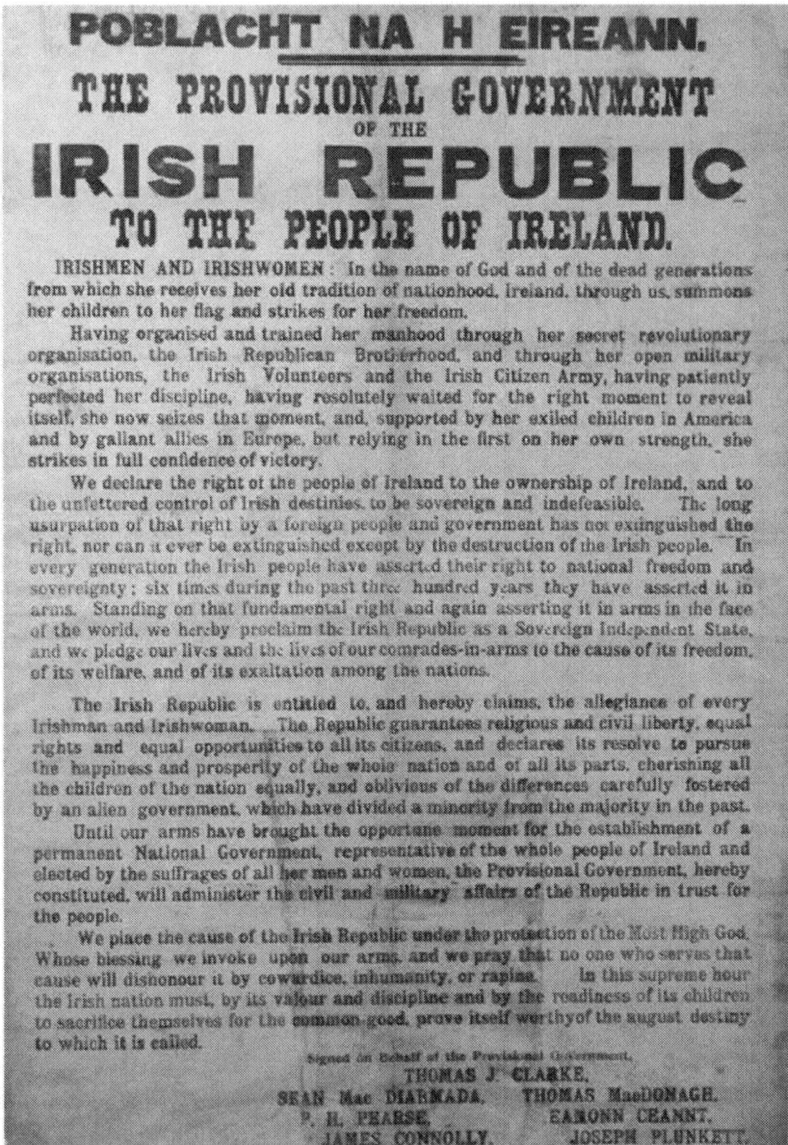

POBLACHT NA H EIREANN.

THE PROVISIONAL GOVERNMENT
OF THE
IRISH REPUBLIC
TO THE PEOPLE OF IRELAND.

IRISHMEN AND IRISHWOMEN: In the name of God and of the dead generations from which she receives her old tradition of nationhood, Ireland, through us, summons her children to her flag and strikes for her freedom.

Having organised and trained her manhood through her secret revolutionary organisation, the Irish Republican Brotherhood, and through her open military organisations, the Irish Volunteers and the Irish Citizen Army, having patiently perfected her discipline, having resolutely waited for the right moment to reveal itself, she now seizes that moment, and, supported by her exiled children in America and by gallant allies in Europe, but relying in the first on her own strength, she strikes in full confidence of victory.

We declare the right of the people of Ireland to the ownership of Ireland, and to the unfettered control of Irish destinies, to be sovereign and indefeasible. The long usurpation of that right by a foreign people and government has not extinguished the right, nor can it ever be extinguished except by the destruction of the Irish people. In every generation the Irish people have asserted their right to national freedom and sovereignty; six times during the past three hundred years they have asserted it in arms. Standing on that fundamental right and again asserting it in arms in the face of the world, we hereby proclaim the Irish Republic as a Sovereign Independent State, and we pledge our lives and the lives of our comrades-in-arms to the cause of its freedom, of its welfare, and of its exaltation among the nations.

The Irish Republic is entitled to, and hereby claims, the allegiance of every Irishman and Irishwoman. The Republic guarantees religious and civil liberty, equal rights and equal opportunities to all its citizens, and declares its resolve to pursue the happiness and prosperity of the whole nation and of all its parts, cherishing all the children of the nation equally, and oblivious of the differences carefully fostered by an alien government, which have divided a minority from the majority in the past.

Until our arms have brought the opportune moment for the establishment of a permanent National Government, representative of the whole people of Ireland and elected by the suffrages of all her men and women, the Provisional Government, hereby constituted, will administer the civil and military affairs of the Republic in trust for the people.

We place the cause of the Irish Republic under the protection of the Most High God, Whose blessing we invoke upon our arms, and we pray that no one who serves that cause will dishonour it by cowardice, inhumanity, or rapine. In this supreme hour the Irish nation must, by its valour and discipline and by the readiness of its children to sacrifice themselves for the common good, prove itself worthyof the august destiny to which it is called.

Signed on Behalf of the Provisional Government,

THOMAS J. CLARKE,

SEAN Mac DIARMADA, THOMAS MacDONAGH,

P. H. PEARSE, EAMONN CEANNT,

JAMES CONNOLLY, JOSEPH PLUNKETT.

WEST MAYO BATILLLION IRA 1921

Left to Right:—
BACK ROW.—Michael Kilroy, T. Kitterick, E. Moane, J. Gibbons, J. Walsh, P. J. Cannon, P. Lambert, J. Kelly, J. Doherty, B. Malone, J. Rush, J. Ring.
MIDDLE ROW:—M. Naughton, J. Hogan, J. Hearney, D. Sammon, J. Keane, J. Connolly, R. Joyce, P. McNamara, W. Malone.
FRONT ROW.—Dan Gavin, T. Heavey, J. Duffy, J. McDonagh, P. Kelly, J. Moran, J. Flaherty, B. Cryan, M. Staunton.
IN FRONT.—Dr. J. A. Madden.

The Men of The West 1916 to '21

Further reading

Bartlett, Thomas, (2010), *A History*, Cambridge University Press: Ireland.

Buckley, Captain Donald, (2008), *The Battle of Tourmakeady*, Dublin: Nonsuch Publishing.

Conway, Vicky, (2014), *Policing Twentieth Century Ireland: A History of An Garda Síochána*, Oxford: Routledge.

Dorney, John, (2013), *Peace After The Final Battle*, Dublin: New Island.

English, Richard, (2006), *Irish Freedom: The History of Nationalism in Ireland*, London: Macmillan.

Herlihy, Jim, (1997), *The Royal Irish Constabulary*, Dublin: Four Courts Press.

Hughes, Harry and Ryan, Áine, (2007), *Charles Hughes: Lankhill to Westport*, Westport.

Leeson, D. M., (2011), *The Black and Tans*, Oxford University Press.

McKee, Tom, (1972), *The Green Flag*, London: Penguin Books.

McNiffe, Liam, (1997), *A History of the Garda Síochána'*, Dublin: Wolfhound Press.

O'Malley, Ernie, The Men Will Talk To Me, Mayo Interviews, Edited by Cormac O'Malley and Vincent Keane, Mercier Press, Cork 2014.

O'Halloran, Clare, (1987), *The Limits of Irish Nationalism*, Dublin: Gill and McMillan.

Parkinson, Alan, (2012), *Friends in High Place:, Ulster's resistance to Irish Home Rule*, Belfast: Ulster Historical Foundation.

Price, Dominic, (2012), *The Flame and The Candle: War in Mayo 1919 – 1924*, Cork: The Collins Press.

Talbot, Michael, (2012), *History of Ireland's Civic Guard*, 'Kindle e-book.

Townshend, Charles, (2005), *Easter 1916: The Irish Rebellion*, Allen Lane, London.

Townshend, Charles, (2013), *The Republic: The Fight for Irish Independence*, Allen Lane, London.

72960409R00175

Made in the USA
Columbia, SC
01 July 2017